SUPERMARKET SUPERMODEL

www.rbooks.co.uk

SUPERMARKET SUPERMODEL

Jim Cartwright

Doubleday

LONDON · TORONTO · SYDNEY · AUCKLAND · JOHANNESBURG

TRANSWORLD PUBLISHERS
61–63 Uxbridge Road, London W5 5SA
A Random House Group Company
www.rbooks.co.uk

First published in Great Britain
in 2008 by Doubleday
an imprint of Transworld Publishers

A CIP catalogue record for this book
is available from the British Library.

ISBN 9780385607384

The author and publishers are grateful for the following permission to
reproduce copyright material: 'The Lion and Albert', words by George
Marriott Edgar © 1933, reproduced by permission of Francis Day & Hunter
Ltd, London W8 5SW.

Addresses for Random House Group Ltd companies outside the UK
can be found at: www.randomhouse.co.uk
The Random House Group Ltd Reg. No. 954009

The Random House Group Limited supports The Forest Stewardship
Council (FSC), the leading international forest-certification organization.
All our titles that are printed on Greenpeace-approved FSC-certified paper
carry the FSC logo. Our paper procurement policy can be
found at www.rbooks.co.uk/environment

Typeset in 11½/17pt Minion by
Kestrel Data, Exeter, Devon.
Printed and bound in Great Britain by
Clays Ltd, St Ives plc.

2 4 6 8 10 9 7 5 3 1

Mixed Sources
Product group from well-managed
forests and other controlled sources
www.fsc.org Cert no. TT-COC-2139
© 1996 Forest Stewardship Council
FSC

SUPERMARKET SUPERMODEL

Chapter One

COLD, SO COLD. I WAS BUTTONING UP MY OVERALL, AND ME fingers were so cold I could hardly do it, I'd come down to get dressed by the fire 'cause it was warmer. The heating was on the blink again. On the way down the stairs in my underwear I felt like I turned blue. I should have put my dressing gown on, but I couldn't see it when I got up and there just wasn't time, no time at all, I was late. Oh it was cold, and it was harder buttoning up too, 'cause I was late and really rushing. I don't like being late, I'm never late for work, I've been close a couple of times but never out and out late.

No breakfast, I'd only just had time to do me hair, I try never to miss that, it was a promise I made to me gran, a hundred times in the morning and night, with me head down to me knees, and then splash my face with cold water, icy water this morning, no creams or lotion, that's what she taught me, and her grandma taught her, and her hair was silk and her skin soft and clear right when she was old.

I got my coat on and left. I should have put a jumper on too, but I'd forgot to bring one down and I just didn't have the time. Oh it's not like me to be late, I don't like it.

I closed the back door. I meant to close it quietly, so as not to wake me mum, she's sleeping so light these days, but with rushing and the cold and the dark I sort of didn't have control and the door slammed shut. I know it seems to sound out louder in the early mornings but it went with a hell of a bang. She's not been well lately has my mum and the last thing I wanted to do was wake her. Then I saw a square of light in the dark of the backyard and I knew I'd gone and left the bathroom light on! Oh I couldn't go back now though, I'd never make the bus, but it would upset her when she got up, should I go back in? Too late – even while I was thinking about it my feet on the ice had made the decision for me and set me off slithering and sliding down our path and on to the road.

Everywhere was frozen solid. I usually walk pretty fast but I had to totter this morning and watch where I walked because when I looked up I felt unsteady. Straight away the cold went for my ears. I should have put a hat on, too late now. The dark road was lit by street lamps, circles of light on the white frost except up the top end where one or two had been smashed out by kids. I could find my way with me eyes closed though, I've lived on this council estate all of my life. Our end's still all right but the top end's going a bit rough now.

I'll probably bump into Bet, she works at our place, she lives higher up, always on the last minute. She came sliding out of her gate as I passed. 'Link me, Linda. Link me before I fall.'

We carried on up the road, slipping and sliding. She's about forty, Bet, hefty and mad and just doesn't care, she's always in a short dress whatever the weather, whatever time of day or night, tights in the winter and bare legs pink or brown or white all summer, depending on the weather, and she has these shorty coats and macs for every occasion and a little fur one for best. I don't know if she chops them down herself or she buys them that way.

'My pegs is my best feature,' she says. 'They staying on show as a distraction from the rest,' and to be honest she's probably right. She's this fine red hair always pinned and piled and shooting all over the shop, a big face and mouth, no neck to speak of and then the rest of her's – how can I say? – round, round's all I can say, and then these very short but sturdy legs with calves like two tennis balls. I was worried about making time for the bus, but every time we speeded up a bit Bet nearly went and she let out this raucous laugh and shriek to wake the street. As we slowly took the corner where a lot of the rougher families lived, we saw an old washing machine in one front garden covered in frost. Bet said, 'Where do they get those from, eh? I've always wondered that.'

'What?' I said.

'Them broken-down washing machines. There's washing machines like that in the front gardens of every rough estate I've ever seen. How come? It's another one of life's mysterious mysteries. Do you think there's a secret showrooms somewhere they all go to where you can get them?' She was off on one now.

'Very exclusive, to be admitted, you've got to have at least two Rottweilers, one that barks all day and one that barks all night, have never paid your rent, have sledgehammered a through wall down without council permission in the middle of the night when your next-door neighbour gets up for work at six o'clock in the morning, have dismantled a motorbike or at least a moped in your back kitchen and never put it back together, have been inside five times and have at least twenty tattoos – and that's just the women.

'Honest, can't you see 'em looking around, picking out their ornamental washing machine? "Oh Alf, imagine that in our front garden, be lovely that as a centrepiece with those car bits you've got and that rusty bike wheel." And the salesman there, "Excuse me, madam, sir, but could I suggest this busted-out television box to go with it, or these, the very latest in garden chic, burnt-out armchair frames?" "Oh Alf, we'd be the envy of the street." "Go on then, we'll take 'em, I can't fault her taste." "Very wise, sir, and to enhance the effect further, I'll throw in some empty milk bottles and cat-food tins and a hundred used tea bags."'

Bet's a real case. Don't know what *she*'s on about though, she's had a kitchen cupboard and a broken fish tank at the side of her house for three years now. She's always like that though. Does all the voices and everything. She's really a very clever woman, reads all the time, she's always swapping paperbacks with my mum, but me mum can't keep up with her, Bet can get through two in a day. Her husband's as mad as her, he hasn't worked for years, he puts his head out the window and shouts after her most mornings, 'Bring home the bacon, Bessie.'

As we shuffled along, I said, 'He not shouting this morning?'

'Nah, bad guts.'

She called him rotten but there must have been something there. She'd sometimes come in with a big grin on her face, someone would say, 'What you smiling at?' and she'd say, 'Beano arrived this morning,' and wink, meaning her and him had well . . . had a bit of a 'session', so to speak.

We skidded and toddled up and on to the main road, laughing all the way. The ice was harder and greyer here and frozen into rigid footprints, and the bigger street lights threw bigger pools of buttery buzzing yellow light on to its surface. We reached the steep brew. We stopped there a while looking down to where the bus stop was, getting the measure of the hill before we navigated it. There was a long queue at the bus stop, curling out of the shelter, and we could see people's frozen breath in front of them and rising all around them. We made our way gingerly down; the ice here was like a hard and smooth sheet and Bet nearly went again, with a big guffaw, and all the queue looked up towards us.

'Don't worry if me legs go up, I've got clean on,' she assured me with a grin, then nearly went again taking me with her. 'I hope you have,' she said.

We carried on down, clutching each other. Suddenly she looked at me. 'You're not normal, you?'

'Pardon?'

'Well, you always look bloody fresh and lovely in a morning. No tutee, nowt. It's not normal in a woman.' I blushed but it was too cold and the blood froze at the cheek. 'Get rough, will you, like the rest of us. Freak.'

We finally made it and tagged on to the end of the queue. Everyone was silent. Everyone seemed almost frozen solid. The first bus must have not even arrived yet, there were two buses' worth of queue here. Everything must be delayed because of the ice; it looked like I was going to be really late now. Suddenly a woman popped her head out from further down the line and said to me, 'How's your mum, love?'

'Oh she's all right. Waiting to go in.'

'Is it *the* op?'

'Yes.'

'Who's she under?'

'Dr Mendleson, I think.'

'Oh, he did me and me sister.'

Someone else in queue piped up. 'He's good, him.'

'Yes.'

'They take everything out. For about three months you feel like a buffalo that's been gutted by Navaho Indians. Then you're all right.'

Others joined in. 'Me friend's just had that done.'

'I've had it.'

'Me too.'

Bet said, 'Is there no one in this queue with a womb? Bloody hell.'

It went quiet again. I was worried about me mum. She'd been ill for a while now, was trying to keep cheerful but it was hard for her and getting her down. There was only me mum and me at home now. Me sister left a few years ago to get married, and me dad's not been with us for a long long long time. She's had to pack in work, so it's not easy moneywise, she's depending on me a lot. That's this recent thing with the lights, sometimes you've hardly got time to get up and downstairs or out the bathroom before she's switching the lights off. 'Save ont' lecky,' she says.

She's not young my mum, should be retired really, she didn't have us until she was in her late forties. She'd given up, wasn't expecting kids, neither was me dad, maybe that's why he took off. So she's always had to work, and she always seemed to get heavy work, packing and humping in a catalogue firm, laundry work, cleaning, and she always seemed to end up where there was the most lifting and shoving things around involved. Why? I don't know – she's only small really, with very fine features and tiny hands. My sister and me have always been tall and have towered over her since we were fourteen but boy can she sling boxes. I wonder if it's all that what's brought on her problem, but the doctor says not, they just put it down to 'women's trouble' and 'time of life' and all that, but I wonder.

Bet kept patting her hands together and blowing out and chattering her teeth and making all sorts of strange and wonderful noises, eeks and short shrieks and sighs, and then blowing and brumming through her lips and stamping her feet. Suddenly she said, 'Sod this for a box of soldiers. I've had it.' Then very loud, 'I'm off. I'm going back home, snuggle back in with the old lad.'

The queue all laughed.

She said to me, 'Any road, Beano might come this morning.' She set off up the road. 'See you, suckers.'

She struggled up the steep icy brew. It took her three attempts to get going at first, holding on to garden privets along the way and pulling herself up. She nearly fell over twice, you could just hear her swearing in the distance. Every time she did it a couple of the old ladies went, 'Ooo,' like they'd been shot, and some of the young kids sniggered. I had visions of her going down flat on her face then sliding all the way back to the bus stop. Then a young postman came and helped her. She had to wait at each gate while he delivered a letter, then he'd help her on. She turned to wink at me and mimed grabbing his backside, slipped round the corner and was gone. Home for another day, Bessie not bringing home the bacon. She's only been at our place about three months, but I couldn't see it lasting, she was always late and taking time off and being rude to the supervisors. I felt sure they'd sack her this time.

I looked back along the queue. Early-morning workers mainly, old dears and a few kids. Grammar-school kids with a long way to go. Three bus journeys. I looked at them and wondered what their lives would be like. I went to the local comp; most of the kids round here did. What a place, wasn't so much about learning as surviving. My sister always says we all should have got a GCSE in survival for just making it; we could have shown the SAS the way out of anywhere, I'm telling you.

Didn't even think about staying on, there was a job there for me so I just took it. We needed the money anyhow. The grammar-school girls were the ones who went on to careers or university and all that sort of thing, we just got jobs, if we were lucky, or crappy college courses, wasted a bit of time, but it got most of us in the end, we were work fodder and felt like it. All I was good at was swimming – I was in the team for swimming – and, for some reason, science, I think mainly for the school microscope, I was fascinated by it. I've always got on with equipment, instruments type of thing; I'm like that at work with the tills. No problem for me, never have been. Though some of the women are scared of them and never quite get the way of them and call for me. Think I might have got it from me gran, she was one of those if you could get the back off something for her she'd sort of fix it in a flash, just saw how it worked and where things went. She was only a mill girl – she couldn't read, my gran – but the engineers at the factory would sometimes send for her to fix the machines. Her fast little fingers would be in and out the machine's innards instinctively handling its parts. Neighbours brought her hairdryers and radios and she'd twiddle them better. No idea how she did it, it was like she was mates with machinery.

It wasn't just the microscope, though, in science, most in science I liked the words, liked science words: 'Ice is crystalline.' Those words 'crystalline substance', 'Celsius'. I like the words better than the words in other classes, even English. 'Molecular'. 'Conductivity'. I can even remember now when we studied ice, lifted it from outside on the windowsill then put it under the microscope. Once I'd had the shock and surprise of seeing the beauty of those perfect patterns, I was sneaking my friends in at break times and focusing the microscope for them till they got the shock, too, of such perfection from a bit of cold sludge. 'Molecules arrange themselves into a crystalline lattice.'

When my sister got a new doll, I got a chemistry set. I was fascinated with it till I stained the carpet, nearly sent the curtains up and dyed the cat. I used to drive my sister mad with it in our beds at night.

'Do you know what happens when you heat magnesium sulphate?'

'No.'

'Do you want to know?'

'Piss off.'

She was good at English though, she had a poem in the paper once:

A Council House Fable

A council house fable,
Two little girls at the kitchen table,
Pigtails and little legs and shiny shoes,
Listening to their mummy's news.

'Daddy's not coming home no more.'
My sister cried, I didn't, I looked at the floor,
I kicked the table, I kicked the table,
I kicked the table till my toes went sore.

I think it was about us. I don't think it was as good though as 'Molecules arrange themselves into a crystalline lattice.' A teacher came to see me mum and Dawn, to try and talk our Dawn into staying on at school, but she had met Ronnie then and just wanted to get a job and get married.

A gasp went up, and the queue suddenly became animated and started moving. The bus was coming round the corner. It looked somehow like a cartoon, all lit up in the dark and cold air, like it was cut out. The ice was still melting on the windows. We trudged on.

Chapter Two

IT WAS THE DRIVER I DIDN'T LIKE THE MOST, SOLEMN TED. He was about fifty-five, with dyed jet-black hair done in a Teddy-boy quiff. Creepy and miserable as hell. And he always watched me walk up the bus, I could feel it, and whenever he braked, he'd often look back at me before he pulled away again. It wasn't like dirty – I mean, when some men look it's, I don't know, afterwards it's like they've had a feel or something. Put hands on you, held you and examined you in their own time for their own use – it wasn't that but . . . I don't know, all I know is I was late.

I rushed down the bus, as though that would get me there any quicker. It was packed, I only just managed to get a seat. A lad in front was reading the *Daily Star*. The old lady next to me said, 'There's a damn bosom on every page.'

I didn't know how they could do it. Firstly, go in front of cameras like that and, secondly, know that people would be looking at you on buses or over egg and bacon all over the country and showing you to their mates and all sorts. I know that where me boyfriend works the blokes cut them out and stick them on the walls in the loo. And what would your family say?

The bus braked and hissed and, was it me imagination, or did it skid and slide a bit? You could feel things like that at the back, I didn't like sitting at the back, like being swung on a tail. There he was, Solemn, peeking; I pretended I didn't notice.

My mum knew him when she was young, he was a bus conductor, and a Teddy-boy even then, had been one all his life. My mum was rollerskating all the time when she was young. She was rollerskating champion of Lancashire at fourteen. When the regular night at the rink was over, the team would stay for practice, and part of it was a rock and roll section and Solemn Ted used to come in when he'd finished his shift on the buses and put the records on for the DJ; he had this amazing rock and roll collection or something, it seems. She said he was miserable as hell but would turn up in these bright rockabilly Hawaiian shirts. Even on the bus sometimes, she said, he'd have one on under his uniform, collar turned up and out, and if an inspector got on he'd quickly tuck it away.

But you had to feel a bit sorry for him, he had this club foot. I've never seen it but I believe he wore a brothel creeper with a special six-inch crepe sole. Funny thinking of me mum young, seeing a young Solemn Ted. I imagined Solemn Ted too, all these years getting down from the bus with his club

19

foot, struggling down, trying to walk to the canteen like all was normal, how he must have wanted to jive.

We were passing the massive disused mills now and coming into town. It used to be a thriving cotton town, ours, but only one or two mills remained and they were divided up into cheap carpet shops and discount bathroom places and gyms, loads of garish signs and posters at the windows, cut-price offers and even a drawing of a Thai boxer. When you passed them, though, they still cast a long shadow at any time of the day. Never much light down these streets. This is where my gran worked, down here in these mills as a girl; wonder what she'd make of the Thai boxer. The last mill chimney in town is here too, going up and up into the sky. Soon after Gran died, I dreamt me and her were sitting right on the very edge of it and she was sharing her sandwiches with me and doing one of her comic monologues, the ones she always did for me that she'd remembered from the music-hall days, and I was holding my breath so I wouldn't laugh and fall back into the chimney hole.

The bus pulled up again. There was the police station, not far to go now. One of my friends from school got on, Wendy, I hadn't seen her for years. She saw me and waved. 'Hiyah,' she called down the bus. She was dressed from a night out. Flimsy dress on, high heels, fully made up, with a much-too-large battered men's bomber jacket on, clutched around her. The sleeves too long for her, you could just about see her mobile phone in her hand. She tottered down the bus to join me. Said to the old dear next to me, 'Budge up, love. She's me long-lost pal. I've not seen her for one hundred years. Budge up. It's friends reunited.'

The old lady wasn't pleased but she couldn't resist the command.

'How's it going?'

'All right,' I said.

'What you got on? Going work? I've just come out cop shop. What a night! We were out all night, got a lift home – but it was only a stolen car, wasn't it? I didn't know, he didn't even know, who was driving it even.'

As she talked to me she had her mobile out all the time as well, checking for or reading text messages or sending quick replies one-handed. 'I might have a record now for all I know. Don't care. Public enemy number one, me. On the way out, picked this up off a bench.' She flicked her padded jacket. 'Could be one of the plods' for all I know. Don't care. I'm freezing. Funny, at night I wear what I want. I don't feel me body at night, me – the less you wear the less you feel it – I can go out in nothing, me, but in the day I cannot take it, I'm froz.

'Been in there all night. We didn't sleep like, just having a laugh with the coppers. Oh it was mad though, we went clubbing in Blackpool. It's going on there every night of the week, then back about two million miles an hour in this car with them bad lads. Then whizz bam wallop, Plod's putting us up for the night. The plod hotel with the plod cup of coffee in a polystyrene cup. What you got on? Going work? Still at Safeshop?' She began to sing the TV jingle, 'Safeshop, the one-stop shop'.

'You been there since school, ant ya? I've had six jobs, me. I wish I could meet a rich bloke-a-man, settle down and get spending. I hates working. I just want money. Me mate's making a packet in the saunas up Manchester city centre, you just twiddle wi' old business bloke-a-mans for a few hours a night an' that, but I don't fancy it. Me mum 'ud go mad, and me dar, though I'd probably meet the old sod in there. He's not been home for five years. Rings in now and again from far-flung boozers and bars of Britannia and surrounding isles. S'posed to have gone on the rigs but I think he's on the run.'

She suddenly turned to the old lady, who had been slowly leaning further and further in to listen. 'Do you?'

'Eh?'

'Do you think he's on the run?'

'Who?'

'Never mind, give us one of your wine gums, Gran, go on, I've not eaten since Rush Wednesday.'

The old lady gave her one.

'What's Rush Wednesday?' I asked.

'I don't know but they like religious references, the old. Come out with us—' Suddenly Wendy stopped and turned back to the old dear. 'Good god, love, they chewy, them, int they! Stone me. They not bits of bus tyre, are they, love? Sodding Nora, they rocks. I'm sorry, love, but I'm going to have to swallow these whole, I value me molars too much. Sodding Nora, love.'

She turned to me. 'She must have teeth of iron and jaws of steel. They do, these old ones, though, don't they? Clampers from the war years. When teeth was teeth an' all that.' She swallowed. 'There they go, down like landmines. Still be digesting on doomsday, them, I'm telling ya. Come on, come out with us.'

'I don't go out much.'

'Don't go out much. Don't go out, OK. Hang on . . . what do you mean, don't go out! You don't go out? What do you do then?'

'Me boyfriend's on shifts so we only go out every other weekend or so.' Why was I suddenly blushing again?

'Where do you go?'

'The Plumb, mainly.'

'That old boozer in town?'

'Yeah, they have a disco at the weekend though, now.'

'Bloody hell, gorgeous. Honest, you go in the Plumb?'

I nodded, with a bigger blush this time.

'We're everywhere, us. Blackpool last night – there's summat every night if you can cadge transport, I'm telling you. If there's summat happening we find it. If there was summat on Venus we'd be there, us. We cadge a lift everywhere, we get everywhere. We never stop. We have a different bloke-a-man every Friday. Swap 'em on Saturday. Come out with us. You still with that bloke-a-man? What's he called?'

'Mark.'

'Mike, yeah. He worked at Macro, din' he?' Wendy suddenly laughed at something someone had sent her on her phone, talking to me at the same time as she typed back a message with her thumb. 'Does he get you cheap stuff?'

'Eh?'

'Martin?'

'Mark?'

'Mike, yeah, him. Does he knock stuff off for you?'

'No.'

'Jack him, come out Friday. You must.'

'I can't.'

'Never say that word while I'm around, I effing hate it with all my heart and soul.'

'I'm working Saturday anyway.'

'So that stops you going out? We never sleep, us lot. Come on Friday, love. Come on, you must. Mozzy comes, and Flic. Blackpool last night. We go all over. Hey, guess who I saw last night, in front of the tower. Welsh Poll – remember her at school, always coming up at playtime speaking in that Welsh accent, saying 'Got a Lil-let?' Her bloody lips were forever chapped, remember? Taff mum, Turkey dad, remember? Bumped into her, she kept saying, "I've seen a shooting star, I've seen a shooting star." I don't know what she was on, probably nothing, probably Welshness. Taff tart. Anyway, come out. We all go. You were always like that though, weren't you?'

'Like what?'

'Bit old-fashioned, like. You were always Goody Two-Shoes at school, like, sort of thing.'

'I wasn't.'

'Well, not completely, but you were so neat and beautiful all the time. Shiny hair and that. You never wore make-up, we were always plastered with it three layers thick, and hair gelled to lard. But you . . . you lived like a nun really, compared to us.'

'I never.'

'I think you did.'

'I came out sometimes.'

'Only rollerskating. You were still following boy bands when we'd all moved on to hardhouse. Tell you what, I'm brasting for a fag.' She leaned over to the lad in front. 'Got a ciggy, pal?'

He looked embarrassed and shook his head and sank deeper into the *Daily Star*.

'Oh you can't bloody smoke on here, can you? I'm off at next stop anyway.' She started laughing at another message just come through on her phone. 'She's obscene, her. Mucky broad. Hey, what she wanted to do to that copper last night, her. It was like a letter in a porn mag. He was only nineteen. Bloody fit, he was too. Something about a uniform, int' there? Does it to you, dunt it, that stiff light-blue shirt, crisp and clean? I love the back of coppers' necks, me . . . Hey, I know what I was going to tell you – do you remember Rosco, Trish Rosco not Rose Rosco? Trisha? She's married now, her, yeah. Wedded up now, the daft cow. He's ancient an' all who she's married, he's about thirty-five or something, a right old toad. Bloody mad, init? I said, "Is he loaded?" She said, "Well, he's got a bit by." What a life, probably bit like yours, probably him and her propped up in bed together as we speak, chewing wine gums and checking their post office book, two auld fossils.' She turned to the old lady. 'No offence, love.'

Wendy got a text message that made her gasp, 'Dirty bastard.' The old lady swayed back in shock. 'Sorry, love, but sometimes you got to let it out. You must feel like that sometimes. When your pension's late or summat, or your perm's plopped.' She points at the *Daily Star* the lad is still reading in front. 'See them knickers? I've got a pair like that, thong back, frilly front. Them there. Oh he's turned over now. Freezing, init?'

She stood up suddenly and rang the bell. 'Oh no, it's not a stop this, is it? Next one.' She sat down again. 'Lend us two quid, I need some cigs to warm me up and get me up that steep brew to our house. It's like running up a slide in your slippers.'

I gave it to her, I don't know why.

'Tar, love. I'll get it back to you. Gi' us your number, I'll put it in me mobile.' She never did.

She hopped off, like a little bird. Seemed to be slipping and sliding above the ice. She was so light-looking and it was like once she'd got going on her high heels she didn't dare stop.

Solemn swung the bus, stiff and hissing, round the big corner. There was a little skid, all the old dears had their hands to their throats in a gasp. But he caught it and steadied the bus and took off down the road. He was a good bus driver all right – should be, he'd been doing it since he was seventeen. A bit like me at Safeshop – would I still be there at fifty-five? I couldn't foresee anything else at present. The bus went into the town centre, most of it emptied, only a few of us left going on up to the out-of-town shopping and industrial estates.

Soon Safeshop came into view. It looked like a spaceship in the distance and in the surrounding darkness of the vast car park. It was even icier underfoot here because there was less people walking over it at this time in a morning, I suppose. Even Solemn didn't watch me walk away as he concentrated on taking the bus off slowly.

Chapter Three

THE COLD HIT ME HARD AFTER THE STUFFY WARMTH OF THE bus and my breath steamed out before me. I seemed to be chasing it as I set off at a run and a trot towards the supermarket. I'd been working here since before leaving school, as a Saturday girl, then just carried on into full time after school. This morning I imagined it was a spaceship and, when I got in, it might take me off somewhere else, somewhere buses ran on time, or it might take me back in time and I wouldn't be late at all, but when I got in, it was the same, and I was still late and rushing and nothing was blasting off this morning. Ken, the night watchman, was getting ready to go.

'Hello, Linda.'

'Hiyah.'

'Late?'

'Is Igor on this morning?'

'She is.'

'Just my luck.'

'What about me? They're talking about going twenty-four-hour I'll lose me job.'

'Oh. I don't think they will.'

I was straightening me hair and smoothing down me overalls, and he picked up my scarf, which I'd dropped in the mad rush to get me overalls on, and he put it in my hand and just said, 'You are beautiful you, you know.'

There was nothing funny in it, Ken's not like that, he just said it as clear as that. I think he shocked himself, he certainly looked that way. I blushed and carried on like I hadn't heard him and then ran from the warmth of the staff room, through the chill of the warehouse, to the enormous rubber doors that led on to the shop floor.

I didn't like being late, not just because I knew the supervisor had it in for me but I just liked being early, getting behind the door here with all the other girls. Waiting for the signal, laughing, giggling, some having a drag on a last crafty fag, some putting on lipstick, and then suddenly we'd all shove against the doors, the great brushes along the bottom scraping the floor, and off we'd go. Released into the space, and the shop-floor vastness, scattering in all directions like a stampede of wildebeest, like a load of extras told to charge or kids out of school at the bell. Don't know why we all rush, some waddling, some tottering, some running, most floating down the aisles on the music we will soon forget is there, having a joke with the cleaners as they come off, short-cutting our way to the tills. You don't really quite know where you are going, you just end up down different aisles, carried by the charge. If you are unlucky you might get yourself blocked by the Carcass sisters on cold meats, two cleaners who are still mopping when the others have done and refuse to move over. Gigantic rumps. But if you take that aisle by mistake you have to see it through, there's no going back. You've got about four inches to squeeze through and that's it, they'd never move any further than that for a mere till girl; they might part six inches or so for the manager, but only just. Yeah, it's a mad checkout girl charge, with a feeling I can't describe, of being a bit special – no, not that, I don't know – of being in before the public, of being privy to something they aren't . . . anyway, whatever it is, it's there first thing but it soon fades off, I can tell you.

Mine was the only empty till in the row and I slotted into it quick as I could, but Igor clocked me with that cold, cold eye. She said nothing but it was noted. Quiet Alice in front turned and winked, chewing a toffee as always; three rows down Julie waved. Behind, Maureen tutted in fun. Mash and Listereenie and Jill-Two waved to me from down the end. Jill-Two has had her hair done. Lily, or Little Lily Lottery as she's known, give me a quick wave, she collects the money for the lottery every week. She was memawing something to me, probably about me money for this week's gamble. Tish, Natt, Melanie and Lucy looked and then away as Igor strolled past. Igor doesn't like anyone. She was one of us up to only two years ago, but since she's been made supervisor she's changed; the only one she likes is Denise on the cig counter and that's because I think they are related or share the same taste in lipstick, or something, it's always bright. Too bright of a morning, it's often smudged into Igor's teeth. To be honest, she's not quite got make-up application sorted. I know it's cruel but she looks like a female impersonator. She's often off filing her nails in Hardware. She didn't used to have the nails. S'pose she couldn't when she was shelf-stacking. They all slag her except me. I don't like calling people names. Me gran said, 'Hate never leaves a hater.'

Opening time is near and Igor approaches the security guard to do the honours, Mr Thompson he's called. Everyone has to call him Mr Thompson, can you believe it? Bet has a routine she does about him. 'Even all his kids call him Mr Thompson. When he got wed it was "Take Mr Thompson to be your lawful wedded Mr Thompson."' She swears she's heard him calling himself Mr Thompson – 'Mr Thompson, you can handle it,' 'Move yourself, Mr Thompson,' all that. There's talk of him and Igor having a little fling, but I don't know. Someone heard, 'Ooo, Mr Thompson,' coming from Soups and Sauces one Christmas. You've got to watch him though, he walks down the end of the till row looking at legs. He has a massive bunch of keys on his belt and if you hear them jangling you tuck your legs in fast.

Igor gives Mr Thompson the nod and he unlocks, with great authority; you'd think he was opening Westminster Abbey. There are two security men, and the other one's called 'Bless'. He can't even get the door open when it's his turn, bless. Igor stands behind him tutting, making it worse, and then either Mr Thompson comes over and sorts it out or Igor takes over. So at any sign that this is going to happen, to avoid humiliation Bless sort of revs himself up and really goes for it, squatting and twisting and getting the key in then out again. It can be funny to watch, if you've got the time, because he's about seven foot, a beanpole. Someone saw him dancing at the works dance, he'd gone out into the corridor to do it 'cause he was shy; they said it was very similar to him unlocking the doors. He's probably in his thirties but red-cheeked like a boy, and he has very thick hair cut into a floppy fringe like a little lad's. I don't know his real name, think it might be Barry. But everyone calls him Bless because when he does anything for you or tells a tale, which are often about helping his auntie, who he lives with, you just can't help saying, 'Bless.'

Besides being a good boy for his auntie and useful for getting stuff from the top shelves for you, he's also a sci-fi nut. He's intergalactic president of some sort of club or other and he collects anything and everything to do with *Star Trek*. He's got some original Mr Spock ears or something he paid a lot of money for. Bet got him to bring them in, pretended she was interested. He put them on to show us, very serious though, collectors' items. Funnily enough, they didn't look comical or out of place on him – in some weird way they suited him. Then Bet put them on to serve customers and she had the place in an uproar. Igor put paid to it of course. Bless is always on about the *Star Wars* trilogy and which do you prefer, *Star Wars* one, two or three, is it . . . ? I can't keep track. He can be a bit boring. I think he's asked me out, it's hard to tell, he just leaves a leaflet for one of his Trekkie conventions on your till, and I think that's it. He's done it to Bridget and Shirley, too. If it's not *Star Trek* club he's on the computer or the net, lost in space. Wonder if he can sci-fi me out of here.

The doors open and in they come, the early-morning customers. The doors are those massive mechanical revolving ones, so you wonder who they are going to chuck out. Once, they jammed, a woman had a faint in summer, blocked everybody in. All these people in there like in a fish tank. No one knew what to do. Mr Thompson was ordering everyone about but he didn't know what to do. It was Quiet Alice who went over and, through manhandling the doors, managed to budge the woman round inch by inch till she rolled out.

Mainly, this time of a morning, it's pensioners – they shop small, baskets mainly – or redundant men, trying to keep a routine, a lifetime of getting up early, or clerical workers all dressed up, rushing in for instant coffee and biscuits for the office or a cake for someone's birthday. Sometimes we all sing for a laugh, heads going down the line, 'Happy birthday to you.' Igor comes skidding down the aisles. Says nothing but just glares. The managers don't mind, I don't think. Adam's been down, when we've done it. He's the young assistant manager, he just laughs. Then you get them just back off holidays, instead of going to bed, straight in for shopping. Some make me laugh, in sombreros, shorts sometimes. Insomniacs come in like walking ghosts.

You get so you can read the baskets, when you've been at it a long time like me. Like Tarot reading but using the goods they've got. Harder with trolleys but with baskets I'm often bob on. You'll do a basket and think, 'recently bereaved' or 'just taken to keep-fit', 'in love at the office', 'forty coming up'.

Sometimes, early, you get the shoplifters. It's all fags and white bread and own-brand lager in the basket but what's in their pockets? Mr Thompson is all over the place when he thinks someone's been at it. He tried twisting a young kid's arm up his back once and got a black eye for it. Bless has a different approach, he's working on an invention to stop shoplifters with a force field or something. He's always trying to get a meeting with the manager to show his plans but he's like the great and powerful Oz, you never see him. He sometimes comes round when Head Office visit, then we all have to call him Geoff and Igor about licks the floor before he walks it.

As I said, the assistant manager's Adam, don't know his second name, but he's all right and a bit the store heart throb, specially for Denise on Cigs and Sweets. Denise is always done up to the nines, and she's saving up for a boob job, her best friend Thinnie told Jill-Two in confidence. A confidence of course lasts about three seconds (if that) on the till line.

Speaking of Cigs and Sweets, Joan works there with Denise but mainly on the newspapers and mags. Joan's all right. She's about the exact opposite of Denise, quietly spoken, very patient and calm – she'd have to be to put up with Denise – fiftyish, grey hair still feathered like she had it in the seventies, and usually in purple polo neck and slacks with a funny little Egyptian symbol pinned on her overalls and big, wide-open eyes. She reads all the horoscopes in all the papers first thing, and she knows everyone's zodiac sign, so if she thinks there's something you should know she'll stop and whisper your stars in your ear as she passes your till. She'd stopped already this morning at Louise and then she stopped at me and whispered, 'Change, be prepared for it. Good fortune brought by someone dark.'

I said, 'I wish.'

She just nodded sagely and moved on.

Maureen from behind said, 'Well?'

'Be prepared for change brought by someone dark.'

'Probably means when Sunbed Ida brings the change bags round,' said Maureen, and we both cracked up laughing, and then the eye of Igor was upon us and we were silent again.

I served a few customers but it was slow this morning. It looks like Liz got Ogden – shame for him really, he's obviously a man who lives on his own, buys a ball of string and five Cup-a-soups and talks for twenty minutes about his piles. Interesting to see how it goes, the slow trickle through early morning building into a mighty torrent come midday, then slacking off a bit and coming back about five o'clock.

I looked out into the darkness and saw two lights approaching outside. Was it aliens? No, it was two headlights, the first car in the car park. As it came into the lights of the supermarket we saw it was a Porsche. The girls craned to look. A man got out, flicking his remote as he rushed to get in from the cold. I watched him pass through the automatic doors like he was used to doors automatically opening for him. He wasn't the usual early-morning shopper. All in black, a handsome older man in young clothes.

I served a few more customers then, from the corner of my eye, I saw that the man in all black had come to my till. I smiled, he smiled. I didn't look at him again but felt him looking at me the whole time. I checked through his things, concentrating on each one intently. A small fresh orange juice. Disposable razors. Shaving foam. A packet of cashew nuts. A woman's magazine. I would have said this was a man-who's-been-travelling-all-night kit, a freshener-up on the journey, but a woman's magazine? At the end he said, 'Ever thought of modelling?' I blushed up from my toes to my hair roots. 'Here's my card.'

Suddenly I couldn't lift my arm to take it. He smiled again and laid it on the conveyor belt and it came down slowly towards me. Then his mobile went. There was an enormous woman pushing him forward as she heaved a frozen chicken on to the belt. He finished the call quickly then rushed away.

'Phone me,' he called back. Then he'd gone.

The big woman said, 'Men, they'll try anything, take it from me.'

Then all I could see was all the girls' heads turning one after the other like a long chorus line, each mouthing, 'Who was that?'

I blushed again. I heard his beautiful car setting off but didn't look. I don't know about modelling, I could have modelled as a red traffic light at that moment. I was dreading the canteen at break time.

Sure enough they had the card off me and it was, 'Hey, girls, check out Kate Moss on the checkout', 'Ooh, look, she's already walking like Naomi Campbell', 'Twiggy of the tills', 'Can they get shopping trolleys down them catwalks then?', 'It'll be kinky'.

'I doubt that,' said Adam, the assistant manager, and he got the card and gave it back to me. I thanked him quietly and thought I'd grab a tray and take the chance to escape to the counter but the tea lady comedy duo, Daf and Flo, was lying in wait.

'What's this we hear Linda, love, Supermarket to Super-model?'

Chapter Four

THAT NIGHT ON THE BUS IT WAS AS DARK AGAIN OUTSIDE as it had been when I came in that morning. Through the window I saw people huddled in the rain against the dark and cold and the drab town, and I wondered, wondered if it really was possible to get out of here. To do other things. I'd never thought of it before. It had never entered me head – just the odd dream, but I'd never let it develop. I saw my reflection in the glass; I didn't know what I saw. I didn't know what he saw, I knew I wasn't bad, but a model? I tried to push it all away, it was too strange.

Down our road the ice was all slush now. It was very empty and lonely just me coming home, passing under the lamp posts again. Past Bet's place – I'd heard she'd been spared the boot but wasn't bothered – I heard muffled sort of hot Latin music coming out from there, Beano music maybe, God knows what they were up to. The only sound in the road, the Latin music distant as I walked through the slush, it made everything seem all the more lonely for some reason. Wish I could be like her and just say sod it for once and just do anything. Whatever I liked.

Told me mum at tea time and she thought it was a con. I lay on my bed and thought, is it? Joan had heard of the model agency; she showed me a picture in a magazine with their name on it. Anyway, I'd decided I wasn't going to phone. It was mad. I got the card out to look at it again, I'd put it away as a souvenir. And I surely would have if it hadn't been for Mark's call.

The phone went downstairs. It was Mark. I told him about it and he said, 'You are not phoning.' Just like that.

I said, 'Who are you to tell me I'm not phoning?'

He just said, 'You're not.'

I hung up on him and straight away in anger, without thinking, dialled the number on the card.

There was no answer. I was just about to put it down, relieved, when I heard the man's voice.

'Yep, Rafe here.'

'It's me, er . . . checkout girl.'

'Wait while I pull over, I'm in London traffic.' I waited, I could hear London behind him. 'Glad you rang.' He talked fast and hard. 'First off, what's your name?'

'Linda.'

'Nice, nice. I'm Rafe, by the way. I phoned my assistant as soon as I left that supermarket and said, "I've found a star." Just keep seeing you in that line looking out the window. What's the second name?'

'Longbottom.'

'Sorry?'

'Longbottom.'

'Oh I see, Linda Longbottom. Could work in a gimmicky kinda way. Gamble, though. Might have to think of a name for you. One word maybe, though that's not the thing so much now, more in glamour that . . . Did you have any ideas?'

I don't know why, but I just said, 'Crystalline.'

'Like it. Like it a lot. Crystalline. OK, now listen, Crystalline. I am going to make two calls now, one to arrange a shoot for you in two days in Manchester – OK? – and one for me to get up there and be with you . . .' On like that he went. On like that, or he'd slip in something like, 'Just going to meet a client, she's back from Paris,' and my heart would skip a beat. I suddenly got nervous and excited at the same time when I heard that. I didn't know why. It all seemed unreal. As he talked I couldn't take it all in, I just kept saying, 'Yes.'

I could hear the traffic and the city chaos in the background, London, and his voice in with it all, then above it. It was so positive; it was energetic, like being on a ride. No one I knew talked like that, it was so immediate, like it was already happening or had happened. Everyone I knew talked with a kind of delay in them. It was always what you were going to do some day, like the brakes were always on. When he hung up I stood and my legs were trembling. What had I started? I wanted to hold on to something, quick. I went for Mum.

*　　　*　　　*

40

'London call on our phone! To a mobile an' all?'

We sat opposite each other at the kitchen table, like we had done when Mum had told us about the operation she was going to have to have, like we did when Gran died, like we did when our Dawn had come home to tell us she was getting married, like we had done as two little pigtailed girls when Mum told us that Dad wasn't coming home no more and cried and Dawn 'kicked the table till my toes went sore'. Now it was my turn to talk. I started again to tell Mum what he'd said. I was surprised – I could remember most of it.

'Will you have to go to London?' she said, with the Northern Mother's mortal fear of the big city.

'Not at first, he's coming up North again, he'll meet me and take me to a photographer he knows.'

'Con. What about paying?'

'He said I'll make it back easily out of my first job.'

'How much?'

'Three hundred pounds.'

'We haven't got that kind of money.'

'I've what Grandma left me.'

'That's for your wedding.'

I lay on me bed. I lay there looking round me room, me sanctuary, all mine since my sister had moved out to get married. Blu-Tack, where old posters had been; they had all been of my favourite boy band, One-plus-two-plus. Paulie was the one I liked best. He was the cute little dark one with the dimples. Used to dream of him and me coming out of clubs in London and stuff like that, walking out of a club in a camera flash . . . London. I'd just been talking to someone in London, about me and a shoot. Me and a shoot. It was a world that only this morning had been as remote to me as the moon and stars. I looked at the little photo-booth picture of Mark and me I kept by the bed. Our hair needed cutting, I was smiling and hugging him, nearly pulling his head off. He's looking serious as usual. We met at Safeshop; he used to work there, in the warehouse. I was still at school, working Saturdays, only sixteen. He was about nineteen, I think. He asked me out, I went. He seemed so much older and he even had a car. He was really my first ever boyfriend. But he shouldn't have said what he did. What had I done? Oh sod it for once. For once I was letting life take me, Bet style.

The only framed picture in me room is a black and white of my grandma in a doorway at the mill. She really was a great beauty, shining hair, pure complexion, stayed with her right through old age. Besides having her gift of the mechanical, they say I look like her. Didn't have her performing gift though, I was always quiet and shy. I loved it when she did those old music hall routines for me. 'Gungadin' and the one about Mad Carew and all that. People said she could have been on stage. There was something about her, she was wasted in the mills. She died when I was about twelve. I still miss her. What would she say? She'd want me to do it. She'd say, 'That's my girl,' and 'You do it, dove, don't miss your chance like most of us do.'

I could hear me mum in the hall on the phone to my sister. I could make out that our Dawn thought it was probably dodgy. When the call was over me mum just shouted upstairs, 'Linda, I'm coming with you.'

Chapter Five

NEXT DAY AT WORK WE WERE ALL BEHIND THE DOOR WAIT-
ing to go in. There was an unusual hush just before the signal
and a bit of sniggering. The door burst open, we spilled in,
and there was Maureen, with a little cardboard-box camera
off the shelves, shouting to me, 'OK, just one more, please,
just one more. Gorgeous. One more.' Everyone started really
laughing. I went into some poses. She kept snapping away.
'Lovely, darling, just one more, over by the bacon shredder.'
I posed around on our way to the tills as she walked backwards.

Igor was waiting, and she was definitely not amused, and
neither were Denise or her friend, Thinnie. They took off and
didn't stay for the joke. I heard Denise thought it should have
been her who was spotted, and it was only because he hadn't
seen her, she had lost out 'cause he was a non-smoker.

I knew I had to ask Igor for time off. I couldn't relax all
morning. My throat was dry with nerves. One woman asked

for cash back and I gave her the price of her goods instead of what she asked for, but we sorted it out. The girls got the whole story out of me, between customers, passing the information back and forth up the line. Wish they hadn't known. I finally saw Igor at the top of Cereals and Soft Drinks. I knew it had to be done. I got some cover from Little Lily, and could feel them all watching me walk up the aisle. Igor was there, supervising a new girl with a price gun, making her so nervous she was sticking the prices on upside down. Igor was just doing her usual, not saying anything, just watching. I stood beside her. She ignored me for a long time. Then I spoke. I almost said, 'Igor'.

'Yvonne?' She looked up but then pretended to be pre-occupied with the girl pricing, poor love had dropped the gun three times already.

'Yes?'

'I . . . er . . . you might have heard . . . sorry . . . I need to-morrow off to . . .'

'Not possible, I've no cover.' I just stood there. She didn't speak. Then she looked at me. 'All right?' she said, then gave a quick 'Sorry,' which she didn't mean, and was clicked out like the price gun.

I just turned and walked back to the tills. I was in tears. I wanted to cry not so much 'cause she'd said no, but because of the way she'd done it and also because I wasn't sure of what I was doing anyway. It had taken so much to reach the decision and, I don't know, now everything seemed to have thrown me back down to reality, I suppose, flat on my face.

All the girls, even while they served, were watching me walk back. Bleep bleep, the tills, bleep bleep and all the eyes on me though I didn't look. Little Lily looked at me. 'You all right, love?' I nodded. 'You're not, are you? Would she not give you the time off?'

I didn't say anything but she knew.

Jill-Two shouted from way down the line. 'What's happened?' The flow of customers stopped, everyone looked.

Lily said, 'They won't give her the time off.'

'And she bloody knew what it was for?'

'Nasty.'

'Uncalled for, that, she's a cruel cow, her.'

'Unbelievable.'

'She gave Denise a day off to get her eyelashes stained.'

'Not bloody fair, this.'

Quiet Alice, who as usual hadn't said anything, suddenly, slowly, took the boiled sweet out of her mouth, called for a stand-in and went up to the office. No one knows to this day what she said, but a couple of minutes later Adam came down and told me I could have the time off.

After work, as I left, the girls all called after me, wishing me the best. 'And keep your knickers on!'

On the bus I got that nervous and excited feeling again, it felt like the brakes were coming off my life and it was going suddenly very fast all on its own.

That night, I was trying to sort out clothes to take. I'd have liked to have got something new but there hadn't been the time and I didn't have the money, especially with the shoot being so expensive. I looked at my body in my underwear. I'd never had to worry about my figure, never given it a thought, always been able to eat what I wanted and it was always loads. In the canteen, it was funny, stuffing down the cream cakes, chips, anything I fancied, while all the dieters gasped in agony just watching. Mum came in.

'Mark still not phoned?'

'You know what he's like.'

'Are you not ringing him?'

'That's what I always have to do.'

'He won't like it.'

I didn't answer. I didn't feel like it. This was what was happening, new parts of me coming up, surprising me.

Chapter Six

IT WAS FOGGY WHEN WE SET OUT TO CATCH THE BUS. MY BIG bag was on one side, my mother at the other. It was Solemn Ted on the bus, could you believe it, though I was glad of him for his solid driving, I knew he'd get us there through the fog. Mum tried to strike up a bit of a conversation with him but he wouldn't have it. When we were getting off she said to him, 'Solemn, you want to bloody cheer up.' He slammed the doors shut and nearly caught us. Mum shouted after him, 'What would Elvis say if he could see you!'

When we arrived in Manchester, we couldn't find our way. The fog made it difficult and I rarely came to Manchester anyway; last time was about three years ago to see One-plus-two-plus. Me mum never came at all. We stopped to ask a man directions; he was really posh. Afterwards me mum said, 'Did he know what he sounded like?'

We eventually found the place. It was a very big building done all in dark glass – dark-glass doors, dark-glass ceilings.

We went up in a glass lift, and my mum held her skirt tight to her knees for fear the floor was some kind of glass too.

Rafe was there to meet us as we stepped out. I got a better look at him this time. Though he was the same height as me, at first his proportions didn't seem right for his height, then I realized he was wearing high stack heels. He was in black again, his eyes were almost black, and though he smiled and wrinkled and changed his face, it seemed permanently the same, unflinching. He reminded me of someone somehow, but I couldn't think who. He wore a ring with a serpent with a big jewelled eye, black too, and his hair was full and, though grey, perfectly clipped like it had just been cut that minute. His whole body seemed strong, not sculptured and shaped but, like, too much energy in it ever to be fat. And when he turned to you it was like being in a full-on beam.

He led us into the studio. He was very charming to Mum; with me he just behaved like we had known each other all our lives. I didn't know what to make of that because I didn't know what to make of anything, I had never ever felt so nervous in my life. There was no excitement mixed in with the feeling this time, just fear.

The studio didn't help; it was just like an old, empty ware-house, with nothing to hold on to, nowhere to focus. Mum said it reminded her of the mills, without the machines. It seemed even bigger because there were only a few of us in there. Besides Rafe and me mum, there was a little bald man with a curly moustache who did hair and make-up – he looked like Hercule Poirot, except he was in tight plastic pants and a

tank top and wore black nail varnish on every other finger
– and the photographer, a really smily and energetic American
woman. She was so energetic and her eyes were so bright blue,
I found it hard to look at her for long and mainly found myself
talking to the red cowboy boots she wore. I opened my bag to
show them what clothes I'd brought. My hands were shaking
so much I could hardly get the zip undone, and though they
were polite about them, the clothes suddenly seemed cheap
and outdated. Rafe wheeled in a rack of clothes he'd brought
himself, just for me to look over, see what I thought, he said.
They were really beautiful things, expensive, a bit flimsy in
places. Mum said, 'Ralph, are you sure about these? There's a
bit of a draught in here.'

We all had a cup of tea but I couldn't drink it. Their conversation was about people they knew. Fashion houses, models,
designers. I felt left out. I was scared to death.

I was dressed. I was made up. The camera was set. I went
out, first thing I saw was Mum with the Yank and Rafe lugging
some heavy lamps into place, Mum taking all the strain as
usual, after that she whipped a tripod over there with one
hand, calling out, 'Where do you want it?' Then I was guided
over and stood on the coloured paper they had unrolled up
the wall and across the floor like gigantic wrapping paper. I
felt vulnerable and lost, like some little puppy dog that was
being gift-wrapped and had absolutely no idea what was going
on or where it was going to end up. I seemed to be standing
there a long time as people talked and moved about and then,
so suddenly it shocked me, the blinds were yanked down, the

lights thudded on, hot, bit blinding at first. I looked down, all I could see were the red cowboy boots, everyone and everything else was unclear behind the lights, and I was so scared.

The photographer said, 'Look up, honey, it's OK, look up into the camera.'

I slowly lifted my eyes and there it was, the camera, it was about all I could see, the lens turning one way then the other, purring as it went, almost hypnotic. It looked at me and I looked at it, and then something amazing happened – I felt at home, I just suddenly felt safe with a machine again, like the till or the old school microscope. It was just the two of us. Others called to me, do this do that, I wasn't really listening, me and the camera were all right together, knew what to do. Watching the lens roll, it could have turned me upside down and I would have gone with it.

Rafe said to me mum, 'She's a natural, she's a natural, I knew she would be. Look at that – it's because she doesn't know what to do she does it so well.'

My mum just said, 'She always took a nice snap.'

We had a quick break, another cup of tea. I was nervous again, with the small talk, I just wanted to get back to it. When we went in there was panic for a minute, none of the lights would work, then someone spotted everything had been un-plugged. Mum had done it! 'Think of your lecky, Ralph.'

At the end I was tired, but happy. I'd enjoyed it and I'd never been told in my life how 'great' I was so many times. I was almost drunk with so much praise, then they popped open a bottle of champagne to celebrate and then I really did go light-headed. Rafe then started officially calling me Crystalline, me mum didn't get it and couldn't even say it. Rafe insisted on paying a taxi to take us all the way home, he gave the driver £50 just like that. Before we got in, Mum asked him how long the pictures would be at the developer's. He laughed and told her he'd be looking at them later.

Just before the taxi pulled away, he said, 'Oops, I almost forgot,' and pushed a bag full of the clothes I'd worn through the window. 'You can keep them.'

I couldn't believe it. The car pulled off and he was waving.

There was an excitement in both of us. Mum didn't say anything to me but I could tell she still wasn't sure about it all or about Rafe. I said, 'Do you like him?'

Though he was charming, though he made her laugh, she said there was something she couldn't put her finger on. Sounds funny, she said, but it was like when somebody gave you something sharp to hold, something that might cut to the bone.

We pulled up outside our home, got out the taxi. Neighbours looking. No one had ever looked before, now we were suddenly on show.

Later, I lay on me bed, champagne in me head. What was happening? Work tomorrow. Could I cope, after all the excitement? Was I changing? Where did all that confidence come from? I'd never known it in anything else.

Chapter Seven

WHEN I CAME HOME FROM WORK NEXT DAY, A BIG BLACK AND white picture of me was propped on the mantelpiece. Me mum was looking at it with tears in her eyes. I sat down next to her and looked. It was me, but it wasn't me, but it was. 'He's phoned, Ralph.'

'Rafe?'

'Aye, he says they are all like this, unbelievable, he said. Wants you to call him.'

I phoned him. When he'd finished I just walked back into the room.

Mum said, 'Well?'

'Job.'

'Eh?'

'Paris.'

'Paris? Con.'

'No, it's not.'

'How do you know?'

'It's £5,000.'

Silence, then, 'English money?'

'Course.'

'Oh.'

'When?'

'Friday.'

'What about your job?'

'It's £5,000.'

'What about Mark? He won't like it.'

'No.'

We both sat looking at the picture.

Next day I phoned work to ask for the next few days off, got Igor the Terrible again, and she told me no. I said I had to and she said, 'Don't come back then.' I wasn't bothered.

Suddenly, frightened free, frightened, free. I didn't know where to go, what to do, pelted round the shops, couldn't sit down, went round the shops on the precinct again and again, like a bird when it's first out the cage. One thing I knew, I had to see Mark. I knew he was on lates at the discount warehouse. I knew he would never phone me. So I decided to pay him a visit that night. I used to pine when he hadn't phoned, until I had to give in and phone him, but now I felt angry at him for not calling me. It seemed so pathetic, childish and hurtful of him.

While I was in the bath Mum came up. 'Your manager's here from work for to see you.' Whispered, like royalty had arrived. I went down in my bathrobe. I could hear me mum watching her Ps and Qs. I walked in. She looked at me like, 'You could have got dressed,' but I wasn't bothered no more.

It was Adam. He'd come to apologize. He'd come on behalf of the company. 'We all know how Yvonne takes her work . . . too seriously, at times, shall we say. You are welcome to come back. But days off are . . .'

'I don't want to.'

I think he was very taken aback, but he said, 'Understood. Well, if you change your mind or you need my help, give me a call any time.' He gave me his card. Then he stood looking at me. Neither of us spoke for a while. Then he broke the silence with, 'Wish you all luck with your career.' Then he went and we heard the front door quietly closing.

'Well, you couldn't say fairer than that,' said Mum.

It was as though the President of the United States had just left the building. She turned on me. 'I hope to God it works out, for your sake. I don't know what's come of you, I don't. Coming down like that, too.'

'Well, he should have phoned to say he was coming.'

'Ohh! Managers is busy, think it's nice of him to make that effort.' I went out; she called after me, 'And by the way, he's in love with you.'

I went upstairs. She'd set me off blushing again, for all my new bravado.

That night I went to the discount store where Mark worked. I had tried to do my hair and make-up like 'Hercule' had, I had decided to put on one of the dresses that Rafe had given me.

55

I don't know why. I even took my coat off as I walked around the back to where he usually worked. It was freezing but I remembered what Wendy had said, and she was right, sometimes the less you have on the less you feel it at first. Round there the big delivery doors were open, it was already flood-lit, and you could see ice forming on the stacked pallets.

Mark saw me, I smiled, some of the love came back, then it was gone again when he did that scowl he always did when we had fallen out. I could tell, inside, though, he was pleased because he thought he had won again. He didn't like the dress. I could tell that too. It shocked him. He was glancing around to see if anyone was about. I knew, if he could, he would have liked to have surrounded me with the pallets, like a fortress. We stood in the cold, silent for a while, shivering, in the distance the echoing noise of fork-lift trucks and men's voices. I told him about the job. I sensed something collapse inside him.

Suddenly a pallet dropped somewhere and made us both jump, and then he had his scowling head on again and his front well and truly up. He said, 'That's it then.'

I nodded. It shocked him, this. I knew he didn't think I'd do it. I saw something flash in his eyes, like he was a little boy, then he walked away. I watched him. His back. Walking away like that, quiet, trying to be tough. I went home and cried.

By morning, after a sleepless night, I had decided I was not going, there was just too much upset, too much change for me, Mark, work.

I got up. My sister Dawn had come round with her new baby. I went down and I told them I wasn't going. Mum said, 'Oh, after all the upset. I don't believe it.'

Dawn gave the baby to Mum and took me into the front room. One of those talk shows was on, a mixed-up family all shouting at each other. She turned the sound down. 'Listen, you go.'

'Eh?'

'Don't miss this chance.'

'But it's all happening so fast. It's not me.'

She looked at me. 'You've got a chance, take it. Don't let anyone or anything put you off.' That was it. She went out. But it was as though she'd slapped me. For a while, I watched the people on TV with the sound off. Then I went upstairs and packed.

Chapter Eight

MUM CAME WITH ME TO THE STATION. SHE ALMOST THREW me case on and off the bus; it was all I could do to stop her heaving it up on to her shoulder like a sailor. She was the same at the train station. At one point, I looked round and she was gone, then I saw her off up the platform carrying some old nun's cases for her. We said goodbye and I sat on the train, she stood on the platform, kept mouthing things to me through the window I couldn't understand, but I knew she was doing it to stop herself crying. She was always like that with us, would keep asking have you got this, and have you got that, and don't forget to speak up and say thank you, and have your manners and all that, but really she was just stopping herself from crying. We didn't kiss and hug after about fourteen, but when I was young she gave great cuddles, long and rocking in her strong little arms. I s'pose as we got bigger it was ridiculous for us, legs dangling to the floor, we could have got her on our knee.

The train pulled out and I waved. Looked back at my little mum, little bow-legged thing, bow-legged with all the burdens. It was quiet on the train, trance-like. I felt in my pocket; it was still there. A card had been delivered as we were leaving. I just slipped it in my pocket. Could be from Mark, but I doubt it.

It was different being on a train in the early mornings rather than on the bus. Different lot of people – businessmen, power-dressed secretaries, city workers. What would they have made of Wendy on here! After the first few stations the train stopped dropping off and picking up, and it opened out to Manchester airport, and then the mobiles started going, one at first, then another as it built up through the carriage. Some were whispering, some bellowing, and I could dip in and out of each of their lives. I thought of my phone. I always kept it well hidden, bit of a chunky thing; some of the girls who had happened to get a glimpse of it called it my Cadbury's quarter-pounder, it was such a chunk. They were selling them off once at Safeshop, I hardly used it. A top-up could probably last me a lifetime – sad but true – and I must be the only girl under thirty who can't text. I never learnt and then suddenly I was so far behind I was embarrassed to ask anyone to show me. Mum's the funniest. If she goes on one, she always holds it away from herself and shouts into it when speaking, then presses it to her ear, like she's using a walkie-talkie in a war or something. You keep expecting her to say, 'Over and out, Tango, Bravo.' She calls them portables. 'Have you got your portable with you?'

There was suddenly something so funny and mad about

being on this train and everyone talking to themselves. Voices all up and down the carriage, everyone talking but not to each other. Bet would have been in her element on here. I could imagine her shouting out, 'Hey, speak up a bit down there, love, we're missing it up here,' or 'You tell 'em, mate,' or 'I do hope that's your beloved wife you are speaking to there, sir,' all like that, or standing up and conducting them like they were a mobile-phone choir. They wouldn't know what had hit them, I'm telling you. I felt like going along the seats gently taking their phones and speaking into them, saying, 'I'm going to be a model in Paris by the way' . . . 'Before you ring McAnny and cancel the eleven o'clock, I'm going to be a model in Paris by the way,' or 'Listen, sorry to interrupt but listen missus, after the school run, before you book that restaurant, I'm going to be a model – can you believe it? – by the way! Over and out.'

At the airport I was nervous, I couldn't remember what to do. I hadn't reckoned on this; last time I went abroad was when I was sixteen, with Mark to Spain, and he looked after the passports and all that. I wanted to ask someone what to do, where to go, but I didn't know how to begin explaining. There was no one about anyway except two coppers with guns; I wasn't going near them. I stood in the middle of this vast, silent space, then heard a mobile going off. It was mine, it was my 'quarter-pounder', I pulled it out and answered. It was Rafe, he was checking I'd got off all right and then, you know what, he talked me through what to do, picking up the tickets, over to the check-in, asked me to give the phone to the girl, and he even booked my seat, with leg room and a window, too, by the time he'd finished with her. When I got through to the lounge and he was sure I knew where to board we said goodbye.

'See you in Paree then, Crystalline.'

'See you there,' I said, and I suddenly had such a thrill inside me I couldn't sit down for the next hour. I looked in every electrical-goods, duty-free, golden-wrapped-chocolate, watch- and sock-shop three times but really looked at nothing, just thrilled and thinking of it all. Once I really did pinch meself and it really hurt and I really was there at the airport waiting to fly to Paris to do a model shoot, and I looked at the girls on the front of all the magazines on the shelves or on the big posters or in the jewellers' windows surrounded by glittering diamonds and gold and I thought, I'm one of them, me, we are models, and I ran off again round the shops looking at everything and nothing and nearly lifted off my feet with the thrill. I could have flown to Paris before the plane – and then like a slap and a hundred pricking needles the nerves would kick in and I'd be going cold and looking for the loos and wanting to go home and lie on me bed and grovel me way back into Safeshop and hide among the tills where I belonged.

Waiting to board, I reached into my pocket and took out the card. It couldn't be Mark, I realized that now, it was in a pale violet envelope, unless his mum had got it for him . . . My heart skipped a little beat, but I knew it wasn't really from him. I turned it over, it wasn't even his writing, it just said 'Linda'. I opened it, and it was from the staff at Safeshop! It was a picture of a bear in a bikini, posing on a beach with a little bear taking its picture with an old-fashioned camera on a tripod. They'd got it off the shelf, I'd seen it before, and they'd stuck some of the pictures on the back from the other day, me posing with a bread stick and in front of the bacon shredder. It was funny seeing the store in the background, it still seemed close enough to take me back in a second, like this was just a day off for the dentist and I was back tomorrow. Inside they had all signed it.

'If they need any "Peg" models I'm the one. Good luck, kidda' – Bet

'Get grub down you at all times, don't go thin' – Daf and Flo

'The force be with you' – Bless

'Have a lovely time modelling' – Gwen (Thinnie)

'Lend us a fiver' – Maureen

'Show leg' – Mash

'See you on the telly' – Listereenie

'Fetch me a male model back' – Lucy

'All the best, luv, you deserve it' – Bridget

'Show 'em how it's done' – Shirl

'Tell them about my busters' – Julie

'xx' – (Quiet) Alice

'Well done and good luck' – Melanie

'Take this opportunity and do all you can to succeed' – Mr Thompson

'Go for it' – Jill-One

'*All bodes well*' – Joan

'*Good luck, lovie, and watch the pennies*' – Little Lily
  Lottery

'*Have a wonderful time*' – Jill-Two

'*Don't forget us*' – Ken

'*All the very best in your new career from the Safeshop
  management*' – Geoff

'*We'll all be thinking of you*' – Adam

I felt my eyes pricking and started filling up a bit, then the
seat numbers were called out and I was in a bit of a tiz with all
the cards and tickets and passport and whatnot.

Chapter Nine

PARIS WAS COLD AND BRIGHT AND LIKE IT HAD JUST BEEN
dusted with clean, powdery snow. Fine French cold, even the
sharp winds came at you stylish. All the French dressed for the
cold but, like, fashionably wrapped and jaunty, not bunched
and hunched like back home. The shoot was right in front of
the Eiffel Tower, would you believe? I had a long white silk
dress on and they did my lips really tarty red and, instead of
snow, they were blowing white feathers. I couldn't quite work
out what it was all about, just stood there nervous, waiting
for the camera. Once it started rolling I knew we'd sort it out
between us. Rafe was watching, big black overcoat and black
gloves, banging his hands together, his stack heels leaving neat
little squares in the snow where he walked.

In between shots, they put a big coat around me and gave
me sips of a hot drink, someone even holding it for me! It was
all for me, all around me – make-up ladies, dressers, someone
to brush your hair, someone to straighten your dress. Even

someone to take you to the loo and bring you back, under a brolly just in case any stray snowflake should fall. No one could understand me at all, even the ones who spoke English. They sometimes repeated things back to me as I had said them, in my accent, which was really funny – I never really realized how broad I was before.

Towards the end of the shoot they suddenly released a load of birds around me. At first I thought they were pigeons, but they were doves, beautiful pure white doves all around me and, as they swirled and flew, I turned with them and went like I was going up too. They were all pleased with me, said it was a one-off shot, couldn't have repeated the birds, and what I did spontaneously was superb. Nobody had ever said anything like this to me before. Not at school, work, anywhere. I felt great. And then it was over, everyone hugging and shaking hands and kissing, and I'd loved it. I thought, five thousand quid, and I must have said out loud, 'I'd have done it for nowt,' because one of the girls said, 'Newt?' I said, 'Nowt,' she said, 'Nowt?' I said, 'Nothing,' she said, 'Nothing?' I said, 'No, nowt's nothing,' she said, 'Newt.' I said, 'Not newt, nowt, nowt's nothing.' 'Newt, nowt, nothing?'– and on like that till we cracked up laughing.

And the photographer came over to me, he was an older bloke, and he said, 'I say it again, Crystalline, you were wonderful today, and part of that is what is inside you, your enjoyment of it, your want to communicate that with us. Never forget the thrill of today, your first time. There is a lot of boredom and tediousness and pettiness and frustration in this job, but if you can hold on to the thrill you found in it today you will be happy. Once you let go of the thrill, it's over in a way, no matter how much money you make.' Then he kissed me on both cheeks in the French way, and his lips were nice and hot against my cold cheeks and he said, 'I am honoured to have been the photographer on your virgin job, right here at the foot of the Eiffel Tower, and I know it is the beginnings of something great.'

And then Rafe was there and guiding me away, and the photographer took Rafe's arm from mine and said, 'Look after her well, *monsieur*, handle with real care, she is something special this one, *oui*?', and he shook his hand but they both held each other's eyes for a second too long or something. I didn't really understand it but I sensed there wasn't much love lost between them, and then the photographer was guiding me to the car, he whispered, 'Darling, be careful on the ice,' looked at Rafe and opened the door for me. Then Rafe was there again and the door slammed, and before I knew it we were off and away. And a lot of times things went fast like that with Rafe, you were here and then you were there.

I was still tingling with excitement when I got to the hotel. It was small but really beautiful – Rafe said he chose it for that – built in some old church or something, high stone arches and coloured glass in the windows, ancient wood doors and polished beams, a romantic place. In fact, it felt a bit skewwhiff with age and sort of painstakingly handmade and loved, bit like sleeping in a genuine antique. Rafe just did everything for me, checked in, got someone to carry my bags.

When I opened the room door he'd filled it with flowers. 'Courtesy of the agency,' he said. I was speechless. He didn't wait for a reply, thankfully, just left, saying, 'Pick you up at eight for dinner.' There was a four-poster bed, and it was just flowers upon flowers, everywhere, the wallpaper was flowers and the flowers they'd sent.

I looked out at Paris, just dipping into darkness now, lights twinkling on and off everywhere, and I thought there must be music playing over it all like in a film and, though I knew it would be cold, I opened the window wide to listen, and there wasn't, of course, any music but I still leant out into the beautiful Paris night and it was delicious to be alive, and I shivered not with the cold but with all the delicate rushes of excitement inside, and possibilities, as I waited for the stars to come out.

We had 'tea' – 'dinner' now. We ate overlooking a river. When it came to the menu, of course I had no idea, all I knew in French was *'Frère Jacques, Frère Jacques, sonnez les matines'* from the kids' nursery rhyme. Never knew what it meant but loved the words, *sonnez les matines*. I was that giddy I almost said, 'I'll have some "Sonnez Laymatine"' but I didn't. Anyway Rafe took care of it all, even to nodding his head in the direction of which fork I should use first and all that. The food was gorgeous, everything tasted so beautiful and light. I said to Rafe, 'Every single dish looks like a work of art.' I wondered what old Daf and Flo would make of it.

Rafe said, 'I'll tell you one thing, you don't eat like a model.'

We had champagne, again. I'd only ever had it at weddings before, now it was every other day – I could get used to this. Rafe asked me if I'd fly to London instead of going home, I'd caused quite a bit of press stir and people wanted to meet me. I just nodded yes to everything. I said to him, 'I've got to start believing it's true soon.'

He said, 'It's true all right, we're going to the top,' and he clinked my glass.

Chapter Ten

LONDON. YOU MIGHT NOT BELIEVE IT BUT I'D NEVER BEEN. I was excited. Another five-star hotel. Another breakfast where I had attention. Attention. Waiters bringing me things, taking things, pulling back chairs, pouring tea, asking, 'Is everything all right, madam?' I should think it bloody well is. Where I had always attended, now I was attended upon. At first I kept thinking I should help stack the dishes, carry something to the kitchen, serve someone across the way, but then I relaxed into it, even asking for things, quiet at first but then more confident. 'Could I have a bit more toast, please?' I think they were amazed at what I ate – cereal, two rounds of toast and marmalade, full English and a muffin.

I'd forgot to phone me mum. It seemed days ago, but it was only yesterday. I phoned from my room while I was waiting for Rafe to come and pick me up.

'Mum.'

'Where you been, you little bugger?!'

'Sorry.'

'I've been worried sick. We kept trying your portable but it was switched off.' Then, 'Are you OK, love?'

I told her what had gone on and where I was. She was so quiet, I was not sure if she was crying. 'You crying?'

She went very silent now and I knew she was. When me mum cries the noise goes deeper inwards instead of outwards until she ends up with her eyes closed and her mouth closed, tears running slowly down her cheeks and the deepest quiet you've ever known. You can't see it without bursting into tears yourself, then you make all the noise.

'Why?' I said.

'I don't know.'

Rafe was taken up in the morning so he sorted a car to take me to the agency's office. The offices were modern and bright, I liked them – all curving counters in pastels and light-wood floors, and along the walls were great big black and white pictures of the agency's most beautiful models. I recognized some of them.

The staff were really good-looking themselves. I imagined even the cleaners were tall and stunning, bending on long straight legs to pad up dust with pastel dusters, graceful with grime, gliding down corridors as if they were catwalks, hoovering in perfect unison, in and out of offices like gazelles, model-walking backwards as they mop – a million miles from the old Carcass sisters.

The woman on reception had a walnut whip propped on

the shelf beside her, like it was on an altar. The walnut whip seemed to be on her mind, as it was the first thing she said to me before she said hello.

'The post girl gave it to me for my birthday, isn't that cute? I'll leave it there for a while, then throw it.'

Once I said my name she knew who I was immediately and managed to make asking me to take a seat and wait sound like a heartfelt apology for me having to waste even a second of my precious life.

Suddenly there were other girls coming, trying to look after me – a magazine? drink? – I didn't always catch their names. They seemed to be called things like Narnia and Amtrex and Butane, but that couldn't be right. It was all coming at me so fast. The seats were modern design, curved and bright like those modern baby-bibs. Styrofoamed and stick-legged, they looked like you'd go over if you sat on them. I sat across two to begin with, to be on the safe side, started on the lip and then budged back bit by bit, but they got surprisingly comfortable once you were on. There were a few others waiting; the chairs kept us all upright and pert and bouncing very slightly, like a row of budgies. Butane came for me and said Rafe was ready to see me. She took me through different corridors, very fast like she'd done it many times before, pausing to hold doors, to get through before the swing, banking round corners, belting down the wide corridors, flattening us against the walls to let someone pass, then off again, smiling and nodding to people as we went. It was like being with a *Blue Peter* presenter on a bobsleigh ride. She guided me on with her head and body movements, tapping a certain door with her elbow, holding another open with her toe and fingertip, all the time talking to me nice, and then she pushed open the door of an office, said my name and vanished. She was the first of many Butanes over the next few days. For a while at the beginning I remembered them all distinctly but after a bit, it's horrible to say, but they all turned into one.

It took Rafe a while to register I was there in the doorway. He was preoccupied, banging things about a bit. He looked little and stroppy, and he was mumbling – first time I'd heard him mumbling in Scottish. There was rage in the room, you could feel it, but it felt like it was pressed under the papers and files and pushing at the windowpanes to get out. When he saw it was me he changed, but I could see his knuckles were white from clenching his fists. I'd never noticed before, they were badly scarred, like they'd been burnt or something. He smiled, it was a big one, but still that smile without the eyes. He indicated for me to sit, and looked up the corridor before he closed the door, as though what had upset him had gone that way. I sat in the chair and sank about six foot into it; there was certainly never a dull moment with the furniture round here. Rafe looked about ten feet tall. Even when he sat on his desk chair he seemed way above me, spinning slightly, then I noticed he had it cranked right to the top, his feet dangling down like a kid's, his toes barely touching the floor as he swivelled. He went through our itinerary. The press were to come this morning, then we'd do a few photographs.

When the reporters came in, Rafe sat right up in the

corner like a black cat. He looked ready to spring if anything out of order was said. There were two of them, one came in after the other, both really really nice. I was shy, but they didn't seem to mind. At the end one of them said, 'It's refreshing to talk to a model who's not pouting all over the place or mumbling into her hair or talking on her mobile every five seconds, or sulking or blowing cigarette smoke all over me.'

The other said, 'You are fresh, fresh – I mean it, really fresh and funny. You are going to go far.'

Rafe said nothing. His face never altered but his black eyes twinkled.

They'd arranged next to take some press pictures outside on location somewhere. As we came through and into reception, another Butane running before us, one of the girls was fixing my big black and white on the wall. Everyone applauded. I blushed – it was like one of the old blushes, blood in a mad rush, burning mad hot, felt like it lifted my hair up about half an inch above my head and burnt it to bracken – but it was lovely to see my picture going up like that, like I'd been accepted and promoted and given a certificate of merit all at once. Then as we passed the reception desk, I saw the woman there sobbing. A couple of people were around her but she was inconsolable. She had eaten the walnut whip. 'I thought, I'm just going for the walnut. There's no calories in that, is there?'

'There's fat,' someone said.

'Is there, oh my God!' It was like she'd been shot. 'Anyway, it came off with some of the chocolate. I got the taste of it and then I saw the white cream, inside, and that was it. I . . . Oh it's all gone, it's all gone. That bitch for giving it to me, bloody bloody bitch!'

As we passed, Rafe stopped and said something to her. I was too far ahead to catch it, but there was no crying after that.

When I was walking up the street with Rafe and the reporter someone stopped me for an autograph. She said, 'I don't know who you are or where you are from, but you look like you are going to be something soon.' You start to think, like, how could I have passed through the streets for years and no one's noticed me before?

The pictures were taken – guess where? Round the corner in a supermarket! They put me behind a till but in glamour clothes. It was weird to be at the till again, everything in me went automatically back into serving mode. I did a bit accidentally and everyone laughed and laughed. I didn't know why so I laughed with them. Later, the papers went a bit mad: 'Supermarket Supermodel' – hey! that was Daf and Flo's line. Never mind. But before that something else happened.

I awoke to the phone ringing. I grabbed it, it smelled of Milky Ways and Turkish Delight – no, that was my breath, too much champagne. Has my tongue turned into chocolate? I was thinking, half in and half out of a dream. It was Rafe, excited, almost in Scottish again. I turned to the clock instinctively, half thinking it was time for work, it was 4 a.m.

'*Trudy!*'

'Uh??'

'Crystalline?'

'Yeah.'

'*Trudy!* Listen, we're going on *Trudy!* Good-morning telly.'

I couldn't think what to say, so I said, 'My mum's favourite.'

'They want you on.'

'Me?'

'Yes!'

'When?'

'Now!'

I sat up on the side of the bed at that.

'They've just been on. There's been a cancellation. If we can get there by six we've got a slot.'

'Oh.'

'I'll swing by and pick you up in half an hour.'

Then he'd gone, left me stumbling in the dark towards the bathroom. I flicked the switch in there and about three thousand tiny lights came on and shot me awake, lights off the marble, off the mirrors; there seemed to be little lights above the lights to light the lights. Sunken bath and a jacuzzi, the toilet paper folded to a perfect triangle, it was all a bit different from running down our stairs in the dark to dress in front of the fire. In fact, I sometimes used to watch *Trudy Time* while I was having my cornflakes and, now I was going to be on it, the thought of this and the trillion lights made everything seem like a dream again.

Even though it was, like, the middle of the night, I thought I'd better phone Mum. She'd kill me if I didn't tell her I was on *Trudy Time*. I tried but it was engaged. At this time?, I thought. She must have knocked it off the hook, she'd done that many times before. I phoned my sister but she wasn't answering, I think she pulls the plug some nights, so she can sleep in, if the baby's been keeping them awake. But I felt a bit angry with them both, like they weren't supporting me in my hour of need on *Trudy*.

We didn't speak much in the car as we drove through empty London streets. I had the quiet of the not-quite awake, he had the maniac quiet of the not-slept.

Next thing I knew, I was in a dressing room, there was a knock on the door. I thought it must be Rafe coming back – he'd gone to get coffees – but it was Trudy herself, she'd come to say hello. I froze up, think I might have been shaking a bit. When you suddenly see people you know from the television it's so strange, I can't describe it proper, it's like two things happen at the same time, 1. it's like they've just climbed out of the telly and aren't real and in a little while must return to Tellyland and 2. it's like you know them really well and somehow share a secret. She was very nice, and so smart, never seen someone so smart of a morning, such a 'clean frontage', as me mum would say – 'I like a telly presenter with a clean frontage.' She could see I was nervous and just kept me talking. I don't know how she did it but she sort of chatted all my nerves out of me. Someone came for her, or I felt she would have stayed longer, she said, 'See you later then,' and it was like I was just going to her house in a bit for tea. Rafe came back and then soon after a girl with a clipboard, bit flustered, bit nervous this Butane, more nervous than me, which kept me calm in a way. I followed her, Rafe clacking after us in his heels. I think it was a bit embarrassing for him, the corridor being so echoing. It was long and straight and seemed to go on for ever, then suddenly the girl stopped and we all almost went into the back of her in a pile-up. She put her finger to her lips and then opened a door in the wall; she had a bit of trouble with it, she didn't know where to tuck the clipboard and kept trying to do it with one hand. The door was very heavy, I had to help. Rafe was coming through too but she indicated that he had to stay there. It was like leaving your dad at the school gates. Then we went through another door, and I was being walked through these narrow flats and wood walls and then it was like being given a soft and gentle shove out of a plane and I was 'on'. Trudy smiled, patted the chair, I sat just as the camera swung round. What surprised me was how intimate it felt – in front of all those people working in the studio, then all of those millions of people watching, it felt the most intimate I'd ever been. More like a chinwag than an interview. Just the two of us in a bright bright room surrounded by darkness. I don't know what I said. I'd had a few things in my head and Rafe had told me some things to say but in the end I just said what I said and it all seemed to all go all right. She laughed out loud sometimes, and then it was over.

Afterwards her eyes were bright and she said, 'Well done' and 'Come again' and 'You'll have no worries' and things like that, and the girl with the clipboard who'd brought me on kept saying, 'Well done' too, as we went back to the dressing rooms, but she took me off the wrong way, out the front and into the darkness, and we had to hop and sidestep shadowy shapes and shadows moving to avoid us and stumble over cables as big as boa constrictors. I glanced back and saw Trudy in her square of light, then we were back again into the blackness and softly tripping around the rolling cameras and the silent shifting folk until we reached a door. It was like a submarine door, this one, and we fought with it for a minute or two before we were out in the corridor blinking like moles in its spanking-bright light. Rafe was waiting and slightly grinning, he just gave me a wink. Then he guided me into the dressing room, sat me down and went back into the corridor, took the Butane to one side, took her to one side and bollocked her, he bollocked in whispers – that was the scary thing with Rafe, I learnt later, he bollocked in whispers. Much worse than shouting. I wanted to say it was all all right and not to bother but when I stood up he just looked at me and quietly shut the door on them.

Trudy popped her head in just before I left. She gave me some advice about handling the fame and said for me to give her a call if I ever needed a chat. I thought she was just saying that, but her assistant came in later and gave me her home number. I couldn't believe it. Rafe took it for safe keeping. There was a winter sun coming through the glass of the building as we left, I didn't feel tired at all now. Just as well – Rafe had arranged a 'brunch' meeting with a designer he wanted me to meet.

Chapter Eleven

WE ARRIVED AT THIS FANCY RESTAURANT. IT WAS A REALLY large place, high ceilings, polished wood floors, big old-fashioned windows to the street. The designer was at a table in the corner, she was only young and seemed to have an old lady's hat on and blusher on both cheeks almost in perfect red circles like Pinocchio. She crackled with energy. We both jumped when we shook hands, like we'd had a nice shock. Rafe had told me she was tipped as the new up-and-coming one to watch – 'Like you,' he said. She was called Lucy, the name of my favourite doll when I was a kid.

'Hello, been dying to meet you, what do you make of it all? Fashionland. False sods, aren't they, most of them? Take today. I've already had a pre-breakfast, a bit of a brekky and a breakfast meeting before this, would you believe, and at every one they've gone mad over my hat. One tosser was even trying to place an order, but I got it off a bag lady in the street this morning, gave her a quid for it. Keep that to yourself. Daft, isn't it? See, I'm flavour of the month right now; if I cut two corners off the cover of an Argos catalogue and sellotaped one over each nipple they'd be interested in it – "What a statement!" "Such verve!" "Oh, darling, we'll take one hundred" – but next month they'll be skinning me alive and spitting on my bones. It's a vicious jungle in Glad Rags.'

Rafe didn't look that pleased. It was the first time I had heard any talk like this.

'Shake 'em up, dear, make mischief, it's the only way to stay sodding sane.'

'As you can see, our Lucy's a bit of a rebel,' Rafe said, trying to finish the conversation by reaching for the menus.

I didn't know what to make of it at all. I liked her immediately, I felt she thought the same about me. She had a really sweet little voice that sort of fluttered and dipped all around us and then swooped in with a sting. 'Take it all with a pinch, love, it's a puke circus' – stuff like that. She was fascinating too, talking about her own life. 'Really and truly I gave the old tramp a twenty note for her hat, I always give when I pass the homeless. I lived rough meself when I first came to London, slept in a cardboard box. Best-dressed box in London, mind! It had curtains and cushions and candles everywhere. It was like an Arabian tent in the end. Amazing what you can find in the bins behind Harvey Nics. Bloody blew away two days later.'

Rafe was doing his best to steer the conversation to something else at every turn.

'What's up, Rafe dearest, afraid I might spike your new

protégée with too much truth and bitters? Don't worry, I like her too much for that but, listen, every pack must carry a health warning. Linda dear, take note: "Fashionland can seriously damage your health."' Then she whispered to me, 'They're not too keen on the sweet little acid drops I let slip, but I don't care.' She laughed, and her hat nearly fell off. 'They've got to put up with me for the moment, I'm too good a bet.'

Rafe still wasn't smiling.

'You're almost too fresh though, they'll have you if you're not careful – heed, dear, heed – have your sweet little pink guts for fancy garters, take it from me. I've seen too many Barbies melt in the fire. God, listen to me, I sound like an ancient old hag, and there's not much in our ages. How jaded, and how quick I've got that way. Don't take me too seriously, love. It's part of the act, the survival mechanism. You enjoy yourself.' She put her hand on mine. 'But you're great, you really are, please don't let the buggers grind you down.'

I didn't know what she meant, but she smiled then and I smiled back, and the lovely food came swirling in right then, and then it was cloths unfolded and cutlery picked up and we all went silent for a while. All this grandeur and it was only dinner – no, sorry, 'lunch', no, brunch. In my old life, lunch was just something grabbed, a quick butty or some fast meal from the canteen, on the plate but still cooking from the microwave, with a shovel of oven chips down the side.

I looked around, again in disbelief, the place was so beautiful, deep dark wood everywhere, full of light from the sun outside, and it was packed. The waiters seemed to be on tiptoe at your table then on silent rollerskates when they left, long white aprons, long white aprons and all you could hear was the gentle tupping of cups and saucers and the occasional cough. Suddenly a mobile phone went off. It was like a siren in there. No one answered it. To my horror I realized it was the quarter-pounder. I couldn't pull it out in here. But I had no choice. Everyone had stopped eating and seemed to be looking at me. I was angry when I answered it.

'Yes!'

It was our Dawn. 'It's me.'

'Yes?'

She was a bit taken aback by my response. 'Mum's ill.'

'What?'

All at once I was out of the world of the restaurant and back with my tribe. My accent got even thicker, I could hear nothing but me sister. 'She's in hospital.'

'When?'

'Early hours of the morning. It's the same trouble, she's not been good for a while now but she wouldn't tell you. It's complicated what's up with her, doctor explained but I don't really understand it. I'm seeing to the kids then I'm going over there.'

'I'll be straight home.'

'I think it's best.'

I turned the phone off and was back in the restaurant. The juxtaposition of worlds hit me hard in the teeth and it was strange, a bit shocking.

Rafe said, 'Anything the matter?'

'My mum. My mum – she's not well. I better get back.'

'Now?'

'I better.'

I was in the hotel room packing. I kept missing things or putting things in then taking them out, couldn't stop thinking about Mum, little in the hospital, legs only halfway down the bed, her faded pink-rose nightie on, no doubt, her lopsided slippers probably still at home on their own, in front of her chair. There was a knock at the door.

'It's me, Rafe. Is it all right to come in?'

I let him in.

'Packing?' he said.

'Trying.'

'Do you know the train times?'

'No, I just thought I'd go there and get one.'

Rafe walked over to the window. 'I don't want you to go.' He didn't look at me, he was looking out the window. 'There's so much happening and so fast.' He took a piece of paper out of his pocket. 'I've got all the details of the hospital, the ward. I managed to speak to a doctor – I had to become your brother, I'm afraid.'

For the first time I felt a surge of something, I don't know if it was anger, more like shock. Surely this was none of his business.

'I've satisfied myself she's fine but I want you to ring and speak to her. I want you to feel all right.'

He held the piece of paper out to me and, before I knew it, I had taken it and was doing what I had been told.

I got through to a nurse. 'Oh, we know who you are, you're Crystalline, you're Mrs Longbottom's girl. She's got all your press cuttings by her bed.'

I blushed and my heart span. I spoke to me mum. She said she was all right, she made out that Dawn was making more of it than it was. 'You know Dawn, she's always dramatical.' She said she would be out soon. She reassured me, said I was to carry on. All she really wanted to know was what Trudy was like.

At the airport I got a call, it was Dawn. She just shouted, 'Do what you like!'

Chapter Twelve

IBIZA WAS FIRST, THEN IT WAS NON-STOP. MONACO, MILAN, we were everywhere. Rafe bought me some new luggage and a new mobile – the poor old quarter-pounder just didn't sit right no more in me Mulberry bag. We gave it a grand good-bye, toasted it at twilight on the beach at Nice then threw it into the sea. What a journey it had made, what a spladoosh it made. Rafe said it was probably registering right now on French Navy scanners as a major landmine. Then I suddenly panicked – I had all my old friends' numbers on there, even Mark's. Rafe said not to worry, I could get them again, but somehow I knew I wouldn't.

I say he got me a new phone, but I didn't hardly see it, he started taking calls for me. Sounds funny but I must admit it did seem easier. He just related things to me at the end of the day; most of it was stuff he needed to sort out anyway. Only thing was I didn't get to speak to my family much, though he kept me up to scratch; Mum was loads better but her operation was going to be brought forward. I asked Rafe to send her a cheque. I didn't know how much money I was making, earning; he said he'd look after it for me.

I was meeting models from all over the world. I felt a bit funny over my accent again. Rafe wanted me to change it at first; I think he dreaded me opening my mouth at times, he'd often answer for me. You know the type of thing:

'How are you liking Rome, Crystalline?'

'Oh, she's getting used to it.'

But when he saw how the press liked how I talked – 'Beguiling, utterly beguiling. *Coronation Street* Crystalline, a pure crystal on a cobblestone', all that – he changed his mind. Rafe had changed his own accent, Scottish, the hardest to change, but he'd done it, forged it how he wanted it with anvil mouth, iron tongue and teeth and throat, wrestled it down, forced it right. Scottish was held back now with jaws of steel, sometimes slipping out here and there like a wild scotchy sprite when he lost his temper or was very sleepy or excited.

Party time was great at first. It was 'You *shall* go to the ball.' Rafe would bring a dress around for me, a beautiful designer creation. I don't know where he got them but they'd be gone in the morning. I said to someone, 'He's my Scottish fairy godmother' and they replied, 'I get the feeling if the prince came round tomorrow, he'd smash the glass slipper and shove it in his face.'

Italy was, for me, where the parties really began, in clubs, on yachts, rooftops, houses – some as big as Safeshop, I swear.

Everything was there. When I say everything I mean drinks, drugs. I only had a glass or two of champagne, stayed away from the rest. I didn't have much choice anyway with Rafe. He wouldn't have let me, he touched nothing. He was like stone where that was concerned. His guiding hands were getting even stronger, they always seemed to be there, moving me to different parts of the room, or out of the door, into a car, a slap on the car roof, 'Take her to the hotel,' and I was gone.

I think the others thought I was mad, I was always leaving just after midnight. Someone would say, 'You're not leaving already?' I'd say, 'Me back's aching from all that standing,' and they'd look dumbfounded and then laugh, and I'd look back and sometimes see the other girls, the ones who weren't completely out of it, watching me in a sort of disbelief. I couldn't understand it, I didn't cotton on, though later I did.

The driver we had in Italy was gorgeous, long black hair; you'd have thought he could be a model. Olive skin and flashing eyes, he shot us up and down those narrow roads, gunning the gears, you couldn't breathe for the length of a street sometimes, but I loved it, bouncing us off the seats, taking the corners, scattering chickens and stall-holders and tourists before us. Taking us up steep, steep, tight cobbled streets at night, bombing under white sheets on the line, fresh and blue in the moonlight, one set, two sets, then there it was, rocking before us, between two houses, a dark Italian deep black-blue sky – 'Elvis-hair blue,' me mum would have called it – with a thousand stars all walled in between two buildings, thought we were going to take off up and into it like a Disney ride. But before you could gasp he cut off into another road just about the width of the car, sparking off the bricks at times, taking us down, down, down, our noses almost on the windscreen, twisting down somewhere, black at the bottom, no lights, and that's how it was.

I remember one party in particular. The driver dropped Rafe and me by the sea. When I say dropped, of course it nearly was, right into the sea. He came to a speeding, lurching halt, just braking, with the front tyres half over the harbour side. That long-suffering little car took about half a minute to settle back on its wheels, I'm telling you, it was touch and go, touch and go.

Then it was down the harbour steps and into a waiting dinghy. You couldn't see hardly anything except the yacht out at sea, white and gold with light, glowing. The dinghy had a motor on it and we took off toward the yacht. Till you got used to it, it was a bit like being on a sloppy mattress. Let's put it this way, I wouldn't have liked to have been coming back on it bladdered. The sea was blacker than the sky, and the sky felt close and cool about us, thrilling, exciting, like the sensation in a theatre, in the black-out just before a show begins. The bloke driving had a little peaked white and gold kind of captain's cap on and this was all I could see for a bit, till me eyes could make things out.

Then we entered the shining beam of light from the yacht. It stretched across the water in gold, a swaying pathway on the sea, each wave seemed to cup and carry its own bit of the light. I felt so overexcited in meself and sort of light-footed, I felt I could have ran right along it and up to the yacht.

We climbed aboard. At first everything looked like it does when you've got tears in your eyes, glistening at each corner point, hazy, dreamt, glazed, slowed down. Then it got really sharp and bright as a diamond, everything in detail, right down to the stitching on the gold épaulettes of the waiters' white white coats. Lights were strung everywhere, lights swinging below lights swinging below lights that were swinging below lights, and lights lighting up lights all around them, and it was reflected off the silver rails and off the shining deck which was like a wooden mirror.

A ship full of beautiful people and beautiful things. Models everywhere, groups of people looking like they were just about to be photographed or had just been photographed. I'm trying to say what it was like but it was really like a dream. Sometimes bits of life are like that and this was one.

Those crisp waiters were everywhere and, on trays aloft, champagne still frothing at the glass top, food too, passed before you, food that's on your tongue and off again, gone like sizzled ice, food that's just flavour really, no need to bite. Posh nosh, 'invisible food', I called it, or food laid out on silver platters looking like a jewellery collection. I must say I longed for a Safeshop canteen chip butty. You bring a chip butty on here, every model would have closed her eyes or fainted over, her mini-stomach cowering behind her liver in fear. Someone would have wrestled it out of your hands and got it overboard and safely into the mouths of the sharks.

We weren't on two minutes when someone offered me drugs. Drugs, drugs everywhere and not a drop to drink – that's not true, there was plenty to drink and that was going down too, but not like the white powder. Models, fields of 'em swaying back and forth and then forward to sniff it up off glass tables or sink-tops or the back of some bloke's hand. Them short sniffs, I can hear them now. You could hear it when you were in the loo sometimes, like the snorts of long, thin pigs. Pills going down, pills going down with champagne. I stayed away. Wealth was there, vast wealth too. You know it when it is, you can physically feel it, makes the air kind of lazy and swaying somehow, and it's like everything and everyone's been cleaned twice, and of course the diamonds are bigger. Besides drugs, besides invisible food, besides drink, sex was also always there, beneath the party like a warming plate.

Tonight we drank more, talked more, met more people. Rafe seemed a lot freer but preoccupied. I was getting tipsy – no, drunk, I was drunk. I looked out into the dark, then back to the light, soft dark to bright light, soft dark to bright light. I thought, you could end up overboard this way, drawn up into the sky, turned in velvet blue-black Elvis hair then gently rolled under the sea. Then thinking how the hell am I going to make it back on that bloody wobbling dinghy thingy. I thought of all these models in their long flowing dresses, all them fine fine fabrics billowing up in beautiful colours, slipping off the dinghy and away, spreading out on the waves like sleeping mermaids.

In the early hours of the morning I noticed girls disappearing with the men. So that was it – no wonder the girls had thought me green, leaving so early. It was the sex game, body contracts being drawn up in dark rooms; careers developed that way, smoozled along. Anyway, I was having none of it.

Later, my empty glass was being filled by a handsome man in his fifties, white hair. I recognized him, he was the one the girls called the Vixen, this was his yacht. He smiled, said a few things, I was too gone to really hear him. Then, funny how it happened, it was like someone had just passed him the salt, there was nothing to it, and I was holding his hand going toward his cabin. He was the richest most powerful man aboard. I saw a group of girls gasp as we passed, astonished probably that the little green Northern lass should be going to the Vixen's lair. Even Rafe was nowhere in sight, or had he known? Made himself scarce deliberately? Turned a blind eye where the Vixen was concerned?

He didn't speak much, started kissing me, so delicate. I'd been used to snogging only, full-on round and rounds, tongues in a bit later, all that. Kissing you do outside the nightclub, at the bus stop. This was something else. He went so softly across my face, my ears – never had them kissed in my life. The kisses seemed to get softer and softer, sometimes so gentle it was just the touch of his breath I felt. At one time he breathed only at a place on my neck for about five minutes. The intensity grew and grew, I couldn't believe it, I was so wet down there just from this. Mark would have been all over by now and we'd be lying back looking at the ceiling. There was no rush from the Vixen, everything slow, soft as silk shifting. But I can't describe it, it was powerful too, sort of possessing. Me clothes, they seemed to shed themselves. I was arching and moving me body to get them off sooner. It wasn't like me, but it was like his hands, his mouth, everything working together. I had given meself up to it. I don't remember how he touched me breast for example, nothing he did seemed separate from anything else. Mark gave them a good feel and squeeze, then moved on almost by rote, but this was part of the whole thing, like a symphony, symphony of sensation. He kissed me down there, and kept collecting the moisture from me in his mouth and scooping it all back into me, tipping it back. It smacked and almost burnt a little, the mixture of us. It was heavenly though, unbearable and irresistible in the same moment. I was hot, I was trembling, he didn't seem to want me to do anything to him. Mark used to wait while I had a go at him, or he might put my hand places, but the Vixen never thought of himself, or was that in a way his pleasure? He was a long time in the air poised above me before he entered. I was arching, arching up towards him, but he waited, waited, then it was all so soft, so easy, again not separate, like he fell into me, and then we fell together, and we were falling, falling, until he caught me up and then started moving. His strokes were all different, in a little then out, then long and full like I was an instrument he was playing – not that I felt used, no, the opposite, valued beyond description, valued, really valued, I'd never felt like that with a man before. Mark was always just in and out in and out faster and faster then over, I could never catch up with him. There was the odd time I thought something was going to happen to me but I got fed up of never going beyond so gave up on it. There was pleasure in what we did but nothing, nothing like this. Soon I was calling out things, making noises, I couldn't help it, I'd never done that before, slipping, rising toward something, I couldn't stop, no way now, on into it, building and spinning and swirling and building, gathering tight then releasing, then tight, then the releasing was less, the releasing less, less, less releasing and tighter, tighter, tighter then off over into a sweet explosion of all the sugars off me, off him, and oh, all the sugar off me off him, him, him. Opening loops of pleasure passing beyond me, I'd gone, and around the room, I'd gone. My eyes were burning, such sweet and reaching pleasure I was crying and my heart just kept opening opening in wider softer swooping loops of lovely pleasure. I held on tight to him, for a long time, he was still inside me, then I let go and lay back on the bed. He didn't finish there but kept on nestling into me, soft kisses but longer time between them now, decreasing in pressure till they stopped, then he took me in his arms. I must have fallen asleep. At one point I sensed him tucking me in – no, that's too strong a word, placing sheets around me, that was it, placing sheets so tenderly around me, like I was something so beautiful, so precious and special. I'd never felt that way. When I woke he had gone, a single flower was there. I went out. I don't know what time it was, it looked like the sun had just come up. The yacht was in dock. A few stragglers were still on deck. At the harbour leaning on his car was our driver, he glanced up when he saw me, beckoned to me and started up the engine. He must have took me to the hotel. I don't remember. You don't remember much when you're floating above the city on a cloud.

We were off to Florence the next day. I asked Rafe about the Vixen but he was silent. I asked some of the girls where he might be, they didn't know, or weren't saying. When we passed the harbour the Vixen's yacht had gone. I thought I saw it in the distance. I said a soft thank you; I've still got that flower somewhere.

After that it was like something had been unlocked, and my sexual self was out. Why not? Everyone else was at it; I thought of Betty and the Beano. Next thing I knew I was up an alley with the boy driver, not the one from Italy but a similar one in Spain. No words, shared a cigarette afterwards, then nod of his head and back in the car. It was different than with the Vixen, exciting though. Everything up for grabs, ancient stone wall scraping me back, young bodies going mad, both of us wet with sweat, his long black fringe over his face, climbing up each other.

I started drinking more. Trying everything – brandy, even beer, and always the champagne underneath everything else, frothing it all up.

I remember a line of us models all swaying at a yacht rail or a rail above a beach or in a club or somewhere, absolutely and utterly and completely sozzled, laughing and laughing and laughing, all about a second away from throwing up. For me, I don't know if it was about fun or about getting away somehow from those strong hands always on my back.

Those hands were beginning to fill me with dread, I was getting so I couldn't stand their touch, couldn't stand them guiding me out the hotel at four thirty in a morning for the next shoot, up the stairs to the plane for the next flight, or while I was walking and at the same time talking into a mobile to some journalist in England, saying the things he'd told me to say or else I felt the hand shift ever so slightly. It had got stronger, the hand, strong so as you felt it could break bones, through clothes and through flesh. I remember there was a time when it made me feel safe but now the more it pressed the more I wanted to twist away from it and run back to the party or back into my hotel room or off over the airport tarmac and back to me mum, me mum, me mum.

Rafe began a campaign, unspoken, to cut my drinking in the bud – 'Half a glass for the young lady, thank you,' 'She'll have an orange juice, if that's all right,' slipping stuff in like that – but he didn't know there was a quarter bottle in my holdall. But when I got back to my room it was, of course, gone.

I very rarely got to speak to home now; Dawn had stopped speaking to me anyway. The last time I rang I heard a horrible thing. Mark had been putting up a massive advert on one wall of the discount store. It was an awkward, dangerous job, but they eventually got it up. When he came down the ladder and stepped back to look he saw that it was a twenty-five-foot picture of me in my underwear. I hear it absolutely devastated him. I didn't like to think of that.

I was starting to lose track of time. My old life had been so routine; now I seemed to be carried along, no day was the same, the jobs just lined up one after another, different places, countries, locations – it began to become a blur. It was an exciting blur at first but at times I forgot where I was and genuinely didn't know what day of the week it was. I know some of the girls crossed the Atlantic three times in four days; not me yet but I could be in two cities in England and one in Europe in that time.

I started one week on a shoot on a demolition site – freezing, wind, hard hats and fancy dresses, walls going down behind us; they wanted that action in the back. It was so loud though, it took a while to stop wincing and covering our ears and be still for the camera. It looked good in the magazine though. They blurred the background in the spread; with us in the foreground it was very dramatic. It was hard to know that when you were in the middle of it all and oh, the noise. Rafe came over at one point to try and give me a message, but it was just too noisy. Days later, rushing for a plane, late, noise again, going up the steps, the engines were going and Rafe mentioned the message again, shouting it, his voice taken, 'That message the other day . . . Your mother's operation's been brought forward. It's on the tenth now.' I took it in, still sounded a while off.

*   *   *

A few nights later, in a hotel, in Poland, very late – I was in bed – I turned the light out. The clock by the bed had red lights, giving you the time, the temperature, the date. The thirteenth. I was almost asleep when it hit me again – the thirteenth! I didn't know what to do, I had missed the operation. What should I do? Was it too late to phone? It was. I'd noticed I was getting so I didn't know what to do in situations any more, I was getting so I couldn't do things, others did everything for me. When I did try it was, like, inept and then like sort of reaching into nothingness waiting for it to be taken out of my hands. I didn't like this feeling, after being so independent at home, but this was even worse – early hours of the morning, in a foreign hotel, unable to speak the language. I didn't want to phone Rafe; in a sort of way I blamed him. He always treated messages from home as trivial; anything not to do with modelling was not important to him. Even if I called him with this he'd tell me to go to sleep. But in our family this was the most major event, bigger than anything. It'd been ringed on the calendar, talked about, worried about, over me mum's head like a dark cloud; it was bigger to me now than anything.

I panicked. I went downstairs and found the clerk, he could hardly speak English. I just started crying. He managed to get the address of the hospital out of me, he arranged for flowers to be delivered in the morning, somehow – Internet, I don't remember – all I remember is I kissed him and piled up all the foreign currency I had on the desk.

The next morning, first thing, I phoned the hospital, but

she wasn't there. The flowers must have tripped down the ward to an empty bed. The woman on the phone told me the operation had been successful and she had discharged herself early. I phoned home, no one answered, and it was engaged constantly at our Dawn's.

That morning's shoot was at the seaside, over rocks. It was a dull and cloudy day with a wind, which is what they wanted. I tried to get my phone off Rafe, but every time I went for him he wasn't around. I tell you he seemed to know when I was after that phone; it was impossible to prise it away from him. I quickly gave up. In desperation I turned to the first person who passed. She was one of the team working on the shoot, she couldn't speak English, I don't think she understood a word I said but she saw I was close to tears and she understood my phone mime. I took off with the phone to the rocks.

I got through to Dawn's house; it was her husband, Ronnie, he seemed pleased to hear from me. He had never bothered with me before, now he was talking away. I had the sense I'd had before when people treated you different because you were famous.

Then I heard Dawn's voice. 'Is that her? Never mind all that, never mind how's bloody Poland! Give it here.'

My heart leapt into my mouth, Dawn on the rampage was a terrible thing. Dawn was great at ding-dongs, I was never very good at them. In the second before she spoke I watched the sea crash against the rocks. It belted all over the place and a white bird seemed flung across the sky. Down the phone I heard a child crying in the background and the telly on. It suddenly struck me, the two completely different worlds we were in, and then she was there.

'Right, you, right, you, you've got a nerve, ain't you, eh! It's all a bit late now, init? You don't ring! You don't even send a card! Nothing, nowt. You think you're above us now, do you, eh? Us and our little lives, eh? You're above us!'

'No . . .'

'We don't matter to you any more.'

'That's not true.'

'I phoned loads of times, loads.'

'Rafe only told me once, I—'

'Don't bloody hide behind him, lady. It was touch and ruddy go for a while.'

'I didn't know.'

'No you didn't. Anyway, this is it, we're finished with you.'

'I wanna speak to Mum.'

'Well, she don't wanna speak to you, do you, Mum?'

And this is where my heart snapped in two. I heard my mum's voice. Quiet. Distant, weary with pain. I heard it and she said . . . 'No.'

'OK, now. Well, goodbye and good riddance.'

The sea hit the rock, hit it hard and went up high, high as me, and fell into the gullies between the rocks, all its mightiness gone, low and slow and trickling back into the sea. Oh Mum. Mum.

It was like I was in a trance for the rest of the shoot – ask me what we did and I couldn't tell you, the same the next day. I know I was on a plane or two, that's all, and I know I drank and I know I drank and drank the planes and hotels and mini-bars dry dry dry. I didn't want to leave too much of a gap for real life to peek in.

I'd come to a standstill somewhere inside, but Rafe was as full on as ever with my career. I was still in the press – stories, photos – and we were still in demand, I never stopped working. Rafe now had America in his sights, or 'Yankee doodle land' as my gran always called it. He decided to clean me up and tightened his regime around me even further. He started to dictate my meal times, what time I went to bed, everything. I wasn't quite as malleable as when we first met, and he was having to watch me full time. I think it became a bit much for him, handling my career, the agency and me. So he moved me in with an ex-lover of his. He sold it to me like we were going to be flatmates but we both knew her job was to get me in shape and to keep tabs on me.

Chapter Thirteen

SUZE DIMPLE LIVED IN A FLAT IN FULHAM. RAFE DROPPED ME off there one day with my bags and left us alone together. It was a nice flat but it smelled like a vegetarian restaurant, and it was all white mainly, except for on the living-room floor, where there was a big blue ball smack in the middle, gently rolling in the breeze from the open window. Suze was friendly enough, smiling and all that in that positive-thinkers kind of way like the psychology experts they have on discussion shows, but I felt scared and under pressure. I think she did, too, if the truth be known. She showed me my room then asked me to join her in the kitchen for a chamomile tea. I sat in the room. It was only small, a boxroom, nicely done and that, bit cold – in design, I mean, though it was cold because the window was open, too. I learnt later that the windows were open what-ever the weather. I got up to close it and caught a glimpse of the view from the window, behind the lace curtains. It was a brick wall. I sat on the bed feeling like a prisoner already.

Suze was about forty-five. It turned out she was a Pilates instructor and life coach. She was coach to a *Breakfast TV* star and a few others who were well known; seems she made a good living. She didn't look too bad, but she looked her age, taut though. Taut, strong body, but the tautness was right deep inside her somehow, and you felt that was what pulled tight her skin and bones, more than any exercise. She had a scar just under her cheekbone in the shape of a diamond. She was always moving her head to angles where you couldn't see it. It was like years of doing this had made it automatic.

We sort of moved politely around each other, but I knew orders were coming down from on high – particularly when she suggested I let her train me, no charge, it would help with the standing on shoots and all that. She was really choosing her words carefully, not wanting to offend but wanting to persuade me and, perhaps more importantly, not to fail Rafe. Anyway, she must have done a good job because I agreed to have a go.

I've never been much good at exercise, probably partly 'cause I've always been slim and never needed it. I went to an aerobics class once with my little mum, absolutely packed solid it was, you couldn't hardly see the instructor. 'Step,' they called it. You had to step up and down on these plastic steps while the instructor shouted at you over loud music. Mum was there at the beginning, lifting and laying out the steps for everyone, you know what she's like – probably got a better work-out doing that than the class. It was boring as hell. The only interesting bit was, with my mum being so small, she got her foot stuck under the step. The instructor kept shouting, 'And up and up, come on at the back there,' and Mum was trying her best, going up on one leg and trying to shake her leg free at the same time. Some of the people behind her who couldn't see the instructor thought that was the exercise and started copying her. The instructor was calling out one thing and half the class was doing this strange twisting step shuffle, and the louder the instructor shouted the more frantically me mum tried to shake free and the more the rest followed. It was hilarious, particularly watching the instructor almost pulling her hair out in confusion. After a bit me mum said, 'Oh sod this for a box of soldiers,' and shook the step off, and all those behind her did the same, all these steps flying all over the place. I rushed her out quickly; we never went again.

I told Suze this story but she didn't get it, kept going on about how it could have led to permanent hip damage for my mother and the other members of the class, all that. After about five minutes of this I was quickly wishing I'd never said anything. Anyway, we started with her exercises; I was pretty pathetic at it, as always. It was stretch this, hold that, all the usual, until she led me over to the blue ball. You are s'posed to bend all over it and that but I just kept rolling off. She kept putting me back on and I was off the other side. Eventually she gave up and we had another chamomile tea.

She racked her brains, she didn't know what to do with me. I could see she was panicking a bit; she'd been given her mission and she wasn't seeing it through. She asked me was there any exercise I liked doing. I said no, nothing, except, well, I'd liked swimming at school. We were down the public swimming pool before you could say cossie and goggles.

It was ages since I'd been for a good old swim. I'd dipped in the hotel pools to cool off and such, but not had a real swim like when I was at school. I was jumping in, dive-bombing, I wanted to race but she wasn't like that; she was doing water Chi Gung or something. When I passed, I splashed her. I regretted it as soon as I'd done it, but it was all right 'cause she splashed me back and we ended up having a water fight like I used to do with Dawn, and we had a really good laugh. Then at the end, I still don't know why I burst into tears – whether it was the sudden release of playing, or thinking of my sister or just everything in general – and she comforted me there in the swimming-pool corner and she was different then, really caring.

And we went home and I said, 'Can we ditch the chamomile?' and she said yes and we had a proper cup of steaming tea and I poured my heart out to her. I told her how I felt trapped, lost, couldn't control myself, it was all getting too much. After that we started to become much more friendly, though she didn't renounce her role as tab-keeper and shaper, she just let it go lax sometimes, turned a blind eye when I sneaked in a bag of crisps, let me stay up from time to time, even have the odd drink.

Work was going well, I was in demand. I got into the routine of staying at Suze's. Early nights, then up and off to work. After I had been there some time though I began to see that she wasn't as together as she appeared or liked to appear.

She had it sorted in many areas of her life, and her clients thought the world of her and that she was the final word, but I saw she still had a problem with Rafe. Whether she still loved him or not I wasn't sure, but he still had control over her. There was something in their past – I just got glimpses of it. She wouldn't talk about it, only things slipped out. I think she was a dancer or something – could have even been a stripper – and he took her under his wing, was going to make her into a model, but it doesn't seem like it happened. They lived together once too, I saw a picture of them from the seventies or eighties, him with long hair and a handlebar moustache, her looking at the camera – a funny look, half unsure, half cocky, almost pleading to the viewer to like her. And there was one leotard she would never throw away, it had something to do with him.

Once after he'd called she sort of lurched forward like she was in pain. Don't know what it was. A few minutes later she was in the kitchen humming, making a smoothie. That's how it was, all vague bits, and she'd never answer a question about Rafe or his past. Only once, we had all candles out in a circle and some reflexology and some wine and some talking about the heart centre or something, and soon everything seemed so soft and secure and we both began opening up and she started smiling and then ever so quietly talking about him.

'No one knows what he was like, he was all energy, a force, raw, exciting. A wild drug. I thought everyone felt that way but he had my mother crying in her Cornwall cottage.' And that was it, whatever that meant – oh, and then she said, 'My heart would give me no pardon,' and then something like 'He reached in and drew me out, there were rolling, rolling liquor bottles and he dragged me out over each bottle like I was on a conveyor belt.' And for then, that was it.

Anyway, I started to listen to her more. She did know her stuff, even if she didn't always apply it in her own life. We were s'posed to be on this diet, she pinned it on the fridge. She stuck to it obsessively except every now and again, usually about one day in the week, she'd go stark staring eating mad and have Mars bars. I wasn't supposed to know. She'd be in different rooms with the doors locked. Funnily enough, that was probably the only damn day I stuck to the diet, for some perverse reason.

We did start to become friends. We sort of didn't let Rafe know though. In fact, I think I was the only friend she had; in fact, I think *she* was the only friend *I* had. I helped her with mechanical things like dissembling and reassembling her food processor. I taught her my Grandma routine, she was always amazed at my skin and hair and slimness, because she had to work really hard at hers. She made her own lotions and beauty potions, jars all over the kitchen units or on the windowsill, apricots stewing with basil leaves on the stove. I don't know if she ever used them, you'd find them going green at the back of the fridge sometimes, unless that was part of the process. Who knows? She said she had a friend who was very high-powered in the government and rich, and he said he was going to back her own cosmetics line. Never saw anything come of it. Sometimes she'd be dropped off late by a big black limousine with shaded windows and afterwards I might hear her humming to herself in her room or sometimes sobbing really quietly or sometimes the next morning the pedal bin would be full of Mars bar wrappers.

She knew all the new philosophies and new-age practices and was always going on courses, or giving them sometimes. She taught me lots of things. She taught me self-defence, she said if anyone comes at you, whatever their size, there was one thing that never failed. She said get your finger and push it in the 'tidgy triangle' just below the throat. All you needed was a little shove and see them fly. She'd seen a few blokes off that way. One guy at a wedding reception got too close and she sent him clean over the buffet table with it. Another time we got talking about sex and she taught me about Kegels, they're s'posed to improve your sex life no end. You squeeze yourself tight as you can, bit like when you are desperate for the loo and have to hold it in, then let them go, on and on like that, work up to a hundred a day. S'posed to strengthen your sex muscles, give you a grip of steel down there. I got to about forty a day then got fed up with it. She could break a pencil with hers – not that she demonstrated, but I believed her.

One day I came home from a shoot disgruntled. I'd had a stroppy photographer, you get them sometimes, bullies, bossing you about. Suze said she would teach me assertiveness. She explained it all to me; she was a good teacher, she had a way of making everything simple. We sat down in front of the window, looking at her windowsill. On it were two plants, one much bigger than the other, it was obscuring the light of the small one. She said, 'Basically, the small plant has three ways of approaching this,' and she turned the little plant one way, to where it was rough and sharp, and bumped it against the bigger one.

'"Move it, you big sprig o' shite, shift over now and bloody pronto!"' she said and pushed at the bigger plant with the smaller one's thorns. 'That's aggressive communication,' she said to me as she turned the little plant to its other side, where it was all soft foliage, which trembled slightly with the sudden turn.

This time her voice was faltering and nervous like. '"Er, I don't suppose . . . it's just that the light isn't . . . I don't know how to . . . sometimes I . . . Oh . . . never mind, I can manage." That's passive communication,' she said as she once again turned the plant, this time to where its single flower was, a little bright clear flower it was too. Now, in a calm, steady but strong voice, she said, '"The way I see it, big plant, is there is plenty room here for both of us. At present I feel cramped by you and can't get enough light. I would like it if you would move over. Thank you." Now that's assertive.'

Suze said she was terrible till she learnt it, either saying nothing or blowing her top, and all women should learn it at school, it was a skill you could learn, like driving or cooking or typing, it wasn't a personality trait. Then she taught me the Assertive Statement.

'It's like this: it's what you think about a situation, how you feel about it, what you want.'

'Eh?'

'It's in three: Think, Feel, Want. Try it with these things.' She turned to the windowsill again.

'Let's say the joss-stick is fed up 'cause it's not been lit for a while, fancies a burn. It could say to the matches . . .' she did the voice of a joss-stick . . . '"I was bought to offer fragrance to the room and make people happy. I feel a bit neglected and unfulfilled. I would like to be lit please." OK, enough examples,' she said. 'You try it.'

She walked me over to the big rubber plant in the corner. 'Right, this plant hasn't been watered for a few days. Speak for it.' She put the watering can beside it. 'Go on, tell the can.'

'I can't.'

She didn't talk to me but to the plant. 'Now, now, a firm calmness, a steady eye contact, posture relaxed, that's it. Now go.'

I don't know where it came from but I just went into it. '"It's been three days now since I have been watered. Though I won't die I feel neglected when I don't get a regular sprinkle. I would prefer to get watered at the same time every day.'

'Yes, fantastic. That's it! That's it!' She was so enthusiastic.

She put some big film music on and we ran round the kitchen. This is what she did with her clients. I could see why they all liked her. And then she taught me my favourite of all, the one Suze said every girl should have in her handbag, Broken Record.

'You just keep acknowledging what they say and then repeating what it is you want, acknowledging repeating, acknowledging repeating. Like, say you are taking back a faulty toaster and the shop assistant says, "Sorry, madam we don't do refunds," you say, "I understand what you are saying but I want a refund for this faulty toaster." She might say, "That's not possible. Anyway, I'd have to contact the suppliers." "I understand you might want to contact the suppliers but my contract is with you and I want a refund today for this faulty toaster," . . . and on and on and on and on like that, till they give up basically.'

She said most people only have so many 'no's in them: keep going and exhaust the lot. She'd set up a sort of assertiveness scrap, set up a situation and off we'd go, whipping out our Assertive Statements and every now and again giving each other a right good going-over with Broken Record. Then we collapsed laughing and had a chamomile. We had a few of these bouts and it sank in nicely. She was clever was Suze.

Next time I was on the phone with Rafe and he was ordering me about or arguing with me or putting pressure on, she's there by my side and she's whispering, 'Assertive Statement,' then 'Broken Record,' then again, like she was bloody ringside. I found I started covering the phone and doing it to her.

'"I am in mid-conversation here, I feel aggravated by your interruptions, I would appreciate it if you would keep quiet."'

Then she's going, 'No, not me, him. Him.'

'"I understand what you are saying but I would like you to remain quiet."'

'No, no, him. Him!'

But concerning Rafe, in the end I said sod it and I let him just say what he wanted and I either did what he wanted or I didn't. I mostly did it. One thing I did achieve with assertiveness, though, was to get my mobile back, for what good it did me – just meant I was on a long cellular lease to him. I kept it off most of the time.

Work was getting more varied. I had been offered work in television adverts; I wasn't sure at first. Rafe wasn't sure either, but I think the agency put pressure on him and he eventually convinced himself with the belief that they might lead to 'lucrative product contracts'. Endorsements was what he was after. I was making good money but not the supermoney yet, endorsing perfume and product lines were real good earners, also as always he had his eye set on 'Yankee doodle land'.

But at the time, I'm telling you, just the whiff of knowledge of Rafe not really wanting me to do something, anything, was enough to make me want to do it a hundred times over and twice a day until Christmas, so I don't know if it was a chance to get at him or a genuine urge to try something new, but we went into it anyhow, hand-selecting the offers as they came in. It was just like modelling really, except you were hanging about a bit longer and mostly moving around, but I enjoyed it.

After the second one I did, I chatted to the director. He'd asked me to do a bit of acting instead of posing, and he liked what I did. I didn't have a line or anything, just expressions. I was already a bit tipsy – there must have been some drink on set – and I did 'The Green Eye of the Yellow God' for him. 'There's a one-eyed yellow idol to the north of Khatmandu...' It all came back to me, even after all those years. When I got to the Mad Carew bits, I did the face like me little grandma had, '... There's a broken-hearted woman tends the grave of Mad Carew...'

I did the whole thing. It really made him laugh. I said my grandma had taught it to me. He was in the middle of telling me he was going into TV drama and that he might bear me in mind, when Rafe was there, hand in my back. I refused to budge this time; the pressure went on but I stayed listening to the director. When Rafe realized he was getting nowhere, he started to drag me off; he had never gone that far before. The director looked shocked. 'Steady on, mate,' he said.

Rafe just glared at him, and for a second I thought he was going to hit him. It was strange for Rafe, this, as he was usually over-charming to these people. He turned back to me. To avoid trouble I let him walk me away.

It was about this time I snuck out to a party in London. Rafe was away and Suze was in bed with a stinking cold or going through detoxification, as she called it. I couldn't believe it, I saw Paulie at the party – remember? My first love, the boy from One-plus-two-plus? When I first saw him I was over-awed. Later I couldn't believe it when he came over to speak to me. 'Crystalline,' he said. He knew me. I always forgot I had this fame of my own, you just got used to heads turning some-times when you went in a restaurant or a shop, but in London people didn't so much as bat an eyelid, or only now and again. Anyway, fame or not, I just couldn't reply. I thought of some of the things Suze had told me about communication but they had gone out the window. What chance have you got when your voice won't work? Only thing for it was a few more drinks. He was drunk and so was I. He stayed with me most of the night. Other people would come over to him but he would say, 'No, I'm talking to Crystalline.'

We stepped out of the club into photographers' flash guns; it was just like I'd seen in my daydreams in my little bedroom at home. I felt like ringing old schoolmates and yelling, he's come down off the wall, my pin-up.

But back at his hotel room, the romance sadly bit the dust. He was out of it – I mean, we were both out of it, but he was out of out of out of it. He struggled to do a line of coke and slid off on to the floor the table was so low. He'd complained about it, he wanted a higher table. By the time they arrived with it he didn't care anyway, he'd managed to get some into his gums somehow, and he fell into a deep snoring sleep on the shagpile, spit going from his mouth into the thick fibres. There would be no Beano delivered this night. I sat alone looking at the fantastic view of London he hadn't even noticed. I had a drink in my hand but I didn't want to finish it, I felt sickened with it all. I did finish it though, I had to.

Next day he was still lying there. I'd got up three times during the night to check he hadn't died. He looked tubby and ill, not like my hero at all. My pin-up. He was suing his manager, living on credit till he got what was his. There was still talk of his solo career taking off, everyone around him spoke in that positive way which at first I so admired but had now begun to find distasteful. It was a talked-up world where everyone is doing wonderful, afraid to look at life in case it's not what they want.

When I got into the streets it was really early morning. London looked that way, fags and rubbish bags and smells, like it was coughing awake, bleary-eyed after a night on the drink itself. I checked my mobile. There were twenty-two missed calls from Rafe.

Back at the apartment, Suze was a mess. She'd been up all night with him calling, she was in trouble, scared, physically scared, sweating: We would have to be more careful; I wasn't to do it again; I was her responsibility.

She was veering from his side to mine, it was terrible to watch. I just thought it best to go. On the way out I heard the Mars bars being unwrapped.

Chapter Fourteen

I WAS SO UNHAPPY. MY CAREER WAS STILL GOING ALL RIGHT but I wasn't. I got a place with another model for a while; it was only temporary, a small flat in Clapham. She was a nice kid but really untidy, the place was a tip: sticky kitchen floors and all that; you'd find toast in the bath, socks on the draining board, knotted-up knickers everywhere. It didn't help to bring any order to my life and, away from Suze, it was easier to stay in bed – no more visits to the swimming baths, or anything – easier to drink, stay out. Rafe didn't know what to do, he'd adopted a new tack the last couple of weeks: leave me to it. I wasn't taking it from him no more, I used Suze's assertiveness training or, if that wasn't working, I'd learnt how to just put on the sullen model's face. He had got cold with me, colder and colder, I don't know what he was trying to do.

I was bingeing on booze a lot more now when there was a gap between jobs. I'd even been late once or twice, which was not like me – I'd overslept or got a bit lost or, one time, even almost forgot about a job. It was difficult with Rafe's new 'leave me to it' attitude, I was feeling it, but I wanted like mad to cope, to cope. I even found myself turning up a bit drunk to a shoot – only a bit, I'm sure nobody noticed – but it frightened me, that, it was one thing having a drink afterwards but not before, never before and I gave up drinking there and then, for about a day and a half, I think. I didn't know what was happening to me at times.

One time I went into the agency and was waiting at reception when a pretty young girl came in, nervous as hell. She had like a country-type accent.

'Hello,' she said.

The receptionist ignored her.

'Hello, I've come for the open interviews.'

'Oh. Have you got photographs?'

'Er . . . yes. They said on the phone just bring snaps—'

Before she'd finished speaking, the receptionist said, 'Put them there.' The girl put them on the desk, and the receptionist looked at them like they were contaminated. 'I'll take them through in a minute. Sit down.'

The girl looked around then started to come over to sit near me.

'Not those seats, those.' The receptionist indicated some other seats away from the main reception, almost behind a partition. She picked up the pictures reluctantly and left. The girl was almost trembling with nerves, I went over to talk to her. She really was beautiful and the trembling made her more so, if possible, almost like a Bambi or a flower in a breeze. She seemed so grateful for someone to talk to and she blurted out her story all at once.

'I've come up from Devon today.'

'That's a long way.'

'I know, but for me it doesn't matter, I want to be a model so much, it's what I've always wanted. My dad wanted to come with me but we couldn't afford it, the two fares. I can't believe I'm here, sitting in this place, it's one of the best, isn't it? I phoned them to ask about going with them and they said they have an open day every second Thursday and to bring some pictures and they . . . and they would have a look at me.' She looked around again like she couldn't believe she was here. She really was so tender.

'How old are you?'

'Sixteen and a half.'

Suddenly this garish gay lad came marching toward her, almost threw the pictures at her. 'Sorry, not for us.' Then as he walked away he said over his shoulder, 'Not quirky enough.'

She had come all that way, they had just discounted her as a person, the whole thing had taken about two minutes. I couldn't bear it. I ran after him, spun him round and head-butted him. Blood shot from his nose. He looked in absolute shock. Then I walked out.

I'd started to do some catwalk modelling. I had wanted to do it for a while but was a bit nervous, it was a real brand-new thing for me, an audience, a show atmosphere, I found it exciting. There was a real buzz once the show was under way. Everyone waiting to go on was a bit like waiting with the girls behind the big door at Safeshop, 'cept here they were having a last line, popping a pill, sucking in their cheeks, doing a mantra, sipping from little water bottles – what was really in them heaven knows. Some were great though, one Chinese model always tickled everyone just before we went on. The show itself was a whirlwind then afterwards you'd be exhausted, sitting in your own booth if you were lucky. I had one, my star was still rising a bit – well, more like risen, stayed still a while and not yet quite dropped.

People weren't quite as interested. I was still making the papers now and again if I did something daffy, or sometimes you'd get a made-up story somewhere. Some girl at a show might come up and show you something about yourself in a magazine, or a picture, or I might get the 'call' from a stony Rafe checking if what he'd read was true or not.

I did a show in Birmingham. It was a massive trade fair. When it was over I got the message that someone was waiting for me. It was Adam, the assistant manager from the super-market. I couldn't believe it. The Safeshop company had a stall at the fair and he was there to help organize it. We talked about all the girls. It was great to hear about them, like drinking pure water (nothing else in the bottle). He told me how I was a legend back there, how they all followed my career, even Igor, how they were all so proud.

I started filling up, I couldn't help it, he was so nice. Even got me to sign the programme from the fashion show. I put,

'I think of you all, love Crystalline.' Then I thought, what am I writing?, and put 'Linda' underneath. And a kiss and then another and another and then another and then I stopped myself, I must have looked a bit manic. He had to go, he wanted to perhaps meet later. I did too but I was scared so I just said I had to get straight back to London. I was scared because, 1. I knew Rafe might appear. He'd taken to doing that now, not telling me he was coming and just turning up, trying to catch me at something, and I didn't want him making a scene in front of Adam and it getting back to them all at Safeshop, especially when it was all so perfect a picture for them. And, 2. I was scared I wouldn't live up to all their expectations, he'd see something in me, I'd say the wrong thing, I don't know.

Later I went off in a corner somewhere and got drunk, it was either that or sob my bloody heart out. Oh Alice, Betty, Igor, oh if only you knew.

Paulie kept ringing. I met him again. Sober in the day, he was white as a sheet and shaky, a chainsmoker. Couldn't bear to wait for anything, shouting at the waiter all the time wanting people to recognize him then not: 'Is that a photographer over there?' – 'No, it's a tourist.' – 'Oh, you never know.'

Then, 'They might be up there.'

'Who?'

'The paparazzi. I saw someone move in that flat. Let's change places.' But he didn't, just took his hat off and tousled his hair.

He'd had a bad time with the band, he told me all about it.

They'd been worked to death, all on about two hundred quid a week retainers. No input, just do as you are told. He'd got sick of it.

Someone came up and asked me for my autograph. He couldn't speak much after that.

I paid the bill – I don't think he knew how to: from the age of seventeen people had done everything for him. He jumped in a cab like he was being chased, but he wasn't, left me on the pavement. If your pin-ups ever start to step out the posters and come down off the wall, make a noose from their own Blu-Tack and hang them.

One morning I was so hung over it was unbelievable. I was making my way home, the whole world was on a slant, I was amazed to see things weren't sliding away and down the street and off the earth. I passed a news stand, and it too, amazingly, was staying where it was. I tottered by, then stopped dead in my tracks and the world righted itself with a clang, I could have sworn I saw our Dawn's face on the front of the *News of the World*. I was going to have to stop this drinking, I was having illusions now. Surely it wasn't, couldn't be, it wasn't . . . it was, it was, it was. I backed up – literally walked backwards like my gran did sometimes when she was imitating music-hall comedians. I even double-taked like she did. I shook my head. Couldn't be. But it was.

I bought the paper. Suddenly I was panting. I went up a back alley beside a takeaway, stood with my back against the dirty hard brick wall for support and read. It said,

Supermodel's sister on the scrapheap

then, inside,

She's swanning about while we're skint

I couldn't believe it. There was the smell of piss up the back alley and that, with the shock, made me feel sick. I wasn't though, I pushed myself back into the hard bricks and let the sensation pass over. I opened my eyes and read on.

As I fumbled with the pages to get to the story inside, I could smell the fried food from the takeaway, heavy, sickening, battering the air in fat. It was like this paper was covered in the cheap sizzle of it, coating the words. What had my sister done? There was a big picture of her holding our Laura, her youngest, some derelict bloody scene behind – it wasn't her home or our house – and then a picture of me mum. Oh, lovely Mum, looking like she was going to cry. It looked like they'd taken it without her knowing. Oh no. What was happening? I was shaking. What was all this? What was going on?

She doesn't care

In black ink, staring out at me. Every line thumped.

Top supermodel Crystalline is flying high, but she has dumped her family, single-mum sister Dawn (*Single now! What's this?*) and her two children and her invalid mother (*Invalid?*). Dawn says 'She's swanking it up there in London, she's never helped us in any way. Recently, my mother was sick – her own mother, and she didn't even come to see her. Even when Mum was in hospital she didn't come. I've been ill, I'm split from my husband. It's terrible.'

The journalist went on to write:

Crystalline, one of the country's top models, has always been one of the nation's favourites. She seems without affectation, and her earthy, demure and common touch have always made her a popular choice. But it appears it is a completely different story at home. When Dawn was asked if she had any message for her famous sister, she said, 'No, she knows what she's done and, as far as we are concerned as a family, the best thing she can do is stay away.' A friend of Crystalline's in London (*Who? Who?? Suddenly I realized had no close friends*) says, 'I've never really heard her mention her family, to be honest. I think it's a matter of going forward, not looking back, it's often the way of it in the cut and thrust of the high fashion world.'

We spoke to Crystalline's agent, who said she is working at present and is unavailable to comment.

I scrunched the paper up, I was angry at first. I scrunched it up in my hands and then I straightened it out again, looked at it in disbelief, then sent all the pages up into the air, and I ran, ran up the backstreet, my £200 shoes buckling on the broken ground, scattering beer cans. A chip tray got caught on my high heel; I just carried on. It was a dead end. I stood facing the bare brick wall and cried and cried. Suddenly my phone chirped: it was a text. I pulled my phone out, dropped it, picked it up, read through the distortion of tears: 'Why? I would say about five grand. Rafe.'

Chapter Fifteen

SOMETIMES THOUGH, SOMETIMES, IT IS STILL LIKE A DREAM, this job. I was in Venice, moonlight, three of us by the canals, then running in the square with silk scarves behind us. I knew one of the girls, she was all right; the other was an American model I'd never met, and she was nice too, it had been a really good shoot. The photographer was French and he had been light and charming in that way only a French male can be, and he'd made the shoot flow, almost like music: here, there, hurrying the pace, slowing it; the breaks came at the right time, the make-up girls flowed in, did their stuff then out. I thought, I'm blessed. I hadn't felt like a drink all day.

The stars were out now and fabulous. There was a hairdresser in jeans and low studded belt, the most beautiful bottom you ever saw. He had been smiling at me and whispering things in Mexican – at least I think it was Mexican: he'll probably turn out to be a Geordie. Then Rafe appeared. I thought he wasn't arriving till tomorrow.

We were all set to go out, the three girls on the town – that was great when you did that, not the parties but just three stunning, tall girls in incredible clothes going round the bars, linking arms, skipping in the squares, causing a stir and a scandal sometimes. I could tell by his bearing that he'd had enough of leaving me to it, now he was back and back in control. He told me I wasn't going out, I needed an early night, he had something arranged for me in London the next day. I could tell he meant it 'cause the Scottish was creeping in. I forgot assertiveness. I'd had enough, I told him to piss off. Then it happened. He slapped me hard.

It echoed around the square. Everyone looked over. I held my face and just looked at him in disbelief, then ran. I ran down streets I didn't know. Just ran. Ran and ran. I ended up on the steps of a church. The old door was locked.

I had to get away from him. I flew out that night, he wouldn't have expected that. Walked out, left the job. There would be uproar.

Some friends of mine, a gay hairdresser and his partner, took me in. I heard Rafe was on the rampage, going mad trying to find me. I heard lots more about him, people were opening up now we had parted, it was all coming out. The rumour was he'd been a criminal at one time, been inside; there were headcase stories. I finally found out what the scars were on his knuckles: he'd had tattoos of 'LOVE' and 'HATE' removed, tattoos he had reportedly done on his own in the backstreets of Glasgow with a pin and school ink. I was scared. I shuddered to think that his serpent ring could have gone down to the bone, taken my eye out. It suddenly struck me – on Suze's face, was that what was under her cheekbone, the kiss of the serpent?

He was phoning everyone I knew. I heard he had burst into a shop he knew I went to, stood outside the changing rooms, convinced I was in there, screamed at the shop assistant when the wrong woman came out. It got back to me that the agency hadn't been happy with him for some time. Was that what that look of fury up the corridor that time in his office had been about? It was like sharp pieces of a steel jigsaw were slamming in tight against my brain. Things were whirling in my mind now and I was really scared. I wanted rid.

I had a model friend whose boyfriend was a lawyer, and he helped me. He wrote to Rafe, but he wouldn't respond except to try and get an address for me out of the lawyer. He wanted me.

I was in a right mess. I needed to get out of the flat but was afraid to go down the off licence. A picture of me, without make-up, clutching a bag with a bottle in it . . . had got into the paper. I wasn't that bothered. I was just there scouring the background of the picture to make sure there were no landmarks Rafe could identify.

I holed up even tighter in my friends' flat. Lispin and Harold, they were great. Lispin's real name was Crispin but everyone called him Lispin, because he had a pronounced sibilant 's', it was really strong. He described it as being 'like the bloody brush on a nightclub drummer's cymbal'.

He didn't care though, he exaggerated it all the more. Harold was his partner and the best colourist in London, shy, ginger, and so little and light and freckled, you could almost see through his skin. They were out working most of the time so my days were weird and lonely. It was a lovely flat though – huge windows, old high ceilings, views all round of city roofs. There was a sort of bedsit at the back of the flat, an old queen lived in there. He only came out once a week, to change his tea towel. When he saw me he'd say, 'She's like the doll on the mantelpiece.' Then he'd say, always like I had just met him, 'I'm Chucky.' Then he'd glare at the boys and say, 'Mr White to these two, "Chucky" to you.'

Then he'd go back to his quarters. They'd always flick the 'V's in unison. He stank actually. They didn't like him 'cause he was their landlord and he wouldn't let them have television on or listen to modern music and he knew everything they said and did and they were expected to clean the tea towels. He said he'd been a female impersonator, till his legs went. He had ginormous short legs, like the back legs of a rhinoceros. It was like having a Carcass sister hugging on to each thigh, I kid you not.

Paulie called me from LA. A producer had said he could launch him in America with what little funds Paulie'd got left. He wondered if I'd do him a favour and come out and be in his video, for free like, for now like, until the single was out and a hit.

Rafe was getting closer. I heard things, I felt things, it was only a matter of time. I felt I was going to crack. I was drinking like mad, there were empty bottles rolling about on the floor. I couldn't even turn to my family. I decided to fly out to see Paulie. But I had hardly any money; it was all with Rafe. I was alone in the kitchen one day and just started crying to myself. It was all too much. Then the bedsit door opened and Chucky beckoned me in.

It was only a small room. He sat with a rug round his knees; he looked like a Toby jug me grandma had had. There were lots of lampshaded lamps of different sizes all around him, maroon mainly, or red and fringed, and they were all full on, making him look pink. It was daytime but the curtains were closed tight. They looked like they'd come from some old theatre or somewhere, they were that thick and velvet and dusty and tasselled. The wardrobe was dark and massive, like you could live in it or travel through time in it, and between that and the bed and the chair there was hardly any space left to get about, just a narrow channel each side. I don't know how he got through, could only go backwards and forwards as far as I could see. There would be no chance of turning round, not with his rhinoceros shanks and tiny feet; he must have had to roll on the bed to change direction. Colourwise, it was a bit like entering a Tarot card. Deep blues and reds and purples, all fading, and billiard-green felt on the shelves, which were covered in knick-knacks, all mismatched – put you in mind of a charity shop window. And it was like there was something soaked into everything, like sweat or gin, and a funny fumey smell, old but sharp – perhaps it was his own rhino-leg smell.

There was nowhere to sit so I just stood before him. His face was big and round but not squashy at all, it was kind of set hard like bloated stone. He took a while to speak; he breathed like a dying man and he moved like he had a high collar on, like you see in the old Sunday afternoon Dickens films. When he wanted to look to the side he had to move his whole body, and nodding up or down was out of the question.

'I've heard all,' he said. 'Now listen, Dolly Ann, listen in. Chucky's got some put by and you can have it.'

'I couldn't.'

'No, no, it's extra to me, it's the teapot money.' I didn't understand, he could see that. 'See up there, up on the shelf there.'

He didn't look that way, it would have meant a whole body shift; anyway, it was like he knew every part of the room by heart, like a blind man.

'Up on the third shelf, left of the centre, between the Edwardian gentleman and the chipmunk on a swing.'

'Er . . .'

'You might see a sombrero, sweep past that, there now, there.'

'Oh yes.' There it was, a teapot with a Union Jack on it.

'It's full of money, that 'un. And I mean bursting. It's dirty money really, mucky. Money I got when I was a rent boy in the sixties. I was saving it for a facelift when I was sixty-four, but it's too late now. You can have it.'

It was all so strange I didn't know what to say.

Suddenly he was up. It was shocking, it was like some

mechanical thing, a heavy machine part swung by momentum, and at the peak of the swing, at the point of no return, he shot his arm out from his body and got the teapot, then landed down again.

He sat panting for a little while, then dribbled a bit, then passed the teapot to me. I was going to look inside but he held up his hand.

'Don't take off the lid, little Dolly Anna. It's bursting with it, it'll burst all over us. And quite frankly I don't really want to see the money again, there's a story behind every pound. Take it, take it. You must join your friend, Mr Paulie.'

How did he know all this! He mustn't miss a thing – no wonder he doesn't want the telly on. I thanked him, but he closed his eyes and did his version of shaking his head, which was to start twisting his whole body from side to side like a whale on dry land. Then he indicated for me to go, and I went.

It was full of all these old tenners from way back when. 'Chucky's mucky money,' Lispin and I called it. I thought you couldn't use them but Harold took them down the bank for me and came back with a grand.

I was off.

Chapter Sixteen

I HAD ONLY EVER BEEN TO LA ONCE BEFORE, FOR A QUICK photo shoot, in and out. What a place! It was warm there, it was perfect teeth there, it was everybody with a dream there, it was truly crazy. Paulie met me at the airport. He'd made a real effort, he was smart – in fact, it was that kind of smart that looked like your mum had got you ready: shiny shoes, everything buttoned up right, hair slicked down – and he was sober. It was the last time I saw him that way. Once the kisses were over I could tell he'd gone as far as he could like this. Coming to meet me had been a benchmark in his mind, and he was itching for something now, some substance, anything. I could see his fingers curling. At one point, as he hurried me to the airport bar, I thought he was going to grab up the airport cleaners' bleach and down it.

Three hours and thirty drinks later we slid through the sliding doors into the blast of America, trying to hold each other up. It was like the sun went off like a flash and we were frozen in a picture and above us in jazzy felt-tip writing it read: 'Paulie and me, two drunks in LA, as lost as each other'. And really nothing stopped whirling after that.

Paulie's project was obviously a rip-off. Some guy called Randy Canyon said he was going to get Paulie back on track and Paulie had complete and blind-drunk faith in him. All the guy needed was some more money, so poor Paulie had given him all he'd got and then some. Paulie asked me to invest. I said forget it, all my money's with Rafe and he's for keeping it. They hadn't even got the song together yet. All Randy had done was show him a rooftop where he would shoot the video. He kept cancelling meetings with us, but Paulie couldn't even remember if he'd cancelled them, or Randy had, or if it was a state holiday. He was just out of it.

One day we got a call from Randy to say he was going to film Paulie and me standing in the 'O' of the Hollywood sign. We met him, a skinny guy in his fifties with parched, thick skin. Each cheek was like a dried-out dog-chew, he had very dry hair tied back in a ponytail – everything about him seemed dry and faded and sucked of moisture, like he'd been staked out in the desert. He swept his hand back over his hair before he put it out to shake mine and suddenly from nowhere there was enough dandruff to stuff a sofa. Soon as he opened his mouth you didn't believe a word he said; his voice had a weird sort of rattle and spit in it. He had two skull rings on, and he said, 'Just mind the rings if you would, little lady, they was a precious gift from one Mr K. "Rolling Stone" Richards

Esquire.' I didn't believe a word of it: they looked like they came from a toy shop.

He drove us up to the Hollywood sign. Seemed he knew a security guard there, an old army buddy of his, and he could get us right up to it, no problem. On the way up I tried to find out some more about him. After a lot of waffle, which I managed to penetrate with assertive questioning, it turned out he was best known for managing a retro punk band called Sperm Kitchen. I just thought, Oh my God – he was making Rafe look like a saint at this rate. To my astonishment he did get us through to the sign. When we arrived and got out of the car to look at it, from the back (where it is rusty, by the way), I pointed out the lack of cameraman, lighting, make-up girl, crew, etc. He said there would be no filming today, Paulie had got it wrong, we were just up here recceing the site and, in fact, while we were on the subject he needed another hundred bucks to secure the best damn cameraman in the Valley. Paulie shook his head like I'd told him to. 'Fifty then,' rattled Randy.

I elbowed Paulie and he shook his head again. I took him to one side and told him he had to have it out with Randy. Suddenly, he went back over to him, like a gun slinger. It was a good start, but then he couldn't get his mind right. So I stepped in with my assertiveness and said, 'As I see it, you have made many promises to my friend, taken his money, and yet nothing has happened. I feel very angry about this. I want you either to show some progress by tomorrow or return his money. Otherwise we will be reporting this to the relevant authorities.'

He seemed taken aback at first then, under his breath, spit and rattle, he said something that sounded like 'Bitch.' Paulie, after all that had been exchanged so far having gone over his head, seemed to hear this and, suddenly, as though jerked by a string from above, he swung for Randy, who didn't even need to move as Paulie missed by miles.

When he saw he was safe Randy went into a kind of leg-trembling Elvis karate stance, waving his hands out in front of him, saying, 'Bring it on, buddy, come on. I am a member of the Black Dragon fighting society of America, taught by the late great and deadly Count Dante himself. No one – I say *no one* – takes a swing at me.'

I was going to let him have one in the tidgy triangle below the throat like Suze taught me, but everything stopped at the sound of Paulie retching. He had made his way over to the sign and collapsed with his head through the 'O' and was throwing up all down the front of it. To his credit, I suppose, Randy helped me heave Paulie out the 'O' and lean him up against the 'L'. Some sort of peace was made in this action and Randy said to forget the hundred bucks, he'd pay, it was on him, and also assured us we would be filming some preliminary stuff soon, and that the recording studios were already booked, it was just a matter of waiting on 'One Mr Rodney Stewart Esquire'. He'd gone a little over time on his new album, but Randy's contact there, a guy called Rifleman, had assured him that Paulie would be in next, no matter who came along. Paulie bucked up at this, particularly the thought of being next in line to Rod Stewart, and he slurred, 'See, I told

134

you he was a sound guy.' Randy flushed at this and before I knew it they were hugging.

Randy dropped us at the foot of the hill. 'You know I love this guy,' he rattled.

'And I love you, man,' slurred Paulie. And as Randy sped off in his car, Paulie called after him, 'And I love Rifleman.' Then he turned to me elated. 'How about that!'

I just gave up, and we got drunk again. Whenever I see the Hollywood sign now I think of Paulie's sick baked into the 'O'.

Chapter Seventeen

I DID LIKE IT IN LA, THOUGH, THE SUN, THE ENERGY OF THE people, the brightness of it. First thing I did – no, getting drunk was the first thing – second thing I did, I set out to clean up Paulie's apartment. It was filthy and poky; right height table though, and that was probably his whole criteria for choosing it, didn't see anything else just focused in on that: 'I'll take it.' Anyway, I started walking to the supermarket to get some cleaning stuff. I couldn't understand why people kept staring at me like I was a ghost. I didn't know then that nobody walks in LA. In the supermarket I was amazed at the giant fruit, the giant tins, the giant cartons of juice. It took two hands to get most things off the shelves, it really was the land of plenty, this California.

The next day, Paulie wanted me to go with him to a meeting; it was a group he'd found which was really helping him. His voice coach out here had introduced him to it. He thought it would help me, too: he was suddenly the sorted-out one, and I needed help. I thought, Oh no, here we go. Are we going to Feng Shui our chakras again like with our Suze?

We had a couple or three vodka fortifiers and then we went to meet the voice coach, who was to take us there. I wasn't prepared for him: he was about ninety-nine, had been a bit actor in B-movies in the forties. He had this deep slack voice. His throat was almost separate from his neck, like a loose, hanging pipe, and on each side it was slack as a turkey's neck. His voice was very slow and very deep and sort of rolled up the long, slack turkey neck, clacking it. You could watch it, see it travelling all the way up bit by bit, climbing the slack rope of his throat, fluttering and smacking at the turkey sides and then on to his enormous slack tongue and out through his big, ancient, slack, flapping, slapping slack lips, and then everything would settle with a sort of gulp that slowly worked its way all the way back down through the slack apparatus to the bottom and then started again. He had slack skin, a slack cardigan over his tall, skinny frame, slack everything. His name was John Sycamore Brewster.

At times it all got a bit scary: his voice was so deep and slow and low suddenly just one tiny corner of the floor would start vibrating, and then you'd feel it tingling in your feet and toes. I thought, one day he's going to bring the whole building down that way, and it might spread to the next house and on through LA, all shuddering and toppling to the ground, not flattened by an earthquake but by old John Sycamore Brewster sitting alone in his upright armchair mouthing a sonnet, with

LA flattened around him, leafing through his B-movie stills, not even noticing.

He was helping Paulie, who he called 'the innocent in the dark woods'. We set off for the meeting, but it took us about half an hour to get out the door and into his car, he walked so slow, and Paulie made it worse. Besides arriving stoned, he had gone into some sort of double trance at being with his teacher and had begun reverently tracing his steps behind him. He looked like he was walking on the moon.

The old car seemed to drive itself. I know that can't be the case but the movements of the old man were so minimal I couldn't see him doing anything. It felt like we finally arrived at the meeting about two and a half years later. Everyone was very welcoming to us though. Mainly there were old people, and old fruits and big black ladies, and the odd young wide-eyed person. Their eyes lit up and sparkled to see us, and the call went round: 'John Sycamore's here' – 'John Sycamore is here.' People were gathering around, leaving their conversations, and a couple of old dears came out from what must have been a little kitchen, wiping their hands on teacloths as they rushed over, calling, 'Oh and Paulie, again!' – 'And a beautiful young lady! Oh, aren't we honoured?' They pawed us and fussed over us all the way to our seats, and big John was mumbling greetings, rocking the wonky old wooden chairs with his reverberations and no doubt rattling the saucers in the kitchen.

The chairs were arranged in a large circle. It was low lit in the meeting house and on one wall was a large black and white picture of the founder, an old lady but with a starlet's head twist and smile, encircled in a kind of back halo light. Seems she was a B-movie actress, too – well, a bit more than that, a B and a half – and an old compatriot of John Sycamore's. Seems she had been much influenced by Freud and a space alien she met on Santa Monica Boulevard.

The group was called the Quester Nesters and they would sit in a circle, with one chair in the centre. One of the group (the Quester) would sit in the chair in the middle and would be talked to by the others, down through various levels of the psyche (the Quest) until they reached the point that was holding them back (the Nest). Then the Quester would explore this nest, fly from it once and for all, and next time round be free to go even deeper, farther, higher until they were free.

The commencement of the meeting was announced, and everyone sat down. Then they all went into meditation for a while, though I noticed one of the old dears took this as an opportunity to pick her nose like a good 'un. Then they requested a 'Quester'. Paulie got up and went for the chair.

Some dame with a voice almost as deep as John Sycamore's took him down first, relaxing him 'deeper and deeper', all that, then another bloke took over: 'You are now through the body and into the mind. I will guide you hence, relaxing, deeper and deeper.' Then another voice. 'Thou art now in the 'hemotions, I will guide thee deeper' – proper committed this one was, going into the thees and thous. No nests so far: was that two to Paulie, none to the 'deeper-deepers' or what? In fact, I was convinced Paulie had dozed off. I knew for a fact he hadn't slept for three days and nights so it wouldn't have surprised me. Then suddenly he began sort of wrestling with himself, his jacket's off, his shirt ripped open to the waist, then he started talking, going on about his time with One-plus-two-plus, suddenly it didn't seem funny any more, the air sort of changed in the room, everyone became sort of intense on him.

He went on about how this sort of minder they had, who they called Goose, always used to check they were dressed and tucked in right before they went on stage. He'd rearrange their costumes, shouting at them, 'Show proper, show proper' (Paulie went into a Welsh accent for this), but all the time the man was goosing them, feeling them up. How Paulie hated this but the Goose was the manager's brother and you couldn't say anything. If you had you might have been out and he didn't want to be out, there were hundreds of young lads queuing up for this chance. He'd hear all the girls screaming out front and then Goose, he'd sort of shove him on with a hand on his bottom.

Then Paulie went into how he'd found out his older sister, who was like his mum, was dying, when he was on tour in Europe, and they wouldn't let him go to her until they'd finished the tour, and she had died by then. She had died by then.

And then his tongue came out one side and he started shaking and crying, and then he lurched forward and threw up. Two of the group were there instantly with a plastic bucket and a glass of water; it must be par for the course. I went to help, and one of the girls, who was young and wide-eyed and trembly, was wiping him with a cloth, a bit too manically for my liking, and saying, 'Well done, oh well done, you have flown that nest.' But he didn't really want any of it, Paulie, he sort of knocked her away. I thought he was going to throw a wobbler but then one of the older women – she looked like the cartoon grandma from the Tweety Pie cartoon – started cuddling him and he relaxed into her arms. Then we got him back to his seat and he seemed settled. He looked up and smiled and everyone applauded.

When everything had settled down, someone requested the next Quester. They all seemed to be waiting for me to volunteer. I was still tipsy from the fortifier so, I don't know why, but I just thought, what the heck. I took the seat in the middle and shut my eyes for the quest. For a while I kept peeping out now and again at their blurred faces, but then John Sycamore took over. I sensed a gasp when he did and realized I was highly honoured, and to the tune of his one-mile-an-hour voice things seemed to get daydreamy and pleasantly out of focus. Questions were coming at me but they seemed miles away – 'Where are you now?' 'What is happening now?' – and then I felt I dropped somewhere and I was with my lovely grandma and we weren't half laughing, and then I went into the snowflake pattern. At first it was like the twist of a microscope took me close and then out again and then I was in the pattern of the flakes, beautiful, indescribably right in them. Like I was vibrating in the white and altering shape along with them, it was amazing.

Then I was aware of me feet and then me body again and, when I opened me eyes, I sensed a real deep hush and awe in the room and they were all looking at me, even Paulie seemed to have surfaced and was looking at me in shock, bolt upright and stunned, and then coming down towards me was old Jack Slack, absolutely overcome. He stopped before me and God knows how he made it but he went down on one knee, calling me the glowing one, he'd seen the glow only once before, on the Grand Mistress, and they all gasped and looked to the picture on the wall. 'You touched that place,' he said. 'Pray, pray give us your true name, the true name that we can intone.'

I wasn't sure then what he meant. I thought of Gran again, and one of the comic monologues she used to do, the one about a little boy called Albert Ramsbottom and a lion, so I said 'Ramsbottom'. He started repeating it but making a lot of the sounds – 'Rrraammmmmmaaasbottom' – you can imagine that his neck flaps were going like the clappers. 'Rrrammmmmmaasssbottom.' They all started chanting it with him: 'Rrrammmmmmmmmmaasssbottom.'

After a while they stopped. 'Please, this is what we have been waiting for for years, we pray of you, give us divine words you heard there, scripture to follow, learnings for life, neglect us not.' I closed my eyes, mainly to stop myself from having a giggling fit. 'Ahh, she goes back' – 'Please reveal.' I suddenly realized I was in a bit of a fix here. All I could think of was 'The Lion and Albert' again.

'There's a famous seaside place called Blackpool
That's noted for fresh air and fun,
And Mr and Mrs Ramsbottom
Went there with young Albert, their son . . .'

Old Jack was really excited now, began repeating things I'd
said and interpreting them in line with Quester teachings:
'We ask for something we can live by' – 'I said verse five,
segment number twelve . . .'

'There were one great big lion called Wallace,
His nose were all covered with scars –
He lay in a somnolent posture,
With the side of his face on the bars.

'Now Albert had heard about lions
How they was ferocious and wild,
To see Wallace lying so peaceful
Well, it didn't seem right to the child.

'So straightway the brave little feller,
Not showing a morsel of fear,
Took his stick with 'orse's 'ead 'andle
And pushed it in Wallace's ear.'

They were ecstatic at this and were calling out bits from it all
over the place – 'Morsel of fear', 'Horse's head handle' – like
they had received great teachings.

'You could see that the lion didn't like it
For giving a kind of a roll,
He pulled Albert inside the cage with 'im
And swallowed the little lad 'ole.'

'Ahhhh, the final extinction of the ego, self devours self,' wailed Old Slack.

I suddenly opened my eyes as though I'd come out of my trance.

John made me stand and everyone applauded. I said, 'I must go now,' and everyone cooed how they understood, but would I come back again and channel Ramsbottom for them? I said I would. As I was leaving, Slack Jack was calling after me, 'You have left us with much to study, and dissect,' and then he turned to the others, 'and we can all practise the somnolent posture until Ramsbottom's next return.'

As I left, I looked back to see him beckoning them to the floor, where they were trying it out. 'The somnolent posture, friends . . .'

And off we went into the night. It took me an hour to talk Paulie round into the truth of it and to get him out of wanting me to show him the somnolent posture.

Chapter Eighteen

WE WERE STUMBLING AROUND LA. PAULIE HAD NEVER DONE anything for himself, so he never carried cash and we were suddenly out of the stuff. He took out his mobile and phoned someone, a friend, he said. Turned out it was someone he'd been introduced to once who'd said call me some time, so Paulie did – that's the barrel-bottom level of acquaintances he'd got himself down to, that and of course Randy ruddy Canyon. It was apparent from what I could overhear that the guy had no idea who Paulie was; anyway, he ended up saying that he was in a bar across town called the Velvet Paw, jump in a cab and come over. We ended up walking it, it was only round the corner but a million miles to an LA-lien.

The guy was called something like Vance Haulage, and loaned Paulie a hundred bucks on the strength of my smile, or so he said. Then we were whirling again, all through the LA night. Wide roads. Gliding cars. Neon bars. Dancing on tables. Cocktails. Everything slanted, everything straight again. A comedy club that wasn't funny. A restaurant where you could draw on the walls. Salad. Someone said a movie star was out on the town, a party forms to hunt his restaurant down. Salad. A comedy club that was funny. Someone was going to punch Paulie in the gob, he's shouting, 'Not in the face, not in the face, give it us in the gut if you must, give it us in the gut, for godsake.' I save him again. Salad. 'Honey, you've found paradise, sun all day, no bugs, no cavities. OK, no one can take an inbreath before twelve in the Valley, but don't you find a smoggy dawn so romantic?' The posse passes, still hunting the star. Someone orders me a sandwich: it's five foot tall, America is sliced on it. A squad car glides by and tells Paulie off for smoking. He shouts, 'One ciggy and I'm in San Quentin.' I save him again. 'Lungs have rights too,' someone calls out. Paulie does one of his puppet swing punches; I catch him. A party in the back of a bar, a party in front of a bar, a party above a bar, I just want to sit at a bar. Are you Vance the Salad then?

Suddenly we are three seconds in the wrong neighbourhood. Gangs of men in back-to-front baseball caps watching from paint-peeling front porches, lizard eyes, everything in the half-dark, Paulie decides he's going to do a drug deal. I save him. Salad. Six-foot sandwiches. Working girls, Paulie thinks they all like him. I save him again. Salad. LA is a salad. I finally have me a salad myself. 'Dressing?' 'No, it's just the way I wear things.' She doesn't get it. 'Dressing?' 'OK.' There's about 55,223 choices of dressing and combinations; I ask for some Branston pickle, they think I've gone mad. I wish I'd never started.

Paulie on his knees, trying to put his hands in the walk of fame. Then can't get up again. He lights up a fag, lets go a long smoke exhalation into the LA air, shouts, 'Never mind drive-by shootings, you can get done for a bloody drive-by exhalation in this town.' People don't think it's funny. I save him again. A lot of neon guitars. A guy called Vance Haulage – haven't we met him before? Lot of people singing. I see a pizza, it's big as a tractor wheel. I hold a gun: it feels very very satisfying, I never knew it would feel like that. 'Give it back now,' somebody says. Before I give it back I cock it and uncock it and unload then reload it and twirl it, that maniacal mechanical knack again. I shrug. Somebody else says, 'Anyone can handle a gun like that got to be in their own mini series.' I see a pizza, it's big as a roundabout in my town. There's suddenly hardly anyone on the street. Everyone's in bed by eleven thirty – 'It's a film town, honey, early shoots.'

Paulie throwing up once more, a woman passing gets excited: 'Gee, is this a reality TV show?' Where are we now? The skies all drifting deep blue and pink. 'Are you Vance Haulage?' – 'No.' – 'Oh.' I'm chasing a policeman, asking him can I hold his gun, oh God. Some girls recognize Paulie, sing to him a One-plus-two-plus song. They recognize him, they recognize him! He's straight away sober and erect, flashing smiles and in heaven, he forgets me instantly, he goes off with them in a taxi, leaves me on the sidewalk with Vance Haulage.

I am in a taxi with Vance, he says we're going to a party then he'll take me home, is that all right? Before I can answer he's kissing me.

'Oh my God, real breasts. They are real, aren't they?'

Before I know where I am he's on the mobile to someone: 'I've got a woman in the cab with me, real breasts.' The cab driver's squinting round now. 'Real, you say?' – 'Real.' – 'Real real?' – 'Real.' – 'Amazing.' Vance is starting up another call: 'You are not going to believe this . . .'

He turns to me abruptly. 'I'm sorry. Don't think me rude, honey.' Then he's back on the blower, 'Yes, yes . . .' The cab driver says to me, 'Don't mind us, ma'am, it's just that they rare these days, they a bit like the new gold in California.'

Enormous pink and white house, with a party in full swing. Inside it's all staircases and chandeliers, Vance is kissing everybody and shaking people's hands off, everyone's patting each other so hard on the back they'll break spines. I don't want no more drink, though, I don't want no more of anything, I'm coming down and it's a crash landing. I recognize some star faces, this is a proper Hollywood party, like you see in the magazines and films. Paulie is going to be crying knowing he missed this. I can see Vance talking animatedly to a crowd, I can see them forming to come look at me. My breasts are going to be in the 'Sights of LA guidebook' soon. I duck out to the gardens. I sit on a bench and cry.

My head started swimming, I was swooning a bit, then coming back. I had had enough, had enough of everything. I was thinking, this was it, the spring was finally uncoiling. The suffering was having its shout, its head. It was the sort of swoon that went sliding, sliding down deep. I could feel

I was losing control and my mind was too out of focus, too drunken clumsy to stop to pick thoughts up or hold them or move things around in there or press things back down again, and I was suddenly sick with my whole life. Looking at me in the garden, you wouldn't know this, you might think it was just some boozed-up woman in boozy tears, but they were tears of everything.

It started sniffily, then weepy, and then I went into that deep cry that you know could go on for ever. You usually stop it, but I was letting it happen, playing a dangerous game opening up and letting it come, and I knew this could be it. It went into that choking cry and, what with the drink, I couldn't stop it. I knew I might bring attention to myself, I was embarrassed, but the draw down was deeper and I couldn't stop it. I bit into my lip but there was nothing that could put the brakes on this. I closed my eyes to try and stop but to no avail: this wasn't just tonight, this was going back farther, deeper, all the way back to London, Rafe, my family, the kitchen table. I couldn't stop.

I half opened my eyes, through the wet misty corners saw a couple leaving. Man was putting a coat over the shoulders of a woman, they seemed to me to be slipping away. I was desperately trying to stop now, almost cuffing myself, but the sobbing just kept coming up and up. If the Quester Nesters could see me now they'd have a field day.

I looked again and the couple had seen me; they stopped on the path. They were coming toward me. I turned away, I didn't want help. I did, I didn't, then they were there.

'Are you all right?'

It was a musical English voice, soft but deeply powered, little lilt of American in it. I couldn't look up. I couldn't answer. 'She's in a bad way.' Again that voice, there was something in it.

'Are you all right?' The man this time, stately, the voice an elderly deep American burr, dark, American oak in it, dark like the wood of the president's desk. 'I'll get her a glass of water.'

Don't ask why, I could tell from their voices, the in and out, their tones somehow, could tell he was her companion for the night, not her lover. A good friend. You could just tell. Love wasn't in the air but friendship was. Good friendship, old friendship, good vintage of a friendship, and for some reason it made me want to cry even more. Think it was the thought of such friendship against my aloneness.

All this and I still hadn't looked up.

'Here, give her my handkerchief,' the man said, then I heard him leave.

'Here, dear, take this.'

The cloth was class, weighty, white, sweet and clean, un-folded heavy. Smelt of the gentlemen of America. Hated to spoil it with my tears, but it could have absorbed the pain of the world.

'Can I help in any way?' That sweet voice again, well spoken, British, the best of London, but something more, some sort of soul in it, it was this something in her tone that made me look up, and through the tears it was a beautiful woman, looked like Jackie Collins. I rubbed my eyes, then again: it *was* Jackie Collins! Then my voice wouldn't work. At first it had been the tears but now it wouldn't work 'cause of the Jackie Collins. The man was back with the water. I took it, hoping it would take away the paralysis. I felt such a fool. I looked at him as I drank, almost afraid to look at her, like she was the good fairy who might vanish with a human stare. His was the face of the man who owned the handkerchief for sure, distinguished, grey above the ears, strong and fit, blue eyes, a man you could depend on. Even through my misty tears I was aware of the solid cut of his suit. The neatly clipped haircut. And all the time, beside him, a sort of glow that was Jackie Collins. A glow I was afraid to look into.

The man said, 'Maybe we should take her inside. Would you like to come inside?' I couldn't speak, but they could tell I didn't want to. Well, Jackie could.

'She doesn't want to go inside.'

I had stopped crying now and felt I would be rewarded with my voice this time if I made the effort. 'Are you Jackie Collins?'

The man answered for her. 'Yes, she is. And your name?'

'Linda.'

'Linda who?'

'Linda's enough for now,' said Jackie, a sort of slight scold for him, bit like being hit with a rose. 'Have you friends in there?' I shook my head quickly. 'We were just slipping away.'

'I have to say I would be crying if we had stayed there any longer,' said the man. Noticed he never shortened any word, gave it its full length and pronunciation, laying every syllable in good clear American.

'Can we give you a ride somewhere?' Her voice again, beautiful. This was Jackie Collins talking to me! Unbelievable. I think, out of nerves and timidity, I would have turned her down but through the second-floor window I saw the breast-hunting crowd looking for me. I accepted the lift with gratitude.

I was overwhelmed with sobby upset still and drunk. Standing up the first time I felt like I had been hit with a shovel and went down again. Then up and the lawn turned to rubber. I was being held and guided on one side by the gentleman and on the other by Jackie Collins! Her books were for sale in Safeshop, I had stacked them myself, they were read eagerly by the girls, Bet loved them – 'Lot of good Yankee-doodle Beano in them, I'm telling you' – brought home from the library by my mum, who always had her name down for the latest one.

It was a chauffeured car, long and sleek with doors that shut with that soft click. With a sweet but not too sweet scent inside, with seats you could sleep on.

'Do you have any idea at all where it might be?' We had been driving for quite a while. They had already asked me the address and I didn't know it. I started trying to describe where Paulie lived but realized I was describing a hundred streets and corners around these parts. 'Paulie's place,' I wanted to say, 'is a dump, where the shower drips cold through green mould holes, where the coffee-table corners are hard with the crystal drift of cocaine and the shagpile carpet heaves its own powder, and it's not Shake 'n' Vac,' but instead I looked out the car window again, desperately trying to find something I recognized, but it was palm trees and dark straight wide streets after dark wide streets. Seemed like everyone was in bed but us.

I felt guilty having them run around like this, but too tired and drunk and lost to do anything about it. The man suggested a hotel. I had to confess I had no money. He offered to pay. The kindness made me cry again – you know, when it's like that, anything nice strokes you at your heart and your throat and you're off again.

Jackie said, 'Listen, it's all right. She can stay at my house.'

The man said, 'Look, I knew you were going to say that. You are too kind, Jacqueline. You don't know anything about her.'

'I know her.'

'What do you mean? You only just met her.'

'Truman, I know her.'

I didn't look over, I still had my face to the window, but I could tell that she was giving him a smile he couldn't resist, and he gave up. He leaned into the driver and said through the glass, 'Miss Collins' home, please, Tod. But you do know that I am accompanying you?'

'You worry too much,' I heard her say.

I must have fallen asleep. Remember arriving, then remember only the lovely white of her house outside and in. A maid, I remember. Recall I didn't know what to do with myself, standing at the bottom of the stairs, wanting to make the most of this amazing meeting, but I was wafting away. Wafted up the white staircase. Wafted into the white of it all somehow. Away. Asleep. Gone.

Morning. I awoke feeling beautiful – was it the white at my eyes? Was it the comfortable bed? Was it the sound of the ocean? No, something else, what was it? Then I realized it was soul music, soul music playing all through the house. I had always liked soul, but I didn't know much about it. I'd had some Soul compilations from Safeshop. Played them in my room. It always did something for me, sent me somewhere.

It was soothing me into the morning, this music, bringing me to the day. I opened my eyes and it was a beautiful room, nearly all white, and before me a mountain of white; I had brought my knees up and with it the thick white duvet. I was smoothing around in all the soul music and the white when I suddenly got the thrill and the fear of remembering I was in Jackie Collins' house. It tipped me out of bed. Then I got that feeling of being a guest in a strange house, hardly breathing, being quiet, trying to make myself not there, moving about ever so delicate, not wanting to disturb anything, almost holding my feet off the ground, leaving no trace. Then a knock on the door nearly made me jump out my skin. Was it someone to arrest me for being in a famous person's house? It was the maid, she was all smiles, didn't speak to me though, it was like she thought I didn't speak English. I suppose I didn't, they wouldn't have heard much Northern round here.

She gave me a folded bathrobe. You could have put it down on the rug and curled right up in it there and then, it was so fluffy; it was like the fluffiness was dying to get out, if I released the cord it would have stood up itself wagging its fluffiness, holding out its fluffy arms for me to step into, it was that fluffy. I took a shower, lovely and warm, as opposed to what Paulie had provided, a juddering, spitting thing and a sliver of rock-hard soap. I really enjoyed it, the scented soap and the warm, warm water all over; it did on the outside what the soul music did on the inside. And after all this I could look forward to the dressing gown, I had the fluff to enter. This was lovely-life LA.

I didn't know whether I should take my time or hurry. I suppose they didn't want me out the house or there wouldn't have been a robe. I wasn't sure what to do. In the end I went out the room and downstairs on the music. It was louder when I left the room, so beautiful. Suddenly it stopped. I was about half-way down the stairs and I realized I was carrying a hangover. It's like the music had kept it above my head and away and now it fell about me like a gravel blanket, irritating everything instantly, putting a coat on my tongue and squeezing each eye. The maid appeared again, smiling, and guided me through to the pool area to sit.

'Miss Collins will join you shortly.' She spoke with measured gaps between words, again like I was foreign. I nodded. 'Would you like something to drink? May I make you something for your—'

She pointed to her head, either she was intuitive, this maid, and she could read a hangover at a hundred paces, or I looked terrible.

I nodded again and said, 'Thank you.' Saw her brow crease up a tad as she strained towards the strange sound.

The pool was enormous, it was just like you see in the magazines, in a real star's house. But it was classical and tranquil here, not overdone. I was just settling into the scene, drowsy in the dream of it between the bleat of my hangover, when I nearly jumped out of my skin. I thought a low flying PanAm special was coming in over my head. I jumped up and looked through the house to see the maid had turned on the blender. It was giant, like everything over here, and she was feeding ingredients and stuff into it. It reminded me of one of those bottomless magician's hats where they put everything in including the hat stand and it's never full.

She brought the drink through with her usual smile, and then went away. As I took my first sip the soul music started up again, so it's hard to know what did the job, but that drink was the smoothest thing I had ever tasted, smooth and soothing, with a little trace of bitterness in there that seemed to draw up the boozy dryness, and with some zings in it here and there that brightened your mouth and turned your tummy the right way up.

I closed my eyes and enjoyed the healing. The music went up a notch or, with soul, is it down deeper a notch? It seems to make you take an extra breath in, even if you've just taken one. It's like a little catch and then ahhhhhhh, you're released into it. It happened, I opened my eyes and she was there. Jackie Collins.

She smiled. She said, 'Crystalline?'

I was shocked at first that she knew that name, then I nodded. She told me Truman had emailed her all that he had found out about me on the net. She knew the whole story. She apologized for him, said he was a good good friend and man but overprotective. He had stayed up all night there, on guard. Set off this morning only after he had checked that Jackie was sleeping soundly in her bed and all the silver was still safe in the drawer. I said I understood and that I liked him and thought he should stand for president. She said he had.

I was glad to find I had a voice in her presence and that I was talking OK, finding something to say. And, after that, all she did was ask me one question and give one line of advice and that was it.

'Is modelling something you want to carry on with?' Surprised, I found I didn't even need to think about it. I nodded. 'Then do it.' And that was it.

After that it was just about being with her. Those few hours in her company gave me a world of wisdom, though there were no lectures or advice or anything like that. I can't describe it proper. It was just like she was an education in herself. She was all the education a young woman needed just by being alive. The way she did things, taking a call, picking a flower, pouring a drink, sharing a joke with the maid, laughing, winking, watching the ocean. She was woman in all her fullness, a rose, beautiful, fragrant, feminine, but that didn't stop her from being powerful and who she wanted to be. It was like I was gathering it from her, getting the fragrance. It was like the good fairy from the films when I was a kid, don't remember her giving much advice, it was just her presence made everything better, the touch of her magic got you on the right track and wicked witches and goblins disintegrated at her jewelled feet.

Suze had been a good teacher, she knew lots of things and could teach you stuff and tell you loads, but she wasn't what she taught, she wasn't it. Jackie was it. She really was everything Suze worked and strained to be, but Jackie was just it. It didn't really matter what she said or did but how she was.

We listened to the soul music and now and again she'd say let's change the track, and it was always right and took us one deeper or one higher or suited the next thing she was going to do. We both did the breath in at one point and smiled.

Too soon it was time to go. She took care of everything, paid for my flight home and got her driver to take me to the airport.

The driver dropped me off at Paulie's to pack. I left a note which said, 'You are a selfish swine and a shallow sod.'

Then I left LA and, resting in Jackie and the soul music, I flew home, flew home on it. I knew what I wanted now, I wanted to be like her. Strong, glamorous, independent, doing what she wanted but still loving and a woman.

Chapter Nineteen

BACK IN LONDON, I REALLY DID FEEL FIRED BY JACKIE. THINGS were good; well I was clean-living at least, that was a start. I didn't feel like getting in touch with everyone straight away, wanted to take my time, let the Jackification complete itself within, let the strength build. No one knew I was back for weeks. Bumped into Lucy the designer in the street, she offered me a room at hers. She had a large place in North London. I took it. It seemed like a hundred years ago now that I'd met her. She was the same, rebellious, eccentric; she had the expression of a little girl on tiptoe looking out the window at a circus parade. She was extreme, sometimes she put big freckles on her face, and she always wore daft hats. Sometimes she'd go out with three on, looking like the Cat in the Hat. She was a really good designer though, always on the verge of breaking through but it never quite happening. Don't know if it was her Two Fingers attitude that held her back – she was a darling of the fashion journalists but not of the establishment;

they'd flirt with her but instead of Lucy playing the game they'd get the two fingers. It was only a matter of time though: they would have to accept her, she was just too good.

Her place was not as you'd expect. It was quite conventional, bland really, mauve walls, nothing much in it, brown curtains, wooden floors, bare light bulbs most places. The only colour was in her studio at the top of the house, a blaze of slung bright colours and fabrics everywhere and wild drawings and materials, and the walls covered in notes and plans and pictures and clothes half made. I used to love going in there, the smell of fresh cloth, too, and the creative energy kind of picked you up and waltzed you round. The house had a nice big living area for parties, it was on two levels, all wooden, one level was like a stage you could launch off. She sometimes got me to wear her clothes and walk up and down there. Sunken living room. No heating though, always cold; people wore coats in the house.

My room was small and sort of long and thin with a tall, narrow window at the end, bit like a nun's cell. But it was calming in that way and uncluttered and what I needed.

Finally I got myself a new agent, not as high-powered as the last, but I wasn't flavour of the month no more and I had a reputation to live down. In fact, I was amazed at how fast things had moved on: new models had come in, you can be so soon forgotten.

I heard some news about Rafe, he'd been sacked from the agency. After the incident with me it seems they had grasped their chance to get rid of him with both hands. He'd gone up to Scotland to try and start up on his own. His need for some cash and the agency's need to protect its reputation had resulted in a settlement being offered to me. I lost loads on the deal. Rafe had itemized everything from the beginning, even down to the first mobile call he'd made to me, the bin bag of clothes after the Manchester shoot and, even, and this was a shock to me, a bill for the hire of an 'extra'. It seems that first autograph I was asked for, in front of the reporter, was set up by him – can you believe it? I lost a lot but I didn't care, I just wanted him off my back and to get going with my life again along Jackie lines.

It was frustrating. It started with really small jobs to begin with, with photographers who knew me and liked me. Some were real duff jobs, but I took them – catalogue work, anything – I needed to build up. It was hard because Rafe had done a hatchet job on me wherever he could; walking off a shoot is taboo in modelling and I'd done it in Venice, no matter the cause. The drink, memories of me exaggerated in the telling and, last but not least, the press had also contributed to my demise – drunk, lost, etc.

God knows what my family thought. As far as I know they didn't care. I was lonely too. I saw a bit of Suze but she was busy trying to raise the money for a health video. She didn't seem too right herself, she was rushing all the time and everywhere, I hardly got time to speak to her, certainly not sitting down. It was just a quick drink in a coffee bar. We'd hardly met and she was leaving, like she was still under

Rafe's watch, like everything we did was furtive. I don't know.

One of the first things I did when I got my first cheque through was send money over to Jackie to repay the air fare and go round to Lispin's, to pay Chucky back. But he'd died, left the flat to the boys, they couldn't believe it. I went to his grave with a big bunch of flowers. It was a funny grave. There had only been the two boys at the funeral and they'd put some of Chucky's knick-knacks round the grave. The sombrero I recognized, and the teapot – the lid had come off and it was half filled with mucky green rainwater. The paint was coming off some of the other things and one had lost its head. Depressing really, a cluster of crazy colour in the grass. The flat was a boon to the boys but blighted by the fact that Harold had been diagnosed HIV positive.

Things were sort of gloomy all round. I was just living quiet in the nun's cell, dull jobs, mauve walls. Lucy was working most of the time, up in the freezing studio in fingerless gloves with a big buttoned old chap's overcoat on and an Ascot hat. I even started to do some of the exercises Suze had taught me, at first to keep warm, but then I started to improve and get into them a bit and follow some of the diet, make smoothies, get in shape.

That's how it was ticking along until I met Li, the Chinese lass from the catwalk days, the one who used to tickle everyone backstage. She tickled me again and persuaded me to go to a party, and there two things happened: I started to drink again and I met Renaldo – in fact, one brought the other with it.

Renaldo was a famous playboy I half knew by reputation. He brought a drink with him when he came to talk to me. He was so attractive, he drew the looks of everyone, such a strong attraction, everything about him – his shirt, his hair, his dark complexion, long eyelashes, the longest I've ever seen on a man – and he was strong-looking, moved strong, like a thoroughbred is strong. If you looked once you had to keep looking, you couldn't just notice him and carry on glancing around the room, you were drawn in, moth to a flame, you stayed till you were scorched, stayed till your wings were burnt off. I had heard things like that about him, but whatever you'd heard you couldn't stop looking. He had dark eyes, and one of those gazes that seems to physically hold you there, stock still. He held out the drink and . . . I couldn't refuse, like when later he asked me for a date, I couldn't refuse, and I began a deadly ride.

It was just so exciting being with him, everywhere we went he seemed to cut it just right, straight through a restaurant to the best table, right across a bar and into the best corner. He took life and made it happen, made it squeal if it didn't shape up. He had the best suits in the world, the fastest car, or at least it felt that way. Every date was like having everything yanked from under you, never getting a footing, like a dangerous adventure, a hunt always, out on the town hunting the life wherever it was, stalking it at speed, fetching it down, devouring it in three, out before the end, turning on a sixpence, a flash in the sky. Hunted down the best meal, hunted out the best party, he was in with your blood and your heartbeat before you knew where you were, an addiction.

One thing you learned pretty soon, was that you had to pay when you were with him. It started with paying your half, then it became, 'Oh, do get this one, Crys, I've forgotten the wallet' or 'You get this, I'll get the next,' but he never did.

At first his focus on you was all intense, all just on you every night, then he was there, then he wasn't, twisting your heart, then he'd turn up with flowers. He had so much going on in his life, then nothing. He'd ask to come over and just lie down all day. He had a company, he even had a PA, but I was never quite sure what he did. And you couldn't ask, he was a man who just didn't answer when he didn't want to, nothing, not even a flicker of recognition that you had spoken.

His kisses were sharp, like being cut, exquisite pain, love-making the same; sometimes he almost threw you away, took you to the wall, the floor. He might ignore you all day, be on his mobile, smoking on his own, not conversing, then he'd suddenly take you with all his might, leave you breathless on the bed, slam the door. Not come back for a day. It was like being in a perpetual tango.

Sundays were deep flaming liquor days; you had to drink brandies with him, otherwise he scoffed, might even leave you for the weekend. I had to read the papers to him, he loved that. I had to be in my underwear, I had to sit across from him in an armchair, and he just listened and looked, both of us burning with brandy.

I was so madly in love with him I would have followed him anywhere. I couldn't help it, I couldn't stop it. I began to wonder if this was the sort of thing between Rafe and Suze. Sometimes it's just wakened up in a woman and you can't understand it but you cannot stop it. That fascination of falling into submissiveness; domination has a seductive power. Once you enter it, in a frightening way you begin to understand the beaten wife who won't leave, the prostitute proud of her pimp, the horror of it but the strange pleasure licking underneath it, addictive, all-encompassing devotion no matter what, the male becomes your single focus. The harder he treats you the more you want of him. Madness. Every part of you screams against it but you cannot resist it. Something ancient in it, historical. Is it back to cavemen days? Is it being dragged by the hair over rocks? Frightening and thrilling, binding but belonging, I don't know but I was in it.

He hated drugs. I've seen him slap girls at parties to stop them taking them. No man would stand up to him when he was in a rage, he was magnificent, like a stallion. We had fights where he held my wrists and I shook and shook and shook while he held me.

It got more and more he saw me when he wanted. I have cried outside looking up at his flat in the rain. He knew I was there; I'd see the curtains pulled to one side. Between times with him I didn't feel alive; only drink took away the edge of the razors. I started missing the odd appointment again, turning up to jobs after having a drink or two. I didn't think they'd notice but they must have done. I got an ultimatum from my agents: clean up or else. Lucy was feeling the strain too, I hadn't paid her rent for a month or two.

It was hard keeping up with Renaldo. I wasn't earning the big money now, and he didn't like me in the same dress twice, and it had to be designer or he'd scoff. Once he tore one off my back; said nothing, waited till we were at the door then tore it off completely. He liked me to wear evening dresses, too, if we went to any occasion, and they had to be designer. Recently he'd taken my last few thousand, to invest it for me, sure-fire thing, etc. Then he told me he'd lost the lot but that was the name of the game, did I have any more? I should have lied but I told him the truth and said I hadn't. He didn't call me for a week. I was pulling my hair out, strand by strand, by Friday.

Chapter Twenty

LUCY SOMETIMES HAD FRIENDS ROUND ON A FRIDAY AND IF I wasn't out I joined them. It was good to be with them, take my mind off things. They were mainly young people in the fashion industry trying to make their way up. It was a bit chilly between me and Lucy, and I ended up chatting to Gab, a young photographer I'd talked to before. We always had a laugh, he knew my story, how my career was diving, and I knew how desperate he was to make his way. I was drunk, as usual. Suddenly he said, 'Listen, Crystalline, listen. What you should do is go back up North, to the supermarket where it all started, do a shoot there after hours when it's empty, just you in there. Then we fire it off to all the mags and get you back up there and me in there.'

We talked ourselves into it, excited, drunk as lords. He had his equipment in the back of the car. We took off. He was driving but shouldn't have been in his state. We'd left with a couple of bottles of wine and we finished them on the way. By the time we got there, bowling up the empty motorways, we were off our heads completely.

We turned into the car park in the dark. Parked up, it felt funny being there and I got a rush of emotion, a wave. All of a sudden I didn't want to go along with it any more, but he had his camera round his neck and was off and out the car. When we got to the door it was already open. It was Ken. He'd seen us on the CCTV. He was a bit awestruck, wanted to say loads but couldn't.

All he managed was, 'Is this your young chap?'

'No, no,' we both said together.

'He's a work colleague,' I said.

Then Ken thought Gab was a famous fashion photographer or something and got all over-respectful, then he showed me the pictures of me from the magazines all around his locker. I asked him if we could go in; he said he couldn't, it would be his job. Then when we told him it was for a shoot, he got excited to be involved. He turned on some lights so we could see our way through to the big doors – oh, the big doors. I told Gab to wait. Then I said, 'Now!' And we went through. Ken must have just turned the lights on, there was a loud thud and then they sprang into life, flicking from one gigantic light to the next, dazzling off the floor, shining on mirrored shelves and illuminating the wares like magic, light shooting round and the whole place massive and empty.

'And then there was light,' said Gab.

He started snapping me straight away. I was all over the place. I sat in a trolley and he sent it spinning, taking pictures as I went round and round, the ceiling turning, the shelves revolving. It took us a while to get into our stride. In the flurry I grabbed a bottle of champagne and opened it. We knocked it back between us, his camera going all the while. Strawberries, chocolates, in the clothes section we kissed, got a bit more carried away. Started snogging, then I'd break away, try some clothes on – holiday gear, skirts, nighties, school uniform, underwear. Snap. Snap. Then we'd be at each other again. It was going a bit too far now, it was too much. He hoisted me up in Cold Foods, my bottom in the freezer. Then Fruit and Veg, doing different things with it, grapes, trickling peach juice on each other's face, licking it off, cucumber and carrot. On like that, on like that. I knocked a stack of cans over. Burst cereal boxes. We ate everything we liked, drank what we wanted, can of stout, the dearest wine on the shelf, chocolate crunchies. Snap. Snap. I ended up so drunk I couldn't see.

We went too far. I was going down the conveyor belt covered in food and drink, in bits of all the clothes I'd tried on. Gab was taking pictures but it had all got too much for him. He looked at me. 'Bloody hell,' is all he said. Ken came running in. Gab took off; he couldn't cope. Ken came over, and I looked up at him bleary-eyed. 'Am I still beautiful?' I said.

I can't remember much else. Ken frantically tried to straighten everything out. Me outside at a phone box. Calling Adam off the card I had saved.

*　　　*　　　*

Then I was in Adam's flat. It was small and neat, in the corner a big ticking grandfather clock much too big for the room, seems it had been passed down through the family. His family was all around too, in pictures. Mum, dad, sister, sister's kids. He was making a cup of tea for me. It was quiet, I felt I hadn't been quiet for months, the spoon on the cup, the sugar bag opening, the sound of the tea being stirred all helped soothe me but also made me feel overpoweringly sad, sad, so sad. Adam was as smart in his dressing gown and pyjamas and slippers as he was as assistant manager on the shop floor; they all looked like Christmas gifts first time worn. He knew how to look after himself, how to live an ordered life, it was apparent in everything somehow, even in the slow sipping of his tea, the saucer by the side. He was 'Supersafeshop man' and I knew I could trust him. Warm tea within, mingling with dirty liquor, the tick of the clock.

We sat in soft armchairs before the gas fire. I talked, he listened, a lovely listening man. I was selective though, it wasn't the full sensational story. He wanted me to contact my mother but I said the time wasn't right, and it wasn't. It was soon dawn and I told him I had to get back to London for a job. That wasn't true. It's just that I was scared back here in my homeland, too close, like the dream, nightmare would be over the longer I stayed, and I wasn't ready for it yet, I wasn't clean enough for the goodness of ordinariness yet. I don't know. He phoned and found out the train times, paid for it I think, I don't remember doing much. He dropped me at the station, he told me not to worry, he was going in early, all would be sorted out at the store. He told me to call him any time. I slept on the train, the ghost train, sleep of the drunk on the train, dark feelings leering like hanging faces, ratcheting round tracks, sharp turns, awake, asleep, spittle and silent eye pressing scream dreams.

Next thing I was back in London.

Chapter Twenty-one

FIRST THING I DISCOVER IS RENALDO HAS FINISHED WITH me. I learn this from an answer-machine message – left by his PA! I hear afterwards that this is how he always does it. What little strength I had is gone now.

As I collapse on a chair, the second message is my agent telling me that I have a bra shoot, basically for a backstreet firm in Coventry. I s'pose fate intended it as a second kick in the teeth, but I didn't feel it, it went in somewhere else, just a distant thud, a stabbing sure enough, but a stabbing on the other side of the world. The death of my career wasn't that important today.

My heart was absolutely broken. Later, of course, it was 'Bastard, bastard,' but for now I could only sit, then stand, then sit, the pain was tremendous. Where does it come from, this pain? It's not like you've been cut into with something, it's not like you are ill, poisoned, but there *is* pain, crippling, unbearable.

No one else was in the house, no one to turn to. I hadn't even changed clothes, but it was an impossibility now, I was suddenly dragging myself around like a wounded deer. I tried ringing Renaldo but I knew it was useless, answer machine after answer machine, voicemail after voicemail. If he didn't want you to get him, you wouldn't. He was a master at this.

I crossed the hall. There was an envelope on the table addressed to me. I opened it, it was from Lucy. It was a nice letter but basically it was telling me she wanted me to leave. I knew it was coming, I accepted it and, again against the big pain, it wasn't much. I made it to the shower and, once the door shut and the warm water fell, that's where I cried and cried. I wanted him so bad.

I tried phoning a few people but no one was about; I had to sit with it on my own. If I went outside, I wanted to come back in; when I was in, I wanted to go out. I was angry, I wanted to kill him, I was broken, I wanted to lie in his arms, burrow right into him. I carried on trying to phone him but I got nowhere. The only vaguely human voice was some woman at one of his companies, a number he'd forgotten he'd given me. She was evasive; I called her a bitch. The anger took me out of it for a few seconds but then the slide back into it was all the worse, an ocean of agony, wherever you went it was there. One thing I hadn't reached for yet was a drink, but I knew it was coming. I just didn't want anything in my body for a while. I thrashed about on the bed for a bit; I fell asleep.

Lucy said, under the circumstances, I could stay longer. I told her I didn't want to, it wasn't fair. I started looking for somewhere else but couldn't find anywhere I could afford. My lovely Lispin said I could go there, said that I could have had Chucky's old place but it had become a sort of sick room for Harold, he was really bad with the HIV, but I didn't think they wanted me there with my problems. I was almost continually drunk now, Lucy just kept out of my way. Cider had become the drink of choice – can you believe it? It was something to do with the sweetness of it and the way it thickened and furred up all your feeling; also, it was cheap. I couldn't eat, in fact I kept being sick all the time. Throwing up first thing had taken the place of my Grandma routines. I needed some work, anything, but there was nothing till the bra shoot.

I heard more about Rafe: the agency he'd started in Glasgow, he couldn't make a go of it, hadn't the money, couldn't raise it. It ended up a glamour-model agency, even called Gorbals Glamour or some such. Someone said it was more like an escort agency supplying call girls. Seemed one girl started playing up and he beat her bad: did she get the diamond on the cheekbone? He ended up in prison. Funny, though, I still didn't feel safe. In some corner of my mind, I felt he was still watching. I dreamt of him springing out of a jack-in-the-box, those tight fists, the knuckles through the skin reading 'HATE' and 'HATE'.

I wanted to phone Suze Dimple, she'd know what to do, but I kept putting it off because I didn't want her to see me in this state. Then I heard she'd committed suicide. Someone I knew saw it in the paper. Swallowed a load of pills, my lovely Dimple gone. I missed the funeral, too drunk, a brain of sour, churning cider, feelings wrapped in rotten peel. I cried three thick apple tears, curled up and sank deeper into the barrel.

Three days later I found out I was pregnant. This was the raw rollercoaster I was on, this is how it kept going. I went after Renaldo this time and I finally tracked him down, by phone only, though. He had nothing to say to the news apart from 'Get rid of it and send me the bill,' and he was gone.

I finally went to pieces. Stopped sleeping altogether. I fell asleep on the bra job, standing up, the photographer threw a cup of cold coffee in my face. I didn't care, I let it run all down me. The make-up girls ran in to wipe me and I just let them, like I was a baby.

I had no fixed abode, I was staying at different people's houses, a week here a week there. People are not so keen on babies in the modelling world, and not so keen on someone throwing up every morning. I'd given up drinking because of the pregnancy but that meant the layers were coming off and I had to face the world and the pain. I was seeing some of the girls I had come up with on cover shots now, making it really big.

I was embarrassed if I saw anyone from those days, the questions, 'What you doing now?' 'Who you with?' Your agent was a means of status; mine was third division really.

Then I got a last chance. Lucy had finally broken through and was doing her first show. She wanted to give me this opportunity to be in it but begged me to behave. My agent, too, made out this was the last chance. I went down there taut as ten wires. I couldn't stop being sick, I'd been sick all morning with the pregnancy.

She had gone really avant garde for this one, had Lucy. We were all in high platform shoes and four-foot headdresses. I kept banging mine on the sink every time I went to throw up. I was a wreck. One of the girls offered me something to calm me down and for the first time ever I took it. God knows what it was but the rest of the show was a blur. I set out to walk the catwalk and the catwalk seemed to go on and on, and on, and I just kept walking it. Next thing I knew I was walking through the council estate where I used to live, in early morning mist and fog – how I got there I don't know to this day. Must have got a train, a lift or maybe I did walk across the country in my platform shoes. Through the fog and the mist I must have looked ten-foot high in the shoes, the clothes, the headdress, lost, weak, stumbling. I finally tripped on a kerb and lay where I fell, couldn't rise; only then did I realize how cold it was. I thought I was going to die.

Suddenly from out the fog a massive figure appeared, panting heavy breath, surrounded by its own mist, dragging one foot, bearing down on me. Was it the drugs? Was it real? It came towards me, I was terrified, I covered me head, I opened me mouth to scream. I must have passed out with fear. I awoke in my mother's lap.

Seems it had been Solemn Ted making his way to work on early shift. He'd carried me in his arms all the way through the estate to our house and given me to my mother without a word. What a strange vision we must have made. Mum just had me, cuddling me, rocking me, and I cried and cried.

I lost the baby. It was a girl.

Chapter Twenty-two

THE DAYS AND WEEKS FOLLOWING I COULDN'T TELL YOU MUCH about. I just stayed with my mum. She kept me close by. People tried to come but Mum politely refused them. 'She's not ready yet, love,' I'd hear her saying down the phone.

I slept in my old room, everything was the same, even the Blu-Tack still there from the Paulie poster. My gran's picture still in the frame.

I don't remember cleaning myself much – must have done, but body care lost any prominence in my life, never got back to the Grandma routine, didn't feel worthy of it. I was nothing. There was guilt, there was shame, I didn't even have the energy for hate any more but if I did have any it was reserved for me, it stopped at me.

I felt a bit better at night, when the lights went on and the swish of the curtain came. I found a big sloppy cardigan, I wore it all the time, it was like I didn't want to have a shape any more. I didn't know what was going on out there, outside our home. I'd sit staring out the window but not seeing anything. Glad when the curtains went across, another swish, another day over. Don't remember eating, tasting anything. Mum never rushed me, she just sat with me, I think she even fed me sometimes. Kissed me on the cheek if she had to go out, on her return, before bed, when I awoke in the morning. I watched telly, telly, telly, waited for the swish, the back of another day, the lamp going on. Not comfort, don't think that, just a different shade to the misery that I appreciated and a sign, a swishing sign that soon be sleep, soon be gone. I didn't look at the papers just in case there was something about me in them.

Our Dawn came round; it was taking her longer to accept me. At first all she said was 'That's my cardigan.'

Later she sat with me. Later we had a cry. Later she told me to get myself together. Later we fell out again. Then made up. Sisters. Eventually, when she saw I had no fight, she just got kind like Mum. My mind was clearing a bit without the drink, all I did was occasionally join me mum of an evening in a Mackeson; she said it would build me up. We had a little chat then, she called them our Mackeson talks. My room was like I'd never been away, but I had been away. It was the same, I was different. I'd cry sometimes and I didn't know why, then I realized it was for the fresh girl who once lay there. She was like another person to me now, someone I'd known a long time ago.

Only person I saw was Solemn Ted passing, going up and down, his Brylcreemed head above the privets. He'd pretend he wasn't looking but there was a kind of glance. Mum said it wasn't his usual way to work, he lived the other side of the estate, but he was coming this way to keep an eye on me. In our next Mackeson talk she told me that me dad had been one of the only ones who'd bothered with Solemn, and he'd never forgot. He was never too fond of Mum, he thought she wasn't right for Dad, but he'd always kept a silent, solemn eye on me. So that was it – and all those years I thought he was eyeing me up. You can get things wrong. I get things wrong.

Mark got married while I was home. I heard about it. I don't know if I felt happy for him, I didn't feel at all most days. I tried to force some feeling one way or another but there was nothing there. If it had been me in white. I'd expected it to be me once. We would have had a little house somewhere by now.

One morning a letter came for me, it was a tax bill. I didn't understand it, it was for thousands of pounds. Rafe said he had taken care of all that. I just left it, I tucked it away in the cardigan pocket. I had to sit on it, tuck it under with the rest of the ache, add it to the pile. I had to. Who would I tell? I caught sight of me little mum out the kitchen window, she was mustering all her strength, pushing up the washing on the washing line with a clothes prop, looked like a pole vault in her little hands. I couldn't add any more to her burdens. It was only morning, there were hours ahead until the swish. I pulled the cardigan tighter round me.

*   *   *

My mum went out one night, rare, visiting a friend in hospital. I was sitting, looking out the window, the street was darkening. I was eager for the dark, as usual, eager for the swish, suddenly I saw Ken passing. I was a bit angry at first – people knew not to call. Then I saw he was agitated, wanted to call but knew he shouldn't. I went upstairs to get ready for bed. I looked down and saw him still there under the lamp post. I went out and asked him in.

He was so sorry 'to have come and troubled me in me time of trouble'. I offered him a drink, tea. He said, 'Have thee nowt stronger?'

All there was was half a bottle of sherry. I poured him a glass. He had something to say but didn't know where to begin. In the end I asked him to spit it out, whatever it was it couldn't be that bad. He said it was that bad, he said he'd had to take the day off work because of the worry of it, first time in twenty years. He had another glass of sherry and then he told me that the night I had spent in the supermarket had gone on to CCTV camera. He'd forgotten until he was clocking off, so he took the video cassette home with him to protect me. He kept forgetting to destroy it. Now his brother had found it; his brother's a market trader, wide boy, fancies himself as a bit of a gangster. Ken tried to get it back, but the younger brother punched him. 'You don't mess with our Idris,' Ken said. 'He's saying he might sell it on the black market, he's saying he might blackmail you, he's saying all sorts.' He was in tears. 'All sorts he's saying.'

He gave me their number, seems they wanted to talk to

me. He was so sorry. He left. On my own, numb as always, but slowly this was cutting into me, still a way off at first, faint, then I began to feel it and see, like shadows, something of the consequences, what this might mean. I drank the rest of the sherry to kill it before it got going and then phoned Gab.

He was shocked, panicked, could finish his career before it had even started. He'd come up. I had to wait a day. When Mum heard someone was going to visit from London, at first she was nervous they were going to take me back into it all, but I assured her he was an old friend. She was glad of it then, thought he might be of help, get me out of myself.

First thing he said was 'You look terrible.'

'Thanks, and so do you,' I said.

He did too. He was on something, I could tell. He looked older, his hair seemed to have suddenly started receding, his forehead was shiny, glistening. He told me he wasn't doing very well at all, his career was going nowhere; it was getting that bad he was thinking of going back to the seaside, where he started as a kid, taking shots of tourists with a parrot – more money than he ever made with modelling and more girls. He was also in debt, to people you shouldn't be in debt to, and that's all he'd say. At this he gave me two photo memory cards, said they were from the Safeshop shoot. He could have sold them to the tabloids for at least twenty grand at one time; he wanted me to have them as the temptation was getting too strong. I took them and put them in my cardie pocket. After that I knew he was still decent and all right and would help me out of this mess. Later he called Ken's brother and then went to see him.

It was late when he got back. I took him up to my room and he told me what had gone on. He was flushed. There were two of them, Idris and his mate.

'They wanted money at first but I convinced them we were broke. I think they knew that really and had a plan B. Here it is.' He paused. 'They won't give the tape up unless we agree to do another, proper one. They want me to direct it. They talk in terms of the money we could make. They'll pay us some up-front, straight away, few grand, each, the rest – the real money – follows after. It's blackmail but an opportunity at the same time. If we don't, they say, though the quality's crap, they will release the supermarket tape and sell it somehow.'

He stared at me. 'What do you think? I . . . I'm up for it but it's up to you.'

For the past weeks I had felt like I was sitting on nails or a slow fire, in agony but not moving. I needed to move in some direction. I didn't care about myself – what did it matter in what direction I moved as long as I moved? I had the tax bill to pay. I nodded. Gab left straight away to sort it out before I could change my mind. It took no time, a day or so, to arrange it.

Chapter Twenty-three

IT WAS THE NIGHT OF THE SHOOT. I STARTED GETTING MADE up a bit, making an effort. Mum was pleased – she thought I was going out. Gab picked me up. It was a cold dark night. We went to the location, a big cash and carry. We waited across the road in Gab's car. It was so cold. They were late. It was almost colder in his car than outside, like sitting in a fridge; he had no heating, it was broken. Eventually a mucky white van rounded the corner. Two blokes got out, real laddish types, one in a flying jacket, jeans, podgy, cocky, with blond highlights, the other with a beard, dumber-looking, slow-moving. Both had had a few pints. We got out to meet them. They came over. The one with the beard stood way too close to me.

'I enjoyed your last film, Miss Crystalline.'

They both started laughing. Sniggering. I flushed a little but didn't blush. That's one side benefit of having no dignity left. Gab was embarrassed about it but high – I could tell when he picked me up – his mind spinning, his eyes wide and hard.

He went to the van to see what equipment they'd got. I could hear them rummaging about among the tools in the back of the van. I had expected a full crew like the old days, I don't know why. Gab came back over to me.

'I think they got the camera off a car boot. They've a hold-all full of cash in there though, must be a good few grand in it.'

The camera came out – seemed they'd got it off some bloke who'd done weddings with it years ago. It was a monster. Paint stains on it. Big sock on the mike like a dirty teddy. Looked like it might work off petrol. It then took them about twenty minutes to unravel all the leads. While they did, I saw they were nervous, like boys.

When we went to enter the cash and carry, they realized they had come without the keys. They had to call the owner. Everyone was freezing. They took out a bottle of whisky and cracked open the top. I was scared. I didn't want them drunk.

The owner arrived in a dusty old Mercedes, lolloping around the corner. A big man got out. I was across the road so couldn't see him too clearly in this light, but he looked Indian but with curly hair, mac and shirt open; he didn't seem to feel the cold. They immediately went to greet him and got a wad of money from the hold-all to give to him. He stuffed it in his coat pockets as he opened up for them. They seemed deferential, wary, Idris trying to cover it with bravado, but it was obvious. They went in, Gab beckoned to me and I crossed the road.

Inside, Idris and Gab checked out the location, the bearded one sorted out the camera, and the owner took off up to a glass booth way above. It was as cold as outside, maybe even colder because massive draughts were running through like cold rivers. It was enormous, a warehouse really, concrete floors, shelves and shelves of stuff going up almost to the roof. I saw the light go on in the owner's booth.

Then the lights started to come on around the cash and carry, long, harsh striplights. The two men gave me a bag. They had managed somewhere to get a checkout uniform. Also in the bag were packets of brand-new stockings and suspenders, and some stilettos. All unlikely for a checkout girl. So for the second time in my life I donned the check-out girl uniform.

They hadn't yet decided between themselves who was going to be the man in the film. Now they were down to doing it you could see they were nervous. I was just frozen outside and inside, no feelings, numb – thank God.

Gab and Idris were arguing about story, script.

'We'll just make it up as we go along, what does it matter? He'll come round the corner,' Idris said.

'See her,' said the other.

'Yeah, see her, up that ladder.' Idris pointed out a long ladder propped against the tinned section.

'He's shopping,' the other said.

They started laughing again.

'You better be able to keep it up.'

'Don't worry about me, mate.'

'This film's got to be longer than twenty seconds.'

'Piss off.'

'Here, have another.'

All that. They decided I should be climbing up the ladder with a can of beans. The bearded one would come round pushing a trolley and see me up there. See up my skirt.

Idris shouted, 'OK . . . start . . .'

'You mean "Action", dun't you?' slurred the bearded one.

'There better be,' said Idris.

They both sniggered.

I came out. I walked to the ladder and started to slowly climb. I suddenly realized I was climbing in deathly silence. I looked down and the two of them were frozen, standing there slack-mouthed, just looking up at me, Idris with the camera on his shoulder.

Gab was trying to get a shot lined up and the bearded one snapped, 'Never mind all that. Carry on up the ladder!'

I carried on; they stood silent, like in a trance. Gab had to nudge Idris to get him to point the camera.

Up the ladder I went, up and up – when was it going to stop? When was it going to stop? My stilettos made it difficult to climb, I either had to do it sort of on the tips of my toes or I had to let the heels slot over the rung and then release them. Climbing, slowly climbing, one rung after the other, I couldn't hold the ladder properly with the bean can in my hand. I was trembling with the cold and uncertainty, aware of them below.

I started to get upset. I felt sick, scared, I started really shaking. Suddenly I began to swoon, righted myself, then swooned again, I was passing out. I looked across, saw the owner in his booth. He looked across at me, we caught each other's eye. He could see the fear in my eyes, the hurt. He came out the booth and down the steps calling, 'STOP!'

He came across, jumped on to a sort of stacker truck, a sort of fork lift, set it going and came up toward me. When he got level with me he lifted me in the cage with him and put his arms around me, put his coat around me and took me down. It turned out they'd forgot to put film in the camera. The owner at this point was fed up with them.

'Here, bugger off, cowboys!'

He threw them out, then he spoke to us. 'They give it bad name. You can make nice film with bit of care. Doesn't have to be all rumpety pumpety. Sweet lady, don't do no more with them.'

He took the money out that they'd given him, he put some back in his pocket then split the thick wodge that was left, handed half to Gab, the other half to me, but I just didn't want it, I couldn't take it. I turned away; anything from them was dirty. I was dirty, could feel myself breaking up, it was like the end of something, the end of some terrible sequence in a film, end of a chapter. I broke down. Trembling legs, lost in his mac, his massive mac that flooded out over the floor. I couldn't find my hands in it to cover my face. He put his enormous arms around me. Gab shot off with the cash.

Even though the owner was just in a shirt, open to below the chest, his body was like a heater, so warm.

'Now then, now then. Listen to me. Everything is all right now. It's all over and gone. What is your name?'

'Cryst . . . Linda.'

'My name is Trinity Patel. Do me honour, Linda, of letting me take you to dinner. Come, please.'

I nodded.

We went to a local Indian restaurant. As soon as we walked in there was activity – a table found for him, chairs pulled back, menus flying in, all that. Not only that, the positive voltage of the place seemed to go up – more smiles, more lights, more music, more colour. But it wasn't that they were afraid of him, or in awe of him or something, they just liked him. It was a real deep kind of like, it was like they were pleased too, like they were curried with pleasure to have him there. I didn't need to order – he ordered near enough everything on the menu, some things twice. When it came he looked over the dishes, his eyes dancing, his face glowing, savouring those last few seconds before he satisfied his appetite. It was like he was almost tickling himself, lifting lids, putting them back, then lifting them again, sniffing, then suddenly he nodded, then laughed and nodded and, like a king at the head of the banquet, shouted, 'Eat, Linda, eat.'

And boy almighty could he eat, but not gluttonous – joyous, it made you want to laugh and bang your fists on the table alongside him and tuck right in there with him, following on after as he glided over the dishes, quick and light, sucking his fingers, rolling his eyes, beaming like a genie.

He talked as we ate. Seemed he was the local cash and carry king. Had an Irish mother and an Indian father. Lived out there as a kid, came over here and started on the markets and now has cash and carries all over, mainly in the north-west but some around the country and also abroad. All I could think was he had the most gentle, the gentlest of eyes, like a panda or something.

After a while I told him about the mess I was in. When I looked up he was crying, massive tears rolling down his cheeks. He couldn't eat anything after that, asked them to take all the food away, clear the table. Then he put a blank cheque down. He told me to fill it in for whatever I wanted, he didn't care if it broke him. After that I couldn't not see him again.

Chapter Twenty-four

NEXT TIME WE MET HE HAD GOT THE CCTV TAPE BACK. 'YOU won't hear from them no more,' he said. I burnt it later, along with the films Gab had given me. It felt like the beginning of the end of something.

Trinity and me started seeing a lot of each other; he was like a jolly magnet you got stuck to somehow, I can't describe it.

He started coming to the house to pick me up. Mum didn't know what to make of it. She called him the Giggling Sheik of Arabeake. She wasn't sure at first, I think she was afraid of me getting hurt again. Then one time I came downstairs and he was cutting her toenails. After that everything had to be all right. He won Dawn over by making the kids laugh and laugh and keeping her in a continual supply of cash and carry stuff, enormous, inexhaustible packs of household items – you could hardly get in her kitchen. The kids used to sit on them to eat their breakfast, usually poured from ginormous cereal boxes. She sold some stuff off, out the back windows to the neighbours. The neighbours called him Wise Man: 'Hey, Dawn, has he been yet, bearing gifts from afar?'

Instead of gold, frankincense and myrrh, it was toilet rolls, soap powder and mirth. He had property all over the place. He had a bungalow in a town by the sea somewhere. One afternoon we had a drive over to look at it.

It was in a quiet place, a street or so back from the front in a sedate little seaside town. It was a small old-fashioned bungalow built in deep-red brick and pebbledash, me mum's favourite. It had a little gate of swirling steel, and one of those seaside gardens of gravel and sand with hard-looking plants in light purples and pale greens, and even an anchor for a rockery. It looked a bit like the bottom of a fish tank. Inside, the bungalow hadn't been touched since the seventies. It wasn't dusty but musty, still all mismatched decoration and a whirling carpet that set your head spinning, tiled coffee tables on shaggy rugs and a drinks bar in studded plastic with the bottles still half full at the back. There was even plastic fruit on the sideboard. He'd bought it fully furnished from distant relatives of the owner who had inherited it. They lived abroad, probably never even saw it. It just hadn't been touched – even the ashtrays were still out, glazed psychedelic fish-shaped ones or souvenir ones with Scottish castles on them. You expected the previous owner to walk back in at any minute, dusting off their garden gloves and pouring a sherry. Trinity thought it was really smart though because he could open the window and hear the sea.

'Listen to waves, Linda, sniff up the air all salted and vinegared.'

He opened all the windows that day. It was a bit draughty but you were OK if you kept close to him, he was like a convector heater. We cuddled up and kissed a bit, even his mouth and lips were really hot; afterward there was a sweet burn on your tongue like you get eating humbugs. I felt really soothed when I was with him and, like, humming a little with happiness, the balm of him, his sing-song voice. He took me on a tour of the place: three small bedrooms all with nylon quilts in purple or yellow flowers and velvet studded headboards. Carpets each a different colour, whirling and swirling in and out the rooms. The bathroom in shell-shaped tiles, shells everywhere, and then the little kitchen with high stools at a breakfast bar and a small back garden. And I nearly forgot, from the front window, if you got on your toes and strained over to one side, you could see the sea. He told me I could live there if I wanted to. When we left and locked up he put the keys in my hand.

That night I thought about it long and hard and I decided I needed to get away from home for a while. I had got some of my strength back, but to really recover I needed to stand on my own two feet a little bit more. I moved in.

Trinity would come down about three times a week. I never knew when, and I quite liked it that way. He gave me money, not regular, just whenever he thought about it, but it were always in wads that lasted me. He called money 'tickets to the bizarre'.

'Plenty tickets to the bizarre for us today, sweet one, get us anything we please.'

I often came in and there was a brand-new dress in the wardrobe, always long and shimmering and sparkling, that's what he liked the best. They were slightly old-fashioned but I didn't mind; no one but him ever saw me in them. We never went anywhere except to the local restaurants. There were only two, one Chinese, one English fare, and they were always half empty anyway and the diners elderly and not interested in the latest trends. It was freeing that it didn't matter, no fashion connoisseurs, press or other models to compete with, no judging looks, no designers present. That all seemed so far away, thank God.

We never went out anywhere, no walks by the sea or anything like that, just ate and lay around. He had no patience with television. He ate only one meal a day but it was massive; whether at home or in a restaurant it was always a banquet. Sometimes at 3 a.m. he'd turn up and we'd eat at the table, or sometimes he'd just throw a blanket on the floor and lay out all the dishes he'd brought, or we'd empty everything from the fridge and cupboards on to paper plates, or the microwave would ping all night with stuff he'd brought from the cash and carry.

He was always warm. Soon as he came through the door, whatever the weather he'd take his shirt off. His skin was very sweet-smelling, a bit like coconut, and lovely and smooth, bit like it was dusted with invisible icing, or like something soft and sugar-powdery was mixed right in with it, bit like what you get on Turkish delight, and he never seemed to sweat or get smelly under his arms. Sex was different, wonderful really, he only had a small penis, tiny even when erect.

'Oh, don't mind me down there, darling,' he'd say. 'There is plenty we can do.'

And there was. We had such fun and laughter, laughter. Never laughed so much in bed. Falling out and getting back in at times, so funny, tears streaming down our cheeks. He'd tickle up warm funny love all around you, a golden cuddling hue. I tried to Kegel him once or twice but there really wasn't anything to hold. But it was good and it was hot as you can imagine. When he was inside me a beautiful heat radiated in a sort of spiral starting small, like a ring on an electric cooker, up and up your body. If it had a colour it would have been glowing red, that's for sure, up and up, sweet heat around your heart and burning your cheeks up and making you pant with pleasure. Funny to be panting and there's no movement.

The sweet scent of him stayed on the sheets long after he'd gone. I'd sometimes wrap myself up in it and smile. Sometimes I'd just lie out on top of him like he was a Li-Lo. Head on his chest. He liked that.

He liked fluffy things too. He'd bring me fluffy things, like pink fluffy slippers, then have me pass them over his light-chocolate body. He liked watching pornography. I used to fall asleep I found it so boring. He liked soft-porn top-shelf magazines too. He read the saucy readers' letters out to me. He was so innocent he thought it was all real. 'Oh, golly,' he'd say.

The magazines were always all over the house; he read them instead of books or the paper. He liked them to hand. It was incongruous in the old people's setting of the bungalow.

It wasn't that he was perverted or anything, he just liked titillation. Would like to have been in a constant state of tickling titillation. After a big meal he sometimes even liked me to brush his teeth, he liked the personal ticklishness of it. He really cheered me up, the colour was coming back to my cheeks, I was getting better.

He would turn up with carrier bags full of money and hide them under the bed. There were loads of them under there. Anything I wanted I just asked him for; you could get absolutely anything when you were in cash and carry. Gifts galore, jewellery, gadgets, flowers, chocolates in big old-fashioned boxes. They piled up in the corner.

After a while though, when he wasn't there I got a bit bored. I was on my own in this small town and, apart from the sea, there was nothing there. So he taught me to drive.

I was the worst driver in the land. Funny, you'd have thought I would be quite good, with my skill on the tills and that, but no, it was all those cars around me suddenly and the traffic lights and signals and people crossing. I couldn't cope with all that and the gears and finding the 'bite' and the constant stalling on the high street etc. In the end he came down in his white Mercedes automatic and things looked up a bit.

He taught me in song; he sang the instructions, 'Mirror signal manoeuvre,' he sang them out as we drove along. He enjoyed the whole thing hugely. If I got trapped and turned a three-point turn into a fifty-two point turn, he thought it was the hoot of all time. When I bumped the car he cried with laughter; if I scraped it, which I did twice, he opened the window and cheered. Cheering along the seafront road was his favourite, he loved it, window down, his head out, his head out and blasted with his favourite salt-sea vinegared air. I think he'd have loved me to go straight down the prom and off into the sea and we'd have glided under there, him guiding me through the fishes and sunk ships, singing out instructions.

But I passed first time, God knows how – perhaps it was because it was a beautiful sunny day, seagulls in the clear blue sky, all that; perhaps it was because the examiner was glad of someone under sixty-five to test in that deserted little town. But it was one of the best feelings of my life. Trinity was waiting for me and he juggled me up and down and round and round in the street. Laughing and squeezing and giggling and kissing me all over my face. He even kissed the examiner and gave him a box of shirts and gigantic supersize soap powder for his wife, and a lifetime's supply of socks or speaking alarm clocks or washing-up liquid or Georgian figurines on a swing – the choice was his. After that he would sometimes take me to work with him. I would be his driver for the day.

He had cash and carries all over the place. The main one was the big one where we met, the headquarters, I suppose. Mai worked there, a Thai woman, she was his right hand really, plain, dark, thick spectacles, really well spoken, no accent whatsoever, always a look of concern. He'd seen her destitute in Thailand, she had literally been left at the side of the road, a bag of little bones begging for her life. He'd wept at the sight of her, picked her up and brought her home. Paid for a boarding-school education. Now she worked with him and she was devoted to him.

Chapter Twenty-five

I SOON BEGAN TO SEE THE OTHER SIDE OF THE OPERATION. Literally, if you had cash you could carry anything out of there. All sorts in the back – pinched stuff, pirated stuff, stuff coming in from all over the world. Trinity was on the phone all the time, two phones at once sometimes. Drugs, too – I soon recognized when he was talking about them on the phone. To try and disguise it he had his own code, spoke in cash and carry terms: Daz or Persil extra for cocaine, speed was Hundreds and thousands, Bisto, heroin. Between calls he would see me sitting in the corner of the office and come and plant big, sloppy kisses all over my face, hold my hand to his chest.

'Now you see another side to the Trinity. I not a bad boy, am I? Am I?'

I often drove him on the rounds of his different premises when he collected rents. Some were residential, some shops, some just storage places. In one house they were making a porn movie. More crew than mine, professional I suppose. I waited in the hall for Trinity; the action was in a room off the living room. What struck me was how strangely silent and clinical the atmosphere was. I could see naked men sat in the kitchen waiting their turn; one was doing a crossword. I felt sick for the girl inside. Then I heard her voice.

'Stop a minute, please. How many more bloke-a-mans?'

I couldn't believe it. Oh no. Wendy. I didn't look further. It turned my stomach so. I ran for the car.

One night Trinity got in the car and gave me a gun. Told me to keep it in my handbag. Mai explained it all later, she was really worried about him. It was a drug war, they came up every four years or so. It was with a man named Sugarstealer, they called him that 'cause though he was really rich, he still lived on a council estate and the garden of his house was high all over with those tall soft purple and white weeds with soft fluffy parcels of seeds called sugarstealers. They blow off in soft streams. I remembered driving him to that one, that sugarstealer house, sitting in the car while he went in, thinking I've never seen such an overgrown garden, and then a breeze passing over it and seeing thousands and thousands of soft sugarstealers shaken free and flying, some landing delicate on the bonnet of the car, or clinging a second to the wing mirrors before spiralling off again in the wind. It would have been really beautiful if you didn't think of them as dirty weeds.

It stays in my mind too because that day Trinity delivered to him about ten stacks of baby food. I remember thinking, so much baby food they must have loads of kids, but no, it turned out that was because of his stomach, Sugarstealer lived off baby food. I caught a glimpse of him through the window, raising his hand in a weak wave to Trinity as he left. You'd think he was a poor pensioner – cardie, vest, slippers – but seemed he was behind much of the criminal activity in town, financed lots of things, bank jobs, drugs, porn, the very hard stuff; the saunas were all his. He looked like a nice old grand-dad, white straggly soft sugarstealer hair even, you wouldn't believe it. Funny, the way they were though, even when there was fighting he'd still have the baby food delivered. Trinity didn't deliver it himself then, but he made sure it got through. It's like, it's all business never personal.

It was horrible though; there was tension for days. Trinity had a couple of bouncers about for a bit. One night though there was just me and him in the cash and carry – Mother's Day it was, I remember 'cause I was wandering the chocolate shelves looking for something for Mum – suddenly a gigantic plastic jar shattered beside me and I was hit in the face with a shower of sweets. It was a shot, a gunshot; another rang out and cut into the tin of Cadbury's Roses beside me.

I hit the floor.

'You idiot!' someone shouted to someone. 'Not her.'

I was terrified, bit like a quiet chaos, a hushed rushing, whispers here, there. I got my gun out, dropped it, it went skidding away across the floor. I was shaking like a leaf, I could hear people running about, mayhem, then for a fleeting flash of a second something – I can't describe it, a sense of recognition of something, a fast flicker gone in the chaos. Oh God, what was happening? I was on my stomach crawling toward the gun, then on all fours like a dog scurrying down the aisles. I didn't know you could shake so much. The gun had gone spinning under some shelving, I reached under for it. On the way back up through the gap in the boxes I saw a figure aiming with a rifle. I looked up and saw Trinity up in the booth, still about his work: it was soundproof – he hadn't heard a thing.

I hit the stack with my shoulder and the boxes toppled on to the gunman, but he was already firing, all it did was knock him off his shot. I saw Trinity fall. I was mad now, all fear had left me. I started shooting the gun, again and again and again, but they were gone as quick as they came and then there was silence, silence like you never knew, then through the still air a sugarstealer floated, down, down, landing gently on the back of my hand.

Trinity was in hospital. He was all covered in tubes at first. We thought for sure he would die. The bullet had blasted through his body and neck and jaw and skimmed his brain; it was a mess. They said a fraction to the left and he would have been dead, so perhaps I saved him. It was little comfort when you saw him, he seemed to be bruised all over, his lovely skin black and blue, pale yellow and red in places. There was a fading old watercolour on the wall of a ship in a sunrise and it was the same colours, it was the same colours. We couldn't bear it, his swollen swollen face, his eyes swollen up shut, we didn't know if they were open or closed. Lots of people came all the time paying their respects; Mum came in, Dawn came. Mai and I stayed almost continuously. One of the bouquets that was delivered was of long purple and white sugarstealers.

'Unusual display,' the nurse said.

I could see Sugarstealer in his slippers, little jar of baby food in a tray on his lap, slowly teaspooning it into the soft skin hole of his toothless mouth, waiting to hear of Trinity's end, but we weren't going to let that happen. Mai and I talked to him all the time, I talked of the bungalow and the sea and food and Mai talked to him about the business.

The police came of course, but we didn't say anything. Mai told me, she had hold of my hand at the time and nearly broke every bone in it, it was so important. 'Say nothing. Listen, you were on the floor the whole time, you saw nothing – nothing, understand?'

'Yes. Yes.'

So I said what she said, but their questioning did make me examine it all again, whatever I was saying to them, the real events, they started in my mind again. There was something, that moment of recognition I had when it was all happening – what was it?

Then it suddenly came to me in a flash, a flash as quick as I had seen it: a pair of stack heels under one of the shelves.

Slowly Trinity came back but he would be in hospital for some time. Mai and me ran the cash and carry together while he was recovering. We were good, too, and legit, we didn't touch the black-market side of things. I picked it up fast, it gave me such confidence. We did everything – I even had a stint as checkout. Organizing, ordering, deal-making: if you could make deals with some of these traders and suppliers, I'm telling you, you could make deals with anyone.

While I was stocktaking I found a box of rare American soul tapes, must have been there for years. I played them, turned the volume up full, had them through the speakers of the cash and carry. I went out on to the floor and opened my arms to be flooded by the sound. I felt full with the spirit of Jackie. Jackified again, clean and strong.

When Trinity came home he was different. Limping, one of his eyes bound in a stare. Never took his shirt off again. No more banquets, he had no real feeling for food any more, ate little; it was almost unbearable to see him picking at things like Pot Noodles and tinned spaghetti on toast. That mighty appetite gone. It was the same with sex; he didn't seem to want to know. It was the same for his work; he let Mai do it, handed everything over to her. He began to sell his properties, he wanted disposable cash, he wanted to pursue a new obsession: me. Not just me for myself, but he'd got it in his head he wanted his queen to be back at the top as a model, and his idea of this was to get me in the top-shelf soft-porn magazines. He wouldn't let me work at the cash and carry no more. I was reluctant to let it go but he went mad. It was the first time I saw temper from him ever. He wouldn't listen. I backed down and went back to the bungalow; he pursued his dream of getting me into those top-shelf magazines. He got me an engagement, his absolute dream come true, a double page spread in the *Daily Sport*. But for me it was a wake-up call. I had to leave.

He understood in the end. Though he'd changed, there was still plenty of heart; it was just too big to be blasted by any gunshot, by anything. We held each other at the front of the bungalow and wept and wept. Just before I got in the car he asked me to wait, he'd almost forgot. He went in the bungalow and came out with all the carrier bags of cash from under the bed. He gave them to me.

Chapter Twenty-six

I MOVED INTO A FLAT NOT FAR FROM THE CENTRE OF MY HOME town. I suddenly realized it was the first time I'd been on my own. Properly on my own. I had money, I had some business understanding now. I had my health back, I was addiction-free, debt-free, I just didn't know what to do next. I was lost. I felt a lot of energy, skills I'd built up, but I didn't know what to do. Not back to modelling, I knew that, and though I'd enjoyed cash and carry, it wasn't for me.

One morning a package arrived. It had been on a bit of a runaround before reaching me, landed at almost every flat I ever stayed at. It was poignant somehow, reading all the addresses off, then seeing them scribbled out and written over, sent on again. Many hands that I'd known must have touched it. Passed it on. I opened it, intrigued. It turned out it was some of Suze Dimple's effects she'd wanted me to have; her relatives had forwarded them on to me. It was a half-finished manuscript she had been working on. It was about how to succeed in life. I know things hadn't ended well for her – perhaps that's why it wasn't finished – but she did know a lot and she'd helped many people. Was she helping me? My thoughts returned to her and I was pleased she'd entrusted it to me. I made myself really comfortable before I started. Put the fire on, made a cup of tea – not chamomile, sorry, Suze – pulled the chair up to the fire and started to read.

Turning the first page was a strange sensation. It was the original, I was sure, perhaps the only copy, and I felt her on that first page. The first chapter was called 'It'. It spoke directly to me. Was a bit like she was speaking to me directly.

Today, sit with yourself and think where you are, look at your body, your mind, what you have around you. Are you happy with it all? If so, gently put this book aside; if not, then we are about to embark on a journey together, only come along if you seriously want to become all you are capable of becoming, because not only are we going to make all your dreams come true, really true, this time they are truly all going to happen. Thrilling, but scary, isn't it? You, you reading, you are going to have it all – yes, you, you reading – but we will also find something else along the way . . .

I totally forgot about the tea, I was excited. Suze knew how to do it. I couldn't wait to turn the pages.

It will come to you, your idea, 'it', that which is yours to pursue, it will come now that you have started reading, in

207

the next day or two, and it will be yours to follow. It will come, it might come in a moment or out of something you never imagined, when you least expect it. Keep open . . . Don't read further. Leave it now a while and return later.

It was hard to leave off but I felt it best to follow. It said not to think about it, but that set me thinking, thinking of all sorts. What's my idea? What am I looking for? It was with me all the time, I kept turning it over in my head. I knew there was something to come. What was it? I had changed, I wasn't the fresh-faced innocent I was at the beginning of this story, I had skills now, I had inner strength, I'd seen life. Jackie had found it. I want something like that. Get Jackified good and proper this time.

In fact, after a day or so it started a bit of tension in my mind. I started wishing in some ways I hadn't read it, but there was no going back now. I gave in and returned to the book. I couldn't resist.

You've come back, you couldn't resist, could you? Nothing's happened yet? Don't fear, it's on its way, all I say is this: when it starts, act. Act immediately, stop whatever you are doing and begin on it! Not later that evening, not when you get home, not after the weekend, no, there and then. There and then. Act.

I carried on doing normal things, picking up a few bits and pieces for the flat, make it more homely, buying food to keep me healthy. I don't know if that was a Suze influence, but all the time it was in the back of my mind.

One day, I was walking down the high street, half there, half dreaming. I was shocked out of my daze by the sight of a homeless lad. He looked like he was going to approach me. I wanted to give him something but had no change, so I turned into a newsagent's to buy something. As always, I looked along the magazines; I knew one of the girls on one of the covers. I took it down to buy. I hadn't bought a fashion magazine for a long time. Two old ladies were in there. One fat, one little and trim.

'Look at that one,' said the little one, pointing at my magazine.

'A veritable skelinkton,' said the other.

'These young models now, they all end up looking like heroin addicts,' said the shopkeeper.

'It's true, what health 'av' they got?'

'What happened to the hour-glass figure?'

'You've still got it, dear, you've gone twenty-four-hour, that's all.'

'Saucy sod. Anyway, better than you, Greenwich lean time.'

We all laughed.

I bought the magazine then stepped out, and the bit of fun was still in my head and the laughter, and then the homeless lad was there, really piercing magnetic eyes, hair falling over his face, more dramatic to me than the faces on the magazine covers, and it hit me, hit me there between the eyes. I think he was expecting something, poor lad, he went from shock to a snarl when I went past him and away up the high street and into the Armani emporium. I bought it, probably the most expensive jacket in the place, one of my carrier bags full of cash gone, the assistant could hardly keep pace with me. Then I was back to the street – yes, he was still there.

I caught him, I held out a fiver. 'Please just do what I say.' He looked bemused, I held out the jacket. 'Step into this.'

He did.

It did something amazing. The expensive, beautifully cut jacket on him, against his shabby, dirty street clothes, his wired body beneath, his wild eyes, like silk over a knife. The two old women came out of the shop. I watched, they stopped mid-chat, suddenly struck, at first by the unusualness of the sight, then just looking. One of them seemed to drop twenty years and, almost in fifties hip talk, said, 'Yeah.' The other nodded open-mouthed. The wild boy just glared at them, then at me. They couldn't stop looking. Must have been like when they put Tarzan in clothes or country-boy Elvis got his first shiny suit. The energy from the juxtaposition was something amazing. I thought we were going to have to get the law to move the old dears on, I really did, then slowly they started walking away, stopping every few yards to look back, then on and round the corner, and then their heads round for one last look and gone.

I gave the boy twenty-five quid and my number, told him there would be another fifty for him if he rang me in an hour.

He never questioned anything, just tucked the money away in a flash, an electric flash of fierce pride. I felt its charge but I never saw where the money went, I saw no movement, he was faster than any poxy stage magician. I held my hands out and he let me hold the jacket while he slipped out of it, and he was back to normal, like the peacock after its brilliant fan. I say normal but he wasn't really, his face was still sharp and haunting. I wanted to kiss it but I thought it might cut my lips to ribbons.

Then I was off. It was like Suze said: my mind was flooded, lit visions swung in excited feeling. The idea was still not fully born, but it was out! It had come out of things said, seen, heroin addicts, wasted models, something about starting with them wasted and working back to health, something about uncut beauty a raw reality. I don't know. I was panting when I got back to the house.

I picked up the book again.

Now it's here, tear forward, don't stop and sit under a tree, never. You know the ones who can help. They will come to mind right now.

Chapter Twenty-seven

I PHONED GAB.

'Get up here.'

'Uh?'

'With your camera. Just come.'

'OK. OK.'

'Tonight, need you tonight.'

Do it, do it, damn do it. If it's now, now, if it's two in the
morning, now, if it's two in the afternoon, now's the time.
Let it lead you how it likes as fast as possible. A wild river
ride or an amble under the stars, just don't get in the way
with fear or excuses or thinking thinking thinking about it.

I went out and bought thousands of pounds worth of designer
clothes – Armani, Donna Karan, Gucci . . . all different sizes.
Sometimes the same jacket twice; the assistants were amazed.
I was giddy but focused, an exhilarating feeling.

Gab arrived and I met him off the train. His skin had broken veins in it now; he was only in his twenties. But I didn't worry 'cause I knew the idea was going to save him, save us both. I told him about it.

'What?'

'We get homeless people—'

'I heard that part, it's the other part.'

'We dress them in designer clothes.'

He just started playing with his camera, his hands were shaking these days; I noticed that. 'Won't work.'

Negatives fall around you like confetti.

'Eh?'

Run through them.

I grabbed his hand and almost threw him in the car.

'Where we going?'

'Following the feeling.'

We just rode. Gab got sweaty. We were getting into the unlit outskirts of town. We saw in the darkness a red fire glowing. Nothing else. I stopped the car.

'Come on then.'

He got out and stood there looking around. It was all darkness, a vague sense of buildings, industrial maybe, but nothing clear, they could have been derelict, a smell of oil and cinders mixed and damp bricks and a choke of smoke from the fire. Quiet, just a wind coming up now and again, rattling something near by, and in the distance you could see it tug at the flames. Our noises were the only noises. I opened the boot and the little inside light came on. I suddenly got a good look at Gab: he was terrified, really terrified, paralysed, white, his eyes darting in all directions then fixed on me, frozen. I felt he needed a slap or something. I grabbed both his hands and kissed him hard on the forehead instead, then quickly started loading him up with clothes, still on hangers some, still in cellophane some. I took what was left and we took off across the darkness to the flames. He had no choice but to follow or stay alone and he stuck close behind me. We set off across the . . . whatever it was . . . it was like hard grass and bricks and stone under us. We were walking lopsided at times, moving towards this fire, and the wind blowing us, rustling the cellophane. I could hear Gab panting behind and his breath sort of whistling, changing as we went over rubble and up and down; it sounded like he was repeating over and over the first line of the nursery rhyme that had been in my head at that meal in Paris all those hundred hundred years ago: 'Frère Jacques, Frère Jacques, Frère Jacques, Frère Jacques, Frère Jacques. Frère Jacques. Frère Jacques.'

As we got nearer we could slowly begin to make out people around the fire. At this point I didn't hear anything more from Gab; it was as though he'd stopped breathing. The closer we got the clearer the figures became. There were about half a dozen or so of them, all around a bonfire, flames dancing, faces lit from below. And there began the legendary bonfire shoot.

We approached steady and slow, arms full of clothes. We must have looked strange. A dog was barking, straining at its string. They all leaned forward into the bonfire light – who were they? A bunch of scruffy no-marks, junkies and drunks – what had I done? – then the next moment the scene looked like an oil painting, each face illuminated by the flames, and they all looked at me and I knew at once I was right, right, right. Each face individual, angular, taut, strong, and their eyes, brilliant eyes.

'What you want? Got anything?'

'Yeah, yes, I've got something.'

I put the clothes down. 'Clothes.'

'Bollocks.'

'They won't last us, look at them.'

I think they thought we were from some charity. I decided to carry on.

Doubt will arise. Let it, then leave it where it lies and carry on.

Then I said, 'I'll pay you to wear them and let me take a few photos.'

'We not dolls, fuck off,' said one of them, the oldest one, forties, fifties maybe; he was probably eighteen, who knows? His face was like sledgehammered, almost concave, but his eyes were burning blue and bright and his hair thick and strong, an electric brush. I tried to quickly take in the others:

a young girl, a few men, another young girl, some others indistinct and 'Sledgehammer'.

'Show the green first,' a young man said. He was blond, had like a sprite's face, looked like it had once been an angel face but had been chiselled, chiselled harshly, looked like it had been chiselled by the wind and weather, hit into shape, cut here and there. It was a face in a beauteous rage, thrown about, formed in a storm.

I put the money down.

Gab pulled me away. 'Are you mad? They'll kill us.'

'No they won't. I know.'

I went back to the fire. The money had gone. Sprite was tearing at the cellophane on a jacket. One of the girls was holding up a mini-skirt. She was slight and wore a dirty baseball cap. Her small body was all taken up in thick, shabby clothes, except for her legs, which were in summer leggings that finished below the knee, and what looked like pumps, once pink, now dirtied away beyond colour. Her movements were so quick and deft she had the mini-skirt on then off then something else torn open. From what I could see of her face it was pale, almost white, with a wide, full mouth and eyes that sparkled but – I can't describe it – this was no twinkle, it was two dark, hard sparks.

Sledgehammer had backed off into the shadows. He said, 'I'm no ponce.'

Another lad laughed.

'What you laughing at?' shouted Sledgehammer.

The lad just ignored him. He had an Armani jacket in his hands. His hair was everywhere, it looked like what you might have paid hundreds of pounds to have styled, but his hair had found its own way. The beginnings of a beard, darkly handsome, big overcoat he had on, could have been a highwayman. He suddenly threw the coat off and put the jacket on. Heavens above, it fit perfect. He let out a laugh, then strolled right around the fire: he looked amazing. The others started then.

One of the girls just pulled a dress on over her head and over what she was wearing, jeans and boots sticking out the bottom, but it still looked good that way. She was tall, short hair like a boy's, a flickering dirty face, fawn-like, then alive with mischief, then the face of a thief, then sultry, all changing as quick as the flames.

Sledgehammer passed and kicked some of the clothes, then sat somewhere else. Another lad and a girl, like apparitions, really tall, still on the edge of the dark, two ghosts. I hadn't noticed them even changing though I'd clocked them when we arrived. They'd appeared nonentities then, just hung back in the dark, two junkies, but now suddenly they stepped forward, and he was in a beautifully cut overcoat; looked almost naked underneath, but something on – vests, I think, I don't know. It was so exciting. His hair was skinhead and his face freckled, I think, and almost see-through. Again impossible to tell how old.

Beside him the girl. She'd let her hair down, her hair long and red, coiling, matted, could have been full of old leaves and bits of wood and apple, burning, I don't know. Her face was ruddy, strong; reminded me of a picture I'd seen in a history book at school. I was remembering words like Celt and Pict and Woden as the fire was stroking her face and hair. She'd put on a long silk dress, the bottom was wet from the grass. She'd kept a black and ripped sweatshirt on and it was all the styles sort of searing together. Strange as she stood just at the outside of the firelight's reach, both him and her on the boundary of light and dark, supernatural somehow.

One man with curly curly Irish hair and a filthy face had slipped on a silk shirt. Another was trying to get a jacket on without letting go of his bottle. Sledgehammer was grunting now, and when I looked he was balancing on one leg trying to get his trousers off. There were layers and layers of clothes, he was swaddled in them, he farted. He started pulling a filthy jumper that was mainly made up of holes up over his head, I got a quick glimpse of his body; it was strong and dirty, cast like a miner's. He glowered at us.

'Wanna see my arse?'

The others were standing about now, forming a scene around the bonfire, a painting again, an incredible sight. I looked at Gab and I could see he was transformed, his fears forgotten in his photographer's inspiration at this picture coming up around him.

Sledgehammer suddenly walked into the scene. He was in a suit. The broken flat face, the eyes burning blue, looked beautiful, true danger, not the designer danger of the scowling pretty-boy models but the real thing.

'Pictures now,' I said.

At this they kind of struck poses hard to describe, really formal, like a tableau, like pictures of Indians and cowboys from the old days. Faces held firm, hard stares, straight mouths, dignified savages. I liked it, it was strong, it had something; it was a million miles away from the poses we took as models, from the usual camera-teasing or the flowing 'Just one more, love, lovely.' It was hard and proud. Gab started taking pictures, he wasn't too sure.

'I need to relax them.'

He started talking to them. 'Over here, look at me. Just move over, love. Look at the stars, will you, sir?' They just ignored him or glared at the camera. Gab said to me, 'What do I do?'

I said, 'Well, how do you pose wildlife?'

He said, 'You don't.'

He seemed to get it. Then a fight broke out, Sledgehammer punching wildly, one of the girls grabbing another by the hair, one of the others laughing, toothless, another drinking; he threw some liquor into the fire and a stream of flame arched out.

Gab was snapping away all around them. He rolled over on the floor at one point, like in a kind of judo roll, and came up snapping, snapped as he rolled, too, as far as I could see. That one would be a trailing, streaming photo. The whole scene was electric. There should have been a photo of him taking the photos.

The fight suddenly calmed down as quick as it had started. No one seemed hurt, there was a lot of swearing and mumbling but no one bore a grudge. They all wandered away. Sledgehammer put his hand in front of the camera, then took it away and glared into it with a big grin, tons of teeth missing.

It was over. They wanted to be left alone now. Some of them threw the clothes back, they started to pile up on the ground. They were restless now, I could feel the agitation. They were looking for something, bored, distracted, wanting to do something else, climb in a hole or get drunk or high. Now I had to keep them together.

'Listen, everyone, there's more money if you do this again, I'll double it next time. I need your numbers, addresses.'

They looked at me blank. No one had numbers, no one had addresses, or if they did, they didn't want to give them. I was determined to keep it together, I gave my number to all of them. Sledgehammer took up the role of leader for five minutes and assured me he'd keep them together. I wasn't sure.

We left on a high. Gab offered me a drink, and I said, 'I can't, not after that,' the rush itself had just made me so high. I didn't want to dull anything but to keep it alive as long as possible. He agreed, but drank anyway.

It was like we'd witnessed something new and amazing, and we bloody well had.

Chapter Twenty-eight

*Action, all action now. Act on, act on and on and on. Don't
stop, you'll lose momentum.*

Suze's words were reverberating in my brain.

'Come on. Let's get down to London. Right now.'

'At this time? there's no trains.'

'I'll drive.'

'I . . .'

Before he'd finished I had loaded all the clothes in the boot,
and we were off. I wouldn't let him look at the pictures until
we could look together. I didn't want to stop, I wanted to make
time, but at the first service station we turned in, both a bit
breathless with excitement and anticipation. We looked at the
pictures through the back of his camera. We didn't speak for a
long time. They were amazing.

We arrived in London just as the sun was coming
up. Bright beams of sunlight knifing up the streets, winking

off windows, turning the empty early morning streets to gold.

'We only need some bells and it's Dick Whittington,' Gab said. 'Can't wait to hit the sack.'

'No,' I said. 'Now,' I said.

'What you on about?'

'I want the pictures. Prints.'

'Aw, come on, Crys. Best I could do is this afternoon, maybe even tomorrow morning.'

'They must be on the editors' desks this afternoon. Come on, Gab.'

'What's got into you? Aren't you tired?'

'Nope. How do we get them?'

'OK. Let me make some calls – but look at the time. There's one place called Insomnia, they deal with all the press all night, never close – they might have a room. I'll try.'

I kissed him. 'I knew you would.'

I realized even assertiveness wasn't necessary when you were riding this energy: it got its own way.

I wasted no time. While he went off to get the prints done, I sat on a dewy park bench and went through directory enquiries on my mobile and got the names and numbers of the major fashion and women's magazines in London. My hands were shaking as I dialled; it was intoxicating, this rush, this surety of purpose. This momentum of doing things straight away was unbelievable. Suze, Suze, if you could see me now. And all around I saw figures moving, waking, the homeless tramps of London town. It was a bit like being homeless myself.

I snuck into a hotel near by and cleaned up, did the Grandma routine: cold water was my foundation, coursing and zinging blood my blusher, a good hair-brushing my conditioner. Went back and changed in the car, put on some of the clothes out the boot.

Gab got back with the photos. 'The guy at Insomnia said to be careful, that's live explosives you got there. He couldn't believe them, said it's like nothing he's ever seen before. And let me tell you he's seen the lot and then some.'

I took them with glee.

'Now can I sleep?' Gab said.

I smiled and gave him a hug and he was gone.

Soon as Big Ben struck ten I was phoning. Most just turned me down flat – they wouldn't even look, meet, meet for a minute, let me leave the shots, even hear me out, nothing. Once I started to describe what I had, I felt them just, well, going. Those that did seem to get it a bit said it sounded exploitative. I said, 'No, no, it's just the opposite,' but I was getting nowhere. I looked in Suze's book.

They will not understand, it is the way. Be persistent now, that is the word. We are passing into persistence now. That is the word. Water wears away rock.

I went on phoning, pleading. I was getting nowhere. Again I looked in Suze's book.

Act on, act on and on, go round a wall, over a wall, or pull it down brick by brick. Change tack, adjust, continue.

I started going round and calling in personally. I went into the offices of a magazine, funnily enough, the same one I had bought that day off the shelves, that day of the idea. I had to get by the receptionist. It was a hopeless task. I did the old Broken Record but she was impenetrable, would not let me pass. Then someone crossed the hall. We half-recognized each other, she'd been a model when I was.

'Crystalline?'

I'd forgotten her name.

'Tilly, it's Tilly.'

She sat with me, she told me her story. She lifted the cuff of her blouse to show me badly raw burnt skin. She had got into drugs, fallen into a fire in a log cabin in Switzerland. Most people's dream of perfect romance, but the dream singed and burnt away. I told her my story, and at the end she just took the pictures.

'At least I can get them seen. Come on.' She took me through. It reminded me a lot of the old days, going through offices, trotting behind Butanes.

'Just wait here a mo, Crystalline. This is the editor's office, I can't promise but . . . She's tough like they all are but . . . well, she's all right, she gave me a break, let's put it that

way, and anyone who can do that the state I was in, well . . .
but . . .'

'Yes?'

'Well, she is tough.'

She was hesitating herself now, I could see. But then she
took a short breath in and tapped on the door and entered.

I waited. Twelve knots of tension started climbing up my
body. Then the door opened. Tilly came out, there was no
chance to speak.

The secretary said, 'Will you go in now, thank you.'

I stood and went in. The editor was sitting on a swivel chair.
She was swivelling it a bit this way, a bit that way and biting
a pencil. I couldn't see her face and then she looked at me
direct.

'What do you think you are doing?'

I went cold. 'I . . .'

'I've never seen anything like this, and I'm going to run it.
If it's not too late I want it in this week's edition.'

Yes. Yes, oh yes, a yes. Yes. Yes. Yessssss.

In the week's wait I went back up North. Suze said:

Keep going. Don't stop to rest. Waiting is a waste, use it.
Break up any tension while you wait with action. Keep the
power whipping through.

I thought I'd better hunt down my models, keep tabs on
them. I'd heard nothing from Sledgehammer, anyone. Where

to begin? I took a trip to where the fire had been, but it was all fenced off now and two big Alsatians were barking and straining at thick chains. No one seemed to want these people 'cept me. I rode about a bit in hope, but nothing else around, bit of wasteland with a burnt-out car in it and the constant barking of the dogs.

I wandered the town then bumped into the first lad I'd met. He was on a corner. He recognized me, but showed no recognition, if you know what I mean. The work was going to have to come from me.

'You never phoned.'

He didn't answer.

'I'll take you for something to eat.'

He laughed.

'I can't go in a restaurant like this. Get some chips from there.' He pointed across the road at a chippy. 'Don't let them know they're for me though, they don't like me.'

I bought the chips and brought them out. We stood on the corner. I expected him to eat them like a wolf, but he chewed really very slowly. I'd never seen anyone eat like that.

'I learnt the secret: make a good thing last,' he said.

'You want to be a model?' I asked him.

'Why not?'

Didn't even want an explanation. I realized how un-encumbered he was, no one to let know, no possessions, no responsibilities, could just walk and follow me into another life in a second if he chose.

I was aware anew of how really striking he was. I told him about the shoot we'd done but somehow he knew – the street grapevine, I suppose.

'I haven't heard from the others I found,' I said.

'You won't, they'll have no means to phone. They've probably not kept track of the days.'

'Will you help me find them?'

'No, I can't help you there, I look after me. That's what I've learnt.'

'You'll keep calling every day or so?'

'You want me to call?'

I looked at him. Saw he had soft blue tattoos between his fingers, hadn't noticed them before – or to be honest, I thought it was dirt. They had long ago lost their shape and clarity.

'Oh, yes, right.'

I gave him £25. He was already walking away, and I hadn't seen the money taken but it was gone. I called after him. 'What's your name?'

'Baron,' he called back without even looking.

It was getting dark. I suddenly felt vulnerable.

Make the move, you'll find the strength.

Where to start looking? By instinct I went down to where the hookers hung out; it wasn't far. It was like a corner of the town, deserted at this time of night, lots of brick walls, lock-ups, warehouses. The corner sort of stuck out into a straggly, dirty, littered wooded bank and motorway. Not much light down there; it was like even the moon wouldn't throw anything in there, get its moonlight muckied. The only illumination was just a sort of thick, humming light thrown from lamps here and there on the walls above graffiti-shuttered units, and as you passed a building sometimes a security light would come on and illuminate everything around you, and figures would pull back around corners, or start into thin alleys.

It was scary down there. The faces were pasty, dabs on the dark. Cars prowling, could feel the car headlights penetrating me, sweeping through my clothes. One brick corner after another. Figures you thought were young were old when you got close but dressed like girls, pigtails in.

I asked one of them, 'You seen a girl with—?'

'Move on.'

'Uh.'

'I said, move on. Don't stand talking, they won't stop if you here.'

Then she grabbed me hard, her fingers like vices, and swung me past her. I scraped along the rough bricks of the wall behind, then carried on. I was going to say something but thought better of it; this wasn't the place for assertive statement, this was vicious.

I turned a corner, there was an alley, a man in a hooded jacket at its dark mouth. 'Crack, love?'

'No.'

The alley wound away thin and wet behind him, it was like a snake, he its hooded head.

'Come on.'

'No.'

'What about some weed for the lady?'

If he'd said Mackeson I'd have probably snatched his hand off, I needed something for this shaking. I moved on. The deeper you went in, the more it was like a maze. Where to next?

Then I came across her. It was the girl, one of them from the bonfire, the one who moved quick, with the diamond black eyes. I saw none of this at first but straight away recognized her dirty pink pumps. She was talking at a car window. I waited. She turned. Saw me. Suddenly, without thinking, I said, 'Leave it, leave. I'll pay you whatever he would have.'

She looked confused but hit the car on the roof and walked with me. 'Eh?'

'The bonfire, remember?'

'Uh, oh yeah.' She was obviously at the end of a high of some sort, but coming down rapid, starting to itch. 'Twenty-five.'

'Is that all you ask?'

'That's right. You pay first.'

I gave it to her.

After that she was hardly there. I knew she was itching to get round the corner to snake alley and the crack man.

'What's your name, your real one?'

She did a little cackle. 'I can't remember. Oh yeah, Gail, I think. I have a different name every night.'

'Can I give you one then?'

'Go on.'

'Sparkie.'

She cackled again, cocky and mocking. 'Whatever turns you on, love.'

And then she looked down and I suddenly saw how young and vulnerable she was. She tossed her head back and I could see she was ready to move, dart even, the crack was calling. It wasn't a look exclusive to desperate street girls, I'd seen its flick so often before, seen its quick and ugly swipe go so many times across the faces of the world's most beautiful women. I put my hand on her to hold her a second.

'How can we keep in touch?'

'Why?'

'There's . . .'

It seemed a ludicrous thing to try and explain here at this time. I just said, 'There's going to be more money for you.'

She just took this without question – well, she didn't want to waste time on questions, she was in the crack continuum where every second away from it is an agonizing hour. 'I've no mobile. I'm in a hostel this week. Could use their phone. We not s'pose to be out. Had to steal these clothes.'

She laughed. She pulled her jacket back. The dress underneath was like an old lady's, Crimplene with big buttons up the front.

I got the number from her, just about. It was like holding back a whippet that had seen the rabbit. I looked up and she was gone. Then suddenly she was fully illuminated in a security light, head down scurrying close to the wall heading for the alley. I called after her, 'The others?'

'Eh?'

'Your friends.'

'No friends of mine.'

She's gone.

Then she put her head round again. 'Try Mill Lane.'

Chapter Twenty-nine

MILL LANE. IT WAS A TERRACE ROW THAT SEEMED TO BE sliding down a cobbled brew, half the houses boarded up or semi-demolished. I wandered down to the bottom one. Then I saw the dog, the one from the bonfire shoot. I recognized it – long bony legs and a sort of lopsided grin that its tongue hung out of. I followed it round and into the backstreet, saw it slink into a backyard then go through some boarding. I walked to the boarding, it was hardboard. I thought there was blood on it at first but it was red paint. At first it just looked like slung paint but then I thought it could have been some kind of symbol. I was going to knock but then it suddenly seemed ridiculous; it was a completely derelict house. I put my head to the gap and looked in: darkness, the smell of wet plaster and damp mattresses and urine. What was I doing here? God, they were scary these places, they were dangerous. Then I recalled Suze's book again.

There will be hard ground to cross. Walk on. To be ground-breaking you must break the ground.

I felt like saying, 'You bloody walk on,' but I knew what it meant: I had to get these people together, the idea demanded it. It had to be this way, nothing less. I could have just launched an agency, said I just used 'real' people but that wasn't the idea that was given to me. This is the way for anything original, I was beginning to understand: no compromise, and dark doors must be passed through.

I took a step in. Something rattled beneath my foot, a rusty corrugated panel, a warning system maybe, and sure enough the dog started barking.

'Shut up, Rolo!' It was a woman's voice. 'Is that you?'

I didn't answer.

'Is that you, Romulus?'

I opened my mouth but at first no voice.

Walk on.

I managed to find some sort of sound. It was a bit squeaky at first till it found a note. 'No, it's . . . It's the woman from the bonfire shoot, the pictures the other day. Were you there?'

Long silence.

'Sorry, it sounds mad, but were you one of the girls at the shoot – the pictures, in the clothes?'

Silence.

'Sorry.'

I was turning to go when I heard movement above, then saw a face at a square in the ceiling. It was the ruddy one, the one with the hair; I knew as soon as I saw it fall and frame the silhouette. At the other side of the square was the panting dog.

'What do you want? Is there any more money?'

'Can I talk to you?'

'If you can get up.'

I looked up to the hole. The way up seemed to be by furniture piled up toward it. An old sideboard, a cupboard with no doors on top of that, a packing case or something, then finally a formica chair with no back. I thought I recognized those chair legs – they were like the ones on the kitchen chairs from Trinity's bungalow, fifties style. It made me smile a second. I called out, 'OK, here I come.'

She guided me up. 'Step on the left corner of the sideboard there, not the other, it's rotted away. Right now, move to the middle a bit, no, no, the other way, that's right. Watch it there, step more in the centre before you put your weight on to step up to the cupboard. Do it quick, one, two and up. That's it, now keep dead still, don't totter or you are over. Right now, right now, this is the tricky bit, this, you've to balance on one leg, sort of turn right round and step up backwards. Lead with your backside for a second or two, that's it. You're doing it, you're right. Watch the wobbling leg. Now sort of swoop and spin, *Now reach up! Reach up* and I'll catch ya.'

And there I was being hoisted up into the hole, the dog sniffing me as I went in.

It was . . . it was disorientating in there at first, not just because of my climb, but 'cause you were like inside but outside at the same time; a whole corner of the roof was missing and stars and night sky through it. There were candles burning and symbols again on the walls, definitely not thrown paint. All over the floor mainly mattresses, forming a sort of eerie landscape in the candle- and moonlight, and an upturned milk crate and a swivel office chair with no back. Lots of bottles and the remains of a fire in the corner and the symbols everywhere over the walls and what was left of the ceiling.

'Sit down,' she said. I'd forgotten she was there.

I chose the swivel chair, regretting it almost straight away. It was damp.

'Can I just say, don't swivel too much. It's on its last swivel, I think – you might swivel off.' She started swivelling her head and her hands. 'Spin in the air awhile then either go smack on your backside or spin off up through the hole in the ceiling and off, off to Mars.'

She laughed and I saw she had one tooth missing, but it didn't take away from her. Her wild look was stunning. Like with all these people, you had to look twice. The first time you saw a dirty, scruffy tramp; if you took the trouble for the second look you saw something else, a raw beauty, and that's what the clothes had done when they wore them – the contrast had shot that beauty up so fast.

The dog came and settled at my feet. He was so mangy, though, I wasn't sure.

'Hey, he likes you, don't often do that, you're honoured.'

I leant down to give him a quick stroke, looking around as I did.

'Don't worry, if the fleas don't get you then the spiders will.' She laughed again. I didn't.

Her hair was so thick. It was matted and greasy and you thought if it was washed it would come up shining copper-red, magnificent and luxurious. She was long-limbed and strong-looking and what me grandma would have described as a buxom lass, not pale like the others, but ruddy with a kind of rough lifeforce, looked like she'd just wielded an axe or run through a forest.

'Make yourself at home.' She laughed again. 'I'd offer you a drink but we've nothing in. Unfortunately finished up the last of the champagne last night.' Laughed again. 'No, really, he'll be back soon. Hope he's got something with him. He's lit one of his candles, that means he usually, usually comes back with something.'

She sat back against the wall and stretched her legs out. They really were long, dancer's or runner's legs, powerful. 'You said something about money.'

It seemed OK to tell her. So I told her the whole thing, plan for the agency, the whole caboodle.

'Models? Us lot?' She laughed again.

'What's up?'

'Well, if you don't know you never will.' Her laugh was a

bit madder this time. 'Why do you think we where we is, we all losers, love, no good for nothing. If you lift that mattress there, there's a hundred cockroaches parked up, waiting to scatter. Do you think I'd be here if I had half a choice? We the ones who know we have no chance.' Laughed again, louder. She went to the mattress. 'Shall I lift it?'

I shirked back in my seat. She laughed again.

'Anyway, you'll be lucky if he does it, he's anti everything to do with everything, him, world's knocked him that way. That's these symbols, driving out the worldly devils and protecting us from harm. Meself, I don't mind them popping in long as it's in the form of booze or food or money.'

'What are they, these symbols?'

'He knows more than me, he's an occultist, he is too. I've seen him change the weather.' The dog was suddenly at the window barking. 'Look – mention him and up he pops.'

We looked out of what was left of a window to see him coming down the cobbled street, tall and willowy and bald. She jumped up and disappeared into the other room.

Then I saw she was on the street running toward him. They hit an embrace and spun each other round, then walked toward the house. Next thing I knew they were coming into the room.

'Yes, yes, we going to be models, she says.'

I was up by now and could see they'd entered, but they hadn't come the 'Chairway to heaven' way in. I was curious to see how they had got in so fast. I stepped into the other room and suddenly there was no room, it was gone, just a staircase still there up the side of the wall, the end of the stair carpet flapping in the wind. Half the house was missing, open to the elements.

'So there is another way up,' I said.

'Oh yes, I just like a laugh. Aw, don't be upset. You've got to remember I'm homeless, and a bit mental, so they say.'

He didn't say anything but just looked at me. He was strange. His complexion was almost transparent, luminous, and his head was completely shaved right to the base, like white wood, and his eyes were like see-through too. Fine neck, fine features, like a monk but a monk of the moonlight. I'd seen that look before, remembered when we went to a monastery on a school trip once. They had beehives and old gardens and winemaking and all that, and someone nicked some of the monastery wine – might even have been Wendy: 'Tastes liked someone peed in the mead, brother.' Someone felt up a monk on the way out – terrible – kept saying, 'I've had a monk. I've had a monk.' But she hadn't.

Later, in the café, there was this fat monk doing the chips. He cracked a joke. You could tell he did it every day a thousand times, particularly to the school trips. He said, 'Hello, I'm the chip monk.' One of the girls – probably Wendy – answered, quick as a flash, 'Oh, thought you was a fry-er.' Got a big laugh. 'Aye, Friar Fuck,' said her mate. Got an even bigger laugh and got us chucked out. But on the coach as we pulled away from the grounds, and all the girls had their navy-blue knickers down and were mooning at the monks, I saw a lone one off on his own pruning a bush or something, and he looked up and directly at me, and he looked like that – see-through face, see-through eyes. I've seen it in holy men pictures, too. One of the models had them all over her booth at the shows, pictures of her guru, and he was like that. And the other place I've seen it is in certain so-called 'slow' people, when they were brought round the supermarket on an outing, standing stock-still, captivated by some label or display. Perhaps they are all three related, but whenever I saw that look it always sent me quiet.

'He'll probably not say anything, but don't take offence.' She talked like he wasn't there. He sat on the milk crate. Reached deep into his pockets and pulled out a hunk of stale, hard-looking bread, milk, a bottle of spirits. She looked pleased.

'Lovely. Do you want some?' she said.

I shook my head. 'No, no, there's hardly enough for you.'

'Oh, we share, always, that's his bidding.'

He didn't take his eyes off me. He took out a knife, I caught my breath. He paused with it and, still not taking his eyes from me, he started cutting the bread. His coatsleeves came up and I could see lacerations going all the way up in a type of scabbed coil.

'He's been beautiful to me, he won't let me on the streets, keeps me off. He'll do anything to keep me from them shaggers out there. He's put this place together for us. It's been the best thing for me, coming together with him, the absolute best. He makes sure I eat, he'll soak that bread in the milk for me, you watch, and we'll eat it after looking through our ceiling at the stars.'

I noticed that what I thought were freckles the first time I saw him were actually holes; there were holes all over his face and in his ears.

'If you looking at his holes, that's where his piercings were. He took 'em all out and sold them last week to get me and him and Rolo a square meal. Weren't it nice? You see, I've got me a good one here.'

He'd stopped looking at me now. I took that as a cue to go.

'Listen, I'll go now. So I can always find you here?'

''Course. We not giving this place up.'

She walked me to the steps outside. 'This way out.'

She was hanging close, really close. I could smell her, it wasn't sweet. I suddenly realized why she was shadowing me – she was after some money without him seeing. I shoved her twenty quid.

It was scary going down the steps, no banister and wide open to the side. I almost preferred the other way.

'Ta ra.'

She was waving vigorously at the top of the stairs, like it was bon voyage and I was off on a ship. Big, vigorous madwoman waves. Or like someone in the war waving at a plane. We had a picture like that somewhere, one of me aunties, black and white, floral pinnie blasted back by the wind, head right back, hand shielding her eyes, waving to the sky.

I suddenly remembered something and called back up.

'Can you direct me to any of the others? The ones who were there that night?'

'I don't know. I know Rattle died. You know, the curly-top one.'

One dead already; it was only a few days ago.

'Police picked up Tell-tale. Won't see him no more.'

She had gone, then reappeared. 'Oh, and Sledgehammer is in hospital.' She pressed her nose flat so I would know who she meant. Then she was gone.

Sledgehammer, that's what I had called him too – good coincidence, there's his name then. I headed off for the hospital straight away. This was not going to be easy.

Just on and on and on, passing through the challenges. Use language to change their shape. Call them challenges, not obstacles, call them puzzles, not problems.

I realized I hadn't asked their names. His was Romulus, I think, that was good, I think. Or maybe I'd call him Cuts: 'Cuts is modelling the latest summer wear for men from Armani' – or Lash, or Monk, Moonmonk maybe. Romulus is all right though, yes, and I'll call her Boadicea. Why not?

They let me in to see Sledgehammer. He was half sitting up on the bed. His face was a little bit flatter, with two more scars maybe. When he saw me he sat up quick, shouting at the top of his voice, 'I told 'em to keep you bitches away, away from me, I told 'em. Don't think you're having me, I'm not nobody's. Keep your appraisals and your forms and your poking noses away from me. Keep your appraisals away. I'm not mad, you hear? I'm not bad – you hear? – but I kill women dead who does appraisals. I flatten poking noses. Do you want to lose your nose, lose your pretty snoz? Keep away or you'll regret it!!'

He was looking at me through blurry, beery but still burning blue eyes. I was shocked at first, then I realized he thought I was from social services or something. I told him who I was, and he perked up when he remembered and calmed down immediately.

'Oh yes, I know you. Put a fiver under the pillow.'

I did.

'Now then, look at the fists. One found the mark, the other missed a trillion mile, swinging for the stars again. Swinging for 'em. You wanna see the other fellow, though, they still scraping him up off the pavement, flat as a cartoon cat.'

I told him he had to be careful now: no more fighting, he was working for me.

I told him the plan, but I don't think he was listening. He kept looking at my handbag. He took my hand at one point, and I felt his rough skin. I don't know why, but it was just so touching, a bit like when a stray dog puts his paw on you. My heart melted. I decided then and there to give him my mobile phone, though most of me felt sure I would never see it again. I knew he'd sell it or lose it or eat it, but somehow it was worth the risk.

'I want to do two things. One . . .' I slipped another £20 under his pillow. '. . . and two, give you this.' I held out my mobile phone. His mouth fell open. 'I am going to leave it with you so that I can call you when I need you to round up the others and come.'

Still slack-mouthed, then he spoke. 'You're leaving that with me?'

I nodded. He suddenly coughed and took it, took it like it was a thing of wonder. He didn't want to talk much after that. I went through the basic controls with him. He just stopped me another couple of times to say, 'You're leaving that with me, yes?'

When I left, I looked back and he was singing into it – 'That's why the lady is a tramp' – then pressing all the buttons, making noises and holding it up to show the other patients.

I suddenly thought, Goodbye phone, but I figured it was worth the risk. And there was always the money drip-feed, which was doing him a power of good and keeping him connected for now. Double insurance – still perhaps not enough to keep a wild spirit captive, but a good try.

It was getting late and I was tired. I set off for home. I was driving through the town centre when I pulled up at the lights beside the big department store. I looked at the mannequins all dressed in high fashion, followed them along, imagined my models 'to be' peeping out from behind the mannequins giving the 'V', when my gaze came to the doorway there was a figure standing, a sleeping bag wrapped around her middle. At first glance I thought it was another of the mannequins, dressed in a strange quilted, bulky new look: it was just the way the figure was standing. Then it hit me – it was another one of the girls from the shoot. She had the sleeping bag coiled around her, but I recognized her.

*Chance is a fine thing. When you see it, don't miss it.
Whatever the cost, pay it.*

A parking ticket would probably be my payment.

I parked up, on double yellows, in the wrong place – who cared? I went over to the store. She was still there.

She recognized me; this was a change. 'Hiyah, I remember you from the dressing-up night, it was a laugh. What you doing? How did them pictures turn out?'

'Great, so great in fact I want to turn you all into models.'

'Hey, even me?'

'Yeah.'

'Bloody hell, I'll need a wash first. What you calling the agency, Half-dead?'

'That's just it – you're more alive than most of 'em, they're not much more than these mannequins.'

'I sleep here two nights a week. I'd do more but you got to keep moving. They don't like you settling. They don't mind me so much though 'cause I never piss in the corner or do the toilet like some of 'em. I've been coming here months, lying among the high-fashion models. I won't go in no Argos or Primark door-holes, no way, I come up here, up town, see what they wearing, settle down wi 'em, and you know, it's funny, I look at them, and I imagine myself in the clothes, I do. And I see myself in the window, then we all come alive and we have a party.'

She beckoned me closer. 'Hey, we could break in if you like. I've been meaning to try it, I think I know a way.' That flash of mischief again across the fawn-like face that I saw in the bonfire flames. 'Imagine getting in there for a night – could sleep in the beautiful beds, lie on the settees, eat lovely food at the lovely tables, watch the massive tellies.'

She took me with her, the power of her imagination was so strong, then it brought a flashback of me and Gab in the supermarket at night.

'Shall we?'

I smiled and shook my head. 'What's your name?'

'Joyce . . . Joyce Clegg.'

'It's a nice enough name, but do you mind if I give you another one?'

She shook her head.

'Fawn.'

'Is that like a Bambi?'

'Yes.'

'My daddy used to call me Bambi. "Come on, Bambi, let's have an early tea and go for a walk in the woods." You shoulda seen my dad – he was tall, he was sensible. He would have lifted me up from this doorway and took me home in his arms.'

There was a shining tear in her eye, she moved her face away and I saw how long and delicate her neck was. She was so graceful, this girl, then suddenly she drew her sleeve across her nose like an urchin, gangly but still graceful, a grubby forest fawn.

She said she'd call me in two days, or she'd be here, or she'd be dead, it was hard to know these days. 'Ta ra.'

Just as I was walking away she called, 'If you go round the corner to outside the theatre you might see Rick, he was there that night, and the other one, the blond one, he's always there, where the fire was.'

'But I went there and there was nothing, just a burnt-out car.'

'That's it, that's his house.'

I walked round the corner and through a square to the theatre and there was the wild-haired highwayman, still in the billowing coat. He was selling the *Big Issue* to the theatre crowd as they came out, and putting on a bit of a show. It consisted of tap-dancing in his big, loose boots, spitting, and singing. Not surprisingly, he wasn't selling many copies.

When I approached he had started shouting at people. 'Do you wear socks? Eh? Do you wear socks? Then you are a puff of the tallest order. Have a *Big Issue* and change your life, sir.' 'Madam, you look like you could do with it. A *Big Issue*, I mean.' 'No offence, sir. Posh twat. Come on then, Queensberry rules.' 'Go on, ger out of it.'

When he saw me approaching him, he thought I was going to buy. 'A customer, I can't believe it. I'm not W. H. Waterstones, I've not much of a selection, but I'm quality, and you can be sure of a smile. Get that down you.' He peeled a magazine off his pile and folded it in a trice with one hand. 'Don't tell me you're changing your mind now, madam, you're my first customer all night.'

I took it and paid with a tenner.

'Now what would you say if I said I had no change?'

'I wouldn't worry, I owe it you anyway – I'm the woman from the photo shoot, the bonfire night.'

''Course you are, but I don't know what you're on about.'

'Remember trying on clothes?'

'Did I? How amazing, was I nice?'

'Yes, you were actually.'

'So what can I do for you except take your money and run? If you have any drugs I'll happily help you work your way through them. If you have your camera and want more snaps I can strike most poses, including action.'

Suddenly he dropped all the papers and did a perfect backflip, his long coat flying, turning in a heavy arch to land covering his face. He flicked it back. I was stunned; so were passers-by.

'Anything else, madam?' He really was devilish handsome and everything that implies, dangerous and thrilling. 'Let's repair to a hostelry. You pay, I'll order.'

All at once there was a small gang of hard-looking men approaching us, slow at first then more rapid.

'Oops, you'll have to excuse me. I'm just about to get the shit kicked out of me.' He took off at a brisk walk.

When you're given choices and you are in this phase, always, always take the risk.

'I must give you my number,' I shouted.

'What was that? Is that music I hear?' He stopped.

'No, it's not that, it's so . . . so that you call me. It's money, it's . . .'

'Write it right across my forehead my dear, but quick, I pray.'

I did. 'It's money, it's modelling, it's . . . Phone.'

'I shall, a promise is a promise.'

The men were upon him by then.

He just grinned at me, then turned to face them. 'Fellows, fellows, can't we enter some kind of talks over this?'

One of them stepped forward with menace; Rick's big, slack boot sailed right into the man's cobblers. It was so cleanly and casually carried out it wasn't like violence at all. No noise either, just a whistle of air through the great, loose boot.

Everything was still for a second, then the man collapsed on the floor. Rick winked at me – 'Forgive me' – took my hand and kissed it, then shot off at speed up a sideroad, his long coat sailing behind him. The remaining two men collected themselves and gave chase.

It didn't seem real until the one with the booted cobblers rolled over and over a few times then crawled to a nearby bench and threw up. I took off quick.

What shall he be christened? Rick's not bad, Tricks not bad, Turpin sounds good. Let's wait and see.

Back to the first port of call, which had now become the last port of call: the scary wasteland. It was even darker, if that's possible, no light anywhere. I could make out the charred metal skeleton of the car. Surely he wasn't in there now. I started across, the grass was sort of wet tonight, sucking bog and sucking fen, it was dragging against my ankles. I got scared, I got to thinking of fat wet rats at my feet, I wanted to go back. I got to the car. I had a little flashlight on my car key-ring so I put that on, shined it in on the car.

He was there, he looked really sweet asleep, like a street angel on the backseat by car-key light. There had been cardboard round him but it had shaken free and was flapping a bit. He looked like an angel in a cardboard crib or a pet brought home, a young pup in the box. He did look young now I got a proper look at him, probably fifteen, sixteen.

I didn't want to wake him. I wrote my name and address and phone number on the box flap, took a hair clip from my handbag and pinned my last twenty-pound note with it, then wrote, 'Contact me as soon as possible.'

I left. I went home, I lay in the dark. I picked up Suze's book.

Hold all together now.

Well, I'd done all I could to keep them together and I had Sledgehammer as final insurance. Now what?

Prepare now, prepare as though it is already all happening, and the waters will run that way and they will. Make the shapes, to catch the dream, to make it real.

I fell asleep and dreamt of city doorways and of black grass, and the moon on a mattress and whistling flying old boots speeding down snaking alleys of buckling dark concrete warmed with the soft burn of crack cocaine.

Chapter Thirty

NEXT MORNING I WAS UP EARLY. I WAS STILL WAITING FOR THE magazine to come out. Meanwhile: '*Prepare.*'

I went looking for an office. I went to estate agent's, took the usual trawl around, saw one in the town centre, one on top of a glass block, one in a shopping centre – modern offices mainly – but nothing felt right. Also bloody expensive, and the old plastic bags had already took a bit of a battering.

Suze's book said:

Don't get distracted now in extravagance. Don't mistake spending as work.

Eventually I found it, just the thing, a unit in a mill. I just liked it and I liked the idea of people coming to see me in there. A model agency in a mill. Wondered if Gran had worked at this one, been in this room here, stood in this place, smoothing her pinnie down, waiting for her wages or seeing the foreman.

To get to the office you had to go up the echoing stone stairs, or there was a big rattling goods lift – room for a football team in there. A guy taught guitar down the hall; up the way someone made cards for all occasions. Above someone taught aerobics and dance, and there was a Thai boxer teaching there too – seemed one came with every mill these days, like the toy in a cornflake packet. It was funny, all this activity all around, it was like being in the centre of a hive. Oh, and running by the back there was a canal, orangey-brown like, but water all the same.

And all the time I was waiting for the magazine. I got the office kitted out – simple: desk, chair, phones. Gab was mad for the magazine's release; he knew it was going to make such a difference to his life. I had him on the phone fourteen times a day. I could chart his progression into the evening by how compos mentis he was. I told him to stop calling until he'd stopped the damn drugs.

The morning it was out, I was at the newsagent's before it opened. It was the one where it had all started, significantly enough. The owner was only just cutting the plastic band on the magazines. I was there before he even got them on the shelf.

'Wow, you're keen.'

Out in the morning mist I couldn't get the magazine open at first I was so nervous. My fingers wouldn't work, shaking so. I finally did it, flicked desperately through the pages, but it wasn't in. I couldn't believe it. I went again, slower this time, the front, the back – no, they hadn't put it in – then suddenly it fell open to the middle and, by God, they'd put it in the centre pages, bless them – bless them twenty-two times over and back again. Oh God, there it was in the centre pages. I never expected a centre-page spread, and it was superb, breathtaking. There they were again, all of them around the fire in the clothes. I twirled in the street.

Gab was on the phone about fourteen-forty times an hour from that point on. He couldn't believe it, felt like people were phoning him from all over the place. The impact was all I had imagined and more. Suze, you gave me a time bomb.

I got a call from the editor. I told her I loved her, she said she loved me, she'd never had such a reaction from the industry. Then I got a call from someone 'on high' in the magazine, a very posh gent, and he loved it.

'You know, this is going to be enormous.'

Next day it hit the papers. It was everywhere. But I was ready, just like Suze said to be, ready and waiting. The phones started going; I was there, in my office, Suze's book open on the desk.

Consider now. Let each option unfold like a flower head.

People wanted interviews with me, with them, more shots for their papers, supplements, but I realized I needed to capitalize in some way.

Push high. Now go to the highest stream.

Something big. A splash.

I needed a show now. That's what struck me, that's what would make the biggest impact the soonest. A fashion show. I phoned Lucy. I knew she had a show coming up, and if anyone would take a risk on us, she would be the one. She started talking straight away about the spread.

'Everyone's talking about it. What have you done, you!'

'Lucy, how about using them in your next show?'

It went quiet.

Don't give up, just try another way. Run on like water, remember.

'You know what it would do. Book us, we're free for this first one, only this one, mind. Get us while you can. You know how you are over the fashion world. Give them a fist in the eye.'

Still she paused.

Another way. Yet another way then. Run, run them all.

'Isn't it true, Lucy, when you first came to London you lived rough for a while?'

'I did.'

'Think what this could do for them.'

'I know that. Gab told me about it all. It is an interesting proposition.'

'Oh go on, Lucy, go for it now. This is the only time it will be like this. Join me in changing things.'

'It'll take some arguing, kicking and screaming, but we can do it. Yeah, we'll do it. You . . . they won't let me down, will they?'

'No.'

'OK.'

'When?'

'You're not going to believe this, but I have two dates for the show. I was going to cancel the earlier one because half the models we wanted weren't available or had been frightened off from working with me, the black sheep.'

Once you are truly under way, be prepared to witness miracles, by the things that gather to aid you, that join up to the parade.

'I could go for it. I've everything ready . . . Do you think you could get done in a day? Like it – coming in without preparation, like a punch. Have them all scrambling to change dates, to cancel appointments to get there – love it, hit them when they are least expecting it, spontaneous spitting spontaneity. Yes, I'm ready, we could announce it on the back of this massive tide you've created. What better publicity? A punch right in the guts. Biff.'

I had her now.

'One thing. It's free, but I get to choose the music.'

'OK. Oh, what you called?'

Off the top of my head. 'Urchins.'

'Brilliant.'

It will not be a chore, you will work with tireless energy.

Right, cowgirl, round 'em up. I phoned the hospital for Sledgehammer. He'd discharged himself days ago – oh no. I tried the mobile, not expecting much and, sure enough, a woman's voice came on. Hello, I thought, here we go, he'd sold it to some unsuspecting someone.

'Hello?'

I hesitated – what do you say? Then I just thought, sod it, and plumped for it: 'Sledgehammer?'

'Sorry?'

Oh no, here we go. I nearly hung up there and then but instead I said, 'Sledgehammer.'

'Oh, Sledge, oh yes, wait a minute.' She shouted at the top of her voice, 'Sledge! Sledge, love! A call.'

'He's just coming, dear. This must be the "call", it's the only one he's ever had. You must be the lady, the lady what give it him. At first we all thought he nicked it, but now I know. I'm the woman does the soup kitchen. He's so proud of this phone, you know, oh my God. He comes in, he hands it to me for safekeeping, instructs me where to put it and when to charge it and to keep it well away from the soup at all costs. He keeps it constantly wrapped in a handkerchief. He's always polishing it and playing with it. Oh, here's the man now.'

'Yep?' he said, like he received a million calls a day. Oh, that Sledgehammer growl, I was so happy to hear from him.

'Sledgehammer, listen, it's happened! You and the others – you are stars.'

Suddenly he shouted to everyone around, 'Hey, you ugly swines, I'm a star.'

Cheers and jeers in the background. The soup-kitchen woman must have grabbed the phone. She said down it, 'Well, he is the most handsomest tramp in Christendom.'

Then Sledgehammer was back on. 'Right, where do you want me?'

'I need you all by tonight. Can you do that?'

''Course I can, 'course I can. You doubting me?'

'No, no. I need everyone here.' I gave him the address. 'Do you know it?'

'I know it!' And he was gone.

I was suddenly alone again in the office, it was quiet all around, just the creak of the Thai boxers' punchbags upstairs, the distant hiss of their breath and the soft pad of their feet. And I felt excited and scared and I started crying. How was I to do it, get a group of homeless people to London for a show tomorrow? I opened Suze's book.

Become someone of strength, behave that way and the quality will follow. That's how it goes. Do you think the courageous don't also tremble? The difference is they still go forward. All qualities are already within. Take the one you need. Swing it about you like a cloak.

I sat there till it went dark. I put the lights on, in the hopes of being a lighthouse for Sledgehammer and my models if they ever came, and I drew out a plan. I felt as long as I stuck to it we could bring it off. It was, I felt sure, a matter of timing, not to leave them with too much time on their hands at any juncture, keep them together in as confined places as possible, then release them for the show. Nothing more could be done then. After that it would be, whatever happens happens. I phoned up and got the train times. I wrote it all out, my plan, then wrote it all out again, with no mistakes, in my best hand. It looked so neat, a cage to contain them, transport us through the day.

Tonight we would stay in here, I'd order in food. Morning, train down – that's not going to be easy. London, I'll have Gab there with cabs ready and we'll go straight to the show. I'll inform Lucy to time it so there is no waiting. I saw on my pad I had underlined each step hard and deep into the paper with each thought. Still, they had to turn up first.

I looked out the window to the street below. No sign of them. In the meantime I phoned Lucy and Gab to set the arrangements. Two hours later still no sign and no one answering Sledgehammer's phone. I was beginning to get worried.

Suddenly, the lift. I heard footsteps in the corridor. I opened the door and stepped out. It was Fawn, she was breathless, she just stared at me, her big eyes full of tears, and said, 'Is this a way out?'

I wished the doubters could have seen her face, and then she leapt into my arms.

I heard the big lift again, and plenty of noise and chaos, the doors opened and out came Turpin, Pup, emerging blinking and skipping like he'd just been born and Sparkie, holding her chest in a fast fluster.

'I hate these things, I hate these things, my nerves is broken now, anybody got anything? This better be worth it else Sledgehammer's dead on the floor.'

They came down the corridor. I beckoned them in.

'Hey up, we all back int' mill,' said Turpin.

Then they were in my office. Quick as kids they were all over the place, feet on the desk, looking in filing cabinets, eating the biscuits.

'Now then, now then,' I said.

Suddenly, leaning in the doorway was Baron, watching us. He looked like James Dean playing a tramp. The others went quiet a while and sort of acknowledged him. He slid in and stood in the corner. The lift rattled again; we heard a voice in the corridor: 'Look where I is now brought. It was a fine day when I met him. I thank Romulus, each morning. Look at this, a mill – why, I remember alls about the industrial revolution, revolting it certainly was, with kids' fingers cut off under the looms, and fat cigars for the bosses, or was they dead kids' fingers they had in their mouths? And all them chimneys smoking up Lancashire. Terrible in the extreme. Romulus knows, I'm sure.'

Then she was in the doorway, Boadicea. She had Rolo on a string.

'Romulus is doing a candle for us. No sweat, we'll be safe

259

after that.' Then she looked at me. 'Where's the money?' Then she looked at the others. 'Look here. Look here, alt' dregs and homeless so and sos.'

'She thinks she's not homeless 'cause she's got half a roof over her head,' Sparkie said.

'Speak for yourself, Slapper,' replied Boadicea.

'Don't come it, you've sold your ass.'

'Never.'

'Lying cow.'

'Hey, hey,' I called.

'Let 'em at it,' called Turpin, grinning, then whooping.

Sparkie was over the desk before I could do a thing. Boadicea had her hands in Sparkie's hair. Rolo was barking, Pup turned a chair over and grabbed his own head. Wondered if this was a typical end of the day down at a London agency. Next thing I knew there was the sound of charging down the stairs and the Thai boxing class was in. They'd heard the commotion, seen the homeless ruffians, thought I was being robbed, and they were saving me. They were leaping and spinning, kicking, whizzing through the air all over the place. Chaos. I started screaming. Turpin was lifting his whistling boot back. Oh no . . . suddenly Romulus was in and holding up an old gnarled stick and everyone stopped. They looked at him.

Then Sledgehammer was at the door. 'Howdedoodee. Said I'd have 'em all here, present and correct, di'n't I, eh?'

Chapter Thirty-one

LONDON-BOUND, EVERYBODY. LONDON-BOUND.

I'd got them all on the train. How? Don't ask. Sledgehammer stopped to talk to every beggar en route: 'We going to London be models.' He had a copy of the magazine permanently open, marching up to the station with it. Others were stopping in shops, getting the magazine down, opening it on the counter and asking for free cigarettes. Turpin offered to officially open an off licence on the way, even though the owner protested he'd been there fifty years. They even got recognized – two trendy girls, hairdressers, I think, stopped and looked at us, then cried out, 'It's them. We saw that spread, you looked great.' You should have seen them all, stunned, then each flushed with pride. I think it was a rare emotion for them. Sledgehammer looked like he had been clubbed with a feathered mojo from above, they didn't know what to do for a second or two. Then off they marched, taller, more confident in their stride. Was this the beginning of that transformation

I had envisioned? On up to the station, heads held a little higher, the rag-tag brigade.

At the station, as we walked through the commuter crowd parted for us. People moving, giving us a wide berth. Some poor sod might be just making their usual way through the morning work crowds, walking head down or on a mobile, and not see us at first, then they'd look up, see what was coming toward them and either freeze, wincing, until we had passed or make the widest circle around us you have ever seen. One woman just leapt to the side, ninja-like. Amazing to see, she was middle-aged too. The screech of the little wheels of her case was like some Kung Fu film soundtrack adding to the effect. And the number of people who quickly stepped into the station shops must have sent business up a hundredfold or more.

People are used to beggars or homeless people one at a time but not mobilized like we were; I was amazed at the power we had. They didn't care or seem to notice though. Only Turpin paid any attention to people, nodding at them, blowing kisses to women, carrying an old lady's bag. She looked terrified he was going to walk on and away with it, but when she reached for her purse to tip him, he was gone, off ahead doing an impression of the train announcer:

'The 8.25 to Euston is at platform five, taking people to be models.'

I know it sounds terrible, but I was just conscious of herding them, of keeping them together. Problem was, I had to go to the loo. I had been holding it since we set off, terrified of leaving them for a second, for fear of what might happen. But it was suddenly too much to bear any longer.

'I'm going to the loo. Will you be all right? Will you all . . .'

'I'll stick 'em together, lady, while you're int' shithouse,' said Sledgehammer.

Thought I heard Baron say, 'Bollocks.'

A chill ran through me as I put me money in and went through the turnstile and into the ladies' loo. I was cursing nature. Me mind was going like a train itself. But what if they disappear? Where are they now? Have I thrown it all away for a 'tinkle', as me mum used to call it? They're probably scattering all over the station right now.

I could hardly pee for it. Wanting to be quick. Wanting to get out. It was like hanging out the window of a high-speed train. I had made the schedule tight so as to make it impossible for them to escape, but goddamn 'tinkle time' I had not allowed for. Would a shepherd leave his flock alone grazing on a hillside? Maybe, but not in the middle of Piccadilly station. And then there was no end on the toilet roll, it was all spun back up in the machine; and then there was the struggle with the door lock. Each thing made me panic more, like in some thriller film. Then there was the hand-dryer, back and under it, side and under it, forward and under it, nowt! In the end I just ran out of there, hands still wet, almost screaming. I could hear the damn hand-dryer kicking into life as I hit the turnstile, nearly vaulted it. Suddenly checked meself. What would it say in Suze's book? I didn't know, but certainly not this. I stopped. I calmed myself before exiting. Straightened up. Breathed in. What was the matter with me? Of course they'll still be there. Of course.

I emerged with dignity but devastated. Of course they had gone. The station suddenly seemed twice as full of swirling people. Where were they? I couldn't see any of them and they weren't exactly indistinct. They'd buggered off, the bastards! What now! London's waiting! A whole show! Lucy! My reputation, for what it was worth! Why did I get involved with these people! They weren't fit to be with normal people! They've cheated me! Yes! Bet they've even robbed me, robbed me somehow on the way through the bog turnstiles! Somehow got their fingers in my purse! It wouldn't surprise me. It would not surprise me.

All these thoughts were boiling up my brain as I rushed the length and breadth of the place, nearly knocking people over. Tramps! Thieves! I even checked my purse, felt an instant rush of shame, felt as bad as the ones who had guided their little cases on wheels in those wide wide arcs around us. Then I felt again the whip and stab and spread of What am I doing? It was a stupid, impossible idea. It was too much for little me to handle! Who did I think I was? I was only a girl, no education, nothing, who did I think I was? If Suze was here now, I'd kick her in both shins and up the backside for getting me into this.

I nearly burst into tears then. This little image came to me, came in my mind, of me mum carrying the weight of things twice her size, Mighty Mouse, the weight of us kids twice her size, bringing us up through the years, and it sort of made me pull myself together and then I went running up the escalator like some TV cop. Nothing there, down again, almost pushing people out the way, nothing there. The announcement for the London Euston train leaving came booming over the station. Then again, they always repeat it. This booming in my brain. Because I'd kept everything so tight, the next train after this would be too late, all would be lost. Then I saw them.

They were just round the corner from the loo. They had tried to stay where I had told them to but seemed the police had moved them on, tried to get them off the station, but they'd just doubled back in the crowds and hid round the corner. Funny how they know to kind of blend away, not be seen when needed. I nearly cried with relief and from the vicious after-sting of all the cruel bitching I had done.

The announcement came again, they all listened. As we ran down the platform I saw one of the guards talking into his walkie-talkie, watching us. Did they notice? Were they oblivious to it? Or did it still hurt but they just didn't show it?

They were all just like kids, looking into the carriages as they rushed past, Romulus moving close by the train, quiet with Rolo, just in case animals weren't allowed. Turpin was out in front, Sparkie was taking a last drag on a fag and flicking it under the train wheels, Pup was trotting along beside Sledgehammer, Sledge pointing things out to him. He looked like a little boy with his granddad. Boadicea was laughing at something, the echo going all over the vast station, then kissing the damn train for some mad reason, then blowing big kisses to no one. Fawn was floating among them, in and out, looking back to me from time to time. Baron at the back was a steady rudder on the mad crew. My clients.

We got into the carriage. Settling in seats, almost emptying a carriage as soon as we got in. Sparkie held open the magazine, crying, 'Never mind, we might stink but look at that, lookey, lookey, look at that.'

I saw what their lives were like, the ever shunned, only attention you got was when you hit someone or got arrested – either not noticed or noticed too much. Another thing that amazed me again was the utter unencumbrance of their lives. No luggage, no preparation, no phone calls to be made; just up and off for them.

The drinking began as soon as it could. I was the bank, of course, and it was buffet car and back, buffet car and back, in a booze boomerang. Though ever watchful, I backed off, just found myself a secure place by the window. It was hopeless to try and impose order: all you could do was pray. Sledgehammer called the train 'Iron horse' and the bar the 'Watering hole'; he took the role of main waiter and provider for all. On his way back from the buffet car, loaded up with drinks, cans in his arms, miniatures in his pockets, half-bottle of wine trapped under his chin, he'd stop and do the Hokey Cokey with the automatic doors.

It wasn't so much a sharing out by Sledgehammer, just an unloading on to the table, cans rolling, bottles skidding and everyone coming over and digging in – everyone except Baron, he got someone to throw him one, giving it the perfect catch every time. He sat apart from the others, one foot up on the seat next to him, looking out the window, calling comments over now and again. Baron was already cleaning up in some way, sort of sharpening before my eyes, looking smarter than the others, already in a Versace jacket. He had asked me before we left the office if he could wear one. There was a strength from him that seemed to be getting stronger, the steel-door strength of the completely and utterly self-contained.

Pup was sitting opposite me, little Pup, quiet, you felt that Pup could just close his eyes and die if he wanted to, I don't know why. Sweet voice Pup, like a little song when he spoke, then it was gone. You savoured it, wanted to hush everyone else up when he said something because you knew you might not hear it again for a long time. He curled up and slept most of the time, panting in like little circling baby breaths, panting his cheeks to pink against the stark white of his skin. When awake, he sat with his knees up, cradling a can, making a can of ale last, seemed to go down his throat a drop at a time. Then you'd look again and he was asleep, his fine hair all out in a mad-angled Tintin tuft.

The countryside shot past. Sun was in at times warming you, then gone and it was cold. I could see this world of the train, of passengers going somewhere legal and proper with tickets, was somewhere they hadn't entered for a long time.

Sledgehammer pipes up, 'Last time I was on a train, last time I was on a train, I was . . . Last time I was on a train, I was . . . I can't remember, old enough, about ten I was, maybe less, maybe more. Might have been handcuffed – not sure – felt like I was but I was with a uniformed woman I was, with cannon-barrel legs and a face like old Abe Lincoln. Smelt like an hospital corridor. Sweat, disinfectant, warm shit, cold potatoes. And a uniform I'll never forget of deep blue, that very deep blue.'

'Elvis-hair blue,' I said.

'No, God bless the King of Rock and Roll, no, was that dark blue of the salt bag in a crisp packet. She never spoke, nowt, not even once. It was contempt, I s'pose, but I was only likkle. My eyes was on a level wid her throat. I thought, what is at the top of that throat there? A dried-out tongue like a bit o' burnt bacon or a cloth square cut from the blue of her clothes, or a thick slug tongue aslumbering, all slimed up wi' contempt for a likkle crooked boy. I would never know. I wouldn't have minded tearing it out and taking a look, but I didn't. Did I cut and run, fans? Sorry, no. Did I not take off through the window and run over the train tops cowboy style? 'Fraid not. I was going nowhere, she had me certain. I thought about the mam I hadn't seen for months, the mam who would certainly hit me before she hit the bottle.

'Talking of trains, all Dad wanted for me was a train set. One birthday he got me one. Wasn't new, that's for sure, been torn up from somewhere, there was bits of felt and lumps of formica on the bottom. Found out later he and a mate had took it up from a toy department display, they'd gone to rob the safes but left with that. It was all I remember him giving me except a clout or two or three. We never lived anywhere long enough for me to put it down. Anyway, it wouldn't lie flat with all the stuff at the bottom, the train came off at every curve.

'Later he got a new family, we went once and stood outside his house, Mam sent us to get some money. I took my train, I remember, I'd cleaned it up with spit and polish and an old Brillo pad and anything I could find. I wanted it gleaming for my dad. He never came out. He saw us though, and I saw him at an upstairs window, a curtain cutting his face in half. As we walked away I pushed the train down a grid and saw it glug slowly away into the sludgy water. I went wicked soon after that, I suppose, ended up on that real train with the hard blue lady, travelling into me own sludgy waters. You can't talk to them if they don't talk to you. You can't listen to them if they don't listen to you. Alls I did do was when she handed me over at the end, I says to her, I says, I says to her, "I'd give you a kiss goodbye, lady, but I know your face would cut my lips to ribbons." It wasn't much, but I was only a likkle laddie boy.'

Sparkie was up and down the carriage, bumming stuff off other passengers, smoking between carriages, coming back. Up again, unable to hold still for a few seconds. Went down the carriage one time and just closed every laptop she could. No reason, that half a grin just going up to her cheek, sparks in her eyes. A few of them, Baron mainly, told her to sit down and stop it with the men. It was a kind of flirting, I suppose, but it was rough and tough. What she was used to. Once or twice she'd just stand up and gaze from one bloke to another, it was like heavy sex stares mixed with hate, stabs. If she'd fluttered her eyelashes they would have cut the tip of your nose off, it was like that, uncomfortable, hard, broken brick sexuality. It got men leaving the carriage or coughing, and moving about and looking at their magazines or laptops. The flirting of street meat. All that brazen power, all that from such a little thing, a flickering bony thing in dirty pink pumps.

With all of them together like this, sometimes it was jolly, sometimes it was dangerous. Hardly any of them stayed in the same seats for long, 'cept sleeping Pup, of course, and Fawn, lovely Fawn, lovely, gentle Fawn. Smiling at me, thrilled with it all, looking out the window, pointing things out, ducks on a pond, two trees hugging, a swing in someone's garden. Big beautiful drinking eyes.

Boadicea kept bursting into song. She had a belting voice, bit like Meat Loaf. She was the only one interested in food and kept asking me for money for burgers and crisps and chocolate and what became her favourite, big round cookies. Back down the carriage with steaming microwaved trays and little brown carrier bags of grub, swinging her hips, her hair bushing out everywhere. She ate in no particular order, a burger could follow a brownie, chips and a chocolate bar could go down together. She was really in the swing of the journey, going from one table to another talking and trying to set up games; must have been some throwback to when she was a kid.

'I spy with my little eye something beginning with T,' she said.

'Train?'

'Table.'

'Tits.'

Laughter.

'No.'

'Tagliatelle in a tray.'

'No. No.' Then she pointed at Sparkie. 'Tart.'

Then nearly a fight. It was calmed by Sledgehammer and a foaming can for each. Mayhem. A kids' outing with maniacs.

Rolo was under the table chewing up plastic cups. Romulus supposedly cured a passenger on the train of a headache by looking at them, staring through hooded eyes and doing deep rhythmical breathing. Boadicea checked with the man and he said it was true. Like a magician's assistant she announced it as true to all; they were amazed and had another ale. The man looked terrified though. I wondered if he had just said it to her to get free of their attentions. Next time I looked he'd left the carriage, and when I saw him again we'd stopped at a station and he was on a bench on the platform, his head in his hands. Boadicea tapped on the window to him, stood up and waved. He ran down the station steps as fast as his legs could carry him, papers falling out of his briefcase but he wasn't coming back.

Outside, landscape passed. Sometimes they all would go quiet, trees in the field would pass, England would pass, mist rolling, wet green land. Then houses and houses. Back gardens of all descriptions. Lives in the gardens. None of them had a home, so I wondered what they thought as home worlds shot past. Kids' toys on the back lawns. Ponds. Pagodas.

271

I don't suppose I had a home, not like that anyway, the prints and paws of people and kids all over it. Mine was minimalist, things still unpacked, I hadn't even put curtains up. No family all over it; these lot were my family at present. Mum had rung and I let it go to answer machine. I didn't want her in on this, she wouldn't understand. She'd worry, and Dawn would fuss and we'd fall out again, no doubt; this was madder than anything I had done so far. Realized how much I had put into it – the plastic bags all lay empty under the bed now. Suze had given me such belief I'd put the lot on this idea, I didn't even have enough for next month's rent and after this, if it didn't work, where would I go? What would I do? I felt the prickle of panic once again. I wouldn't mind a page of Suze's book right now, but I couldn't get it out here, they'd have it in bits and passed over their heads and out the windows and streaming off away down the tracks. Like giving the bible to monkeys.

Turpin was gallantry itself. Any ladies coming through he was there, helping them lift and lower bags, carrying their hot tea, balancing the steaming cups right to the table. Or he'd be in the next carriage and you could just hear women laughing. He'd have a story made up out of anything. I say story – lies really, I suppose, yarns, but so beautifully woven and threaded through each other and then thrown out before you, before you even knew where you were. Not the slow Sledgehammer way of putting up the scaffolding of a story, these were spun tales, silken, smooth, sexy, with a whipping, breathtaking end or a gag to literally make you wet yourself.

Sledgehammer wouldn't even compete. If they set off with a tale side by side, soon as Turpin overtook him Sledgehammer would concede defeat by going quiet but then letting go with a rip-roaring burp.

The ticket collector, a miserable little man, came in and down the carriage. He was giving a young girl a bad time for not having the proper ticket. Turpin clocked it and went quiet. When the ticket collector got to Turpin, his feet in the big whistling boots were on the table. By the time I saw it coming it was too late – the ticket collector went straight for the boot bait, as I feared he would . . .

'Remove those boots from the table.'

There was suddenly silence among them. They all pricked up their ears.

Sparkie stood up. Sledgehammer did a slow cowboy turn. I could feel it all gathering around me. I could see it coming, like a crash, but for some reason I couldn't move, couldn't get there in time, like in a slow-motion dream. My eyes were just pinned to the little trumped-up chap.

'Pardon me?' said Turpin.

'Remove boots from table.'

'Tell you what, Tickerty, if you're so fond of your table, why don't you remove it from under my boots?'

'I won't ask you again.' He seemed to be reaching for the boots.

Suddenly Turpin's voice was there, low, cutting and quiet, a whisper used like a razor. 'Come on, Tickerty, take a pot shot. Take one, I'll send you on an away day you'll never forget.'

I was about to speak but was drowned out not with the noise but with the energy of them all around me. I felt them unite in an instant; one second all out for themselves, the next a force. I was scared, together they were capable of terrible damage, I knew. The stupid little ticket man was attempting to hold his ground. 'I . . . I won't tell you again . . . I . . .'

But there was stuttering from him, cold sweat from him, shaking, he was holding on tight, though. Oh Christ, don't be brave.

Then Baron was up, Baron finished it really, thank God, just stood up, let out a strange soft whistle. I can't describe it, it went straight to your stomach, took your legs, it had real cowboys in it, real gangsters, real alleys and knives, not books or films. It was the soft whistle of 'this is real'; it caused the trembling ticket man to look across at him, and it was in the eyes, it was the not caring, two cold, cutting coins, nowhere for light to glint. Too much for the ticket man to take, and he was gone. He walked without looking back. Straight down the aisle, ramrod straight but trembling like hell. An ego on a little bobbing stick. But I knew there was more to come.

Next thing he was back with the guard.

'I believe you have threatened a member of my staff. We are going to have you escorted off the train at the next station.'

'What say . . . ?'

I had myself together now, prepared; I was up and between them.

''Scuse me, sir. These people are travelling with me.' He looked amazed. 'May I have a word with you between the carriages? Thank you.' They followed me out of the carriage.

As the door closed behind us I glanced back through the glass, tense, afraid they might be pulling the carriage apart, but they were all sitting quiet and glum like naughty schoolkids.

I told them both the story of who we were, what was going on, how much it meant. The older man seemed genuinely interested but the ticket man kept tutting out loud or looking through the window; he really was a nasty little tyke. I wished I had the whistling boots on meself and I could plant one firmly up his backside and send him out through the window and into the whizzing trees and pylons.

I decided this wasn't the time for assertiveness but for pleading. I ended with something like, 'They're boisterous – it's to be understood in the circumstances. Please don't take this chance away from them. I guarantee that I can keep them in check for the rest of the journey.'

The guard got to kind of stroking his chin. Tickerty was nastier than ever now, no give at all. He was insisting on their expulsion. On and on. If he carried on any more I was getting ready to speed past pleading, shoot through assertiveness and then go mental. I was fighting for something important here. Then the older guard suddenly touched him on the shoulder. Said to me, 'We'll give you a chance, but any more trouble and I'll phone forward for the police and you're off at the next station.'

Tickerty's face nearly popped but he said nothing.

I prayed they wouldn't walk back through our carriage in case they kicked off again; the guard turned as though he was going to and then suddenly they went back the other way.

I went back into the carriage.

'We've got to behave. Stay in the seats now, be quiet. If we get thrown off it will jeopardize everything. Worse still if anyone is arrested – that's it.'

They didn't say anything, their expressions didn't even change, but I knew I had been understood. There was just the chuggedy-chug and switching clack of the train after that.

I sat by the window again. After the intensity of the situation and probably all the tension that had gone before I felt really, really exhausted and, for the first time in ages, I wished someone was there with me. So deep was the sudden tiredness I began to doze, and just before the doze it was really obvious who I should be with, but I couldn't figure it out. Like I kept knowing and then instantly forgetting with the click-clack of the train, but the feeling was of someone solid and soothing, and that feeling went all around me, swaddling me, like that phrase I remember from RE: 'they wrapped him in swaddling clothes', softening me away in a sleep. I kept trying to resist, pulling myself out of it, but then was drawn back in. And it was in this way I heard their voices, they must have been talking among themselves. Pup was speaking.

'I slept in a pram once, when I first went on the streets. I was so small when I first hit the streets, curled up in an old pram. Used to wheel it round and park it at prime spots. Parked down by the canal one night. While I was kipping someone must have taken the brake off. I went into the water still sleeping, till it licked my chops. I didn't even want to wake then, I was turning round really slow in there, sky going round, canal was cold but kinda cosy, turning, turning nice and easy, nice and easy it went like sloppy dogs swimming round me, swimming me slowly under, lapping my legs and hands and cheeks. But then I thought I better come away and out and I did.

'I love sleeping. At school you'd always find me under the desk. Quiet and warm. Funny, things went in though. The teacher balled me out for kipping through his class but when he tested me I could do all the times tables and formulas and even told him what he said to himself when no one was listening. Strange that, all gone now. Might be a dream anyway. This might be a dream anyway. Sleep and wake all mixtured.'

Then Boadicea was speaking, slurry and drunk and slow. 'Of course, Romulus, by gum I knows him, he never travels, not in a bodily sense, though he has been all over the universe in my opinion. Take it or leave it but sneer not. Once or twice I've woke early to see him appear, seemingly fresh from out-side, and it's muddy and wet out there but he's no muck on his boots, his bald and gleaming head is dry. And I've found dust before now on his coat tails – purply, powdery, not of this planet, I'm sure. And plants in his pockets a colour not seen on this earth, cabbagey-moon cream leaves, the roots still full of white dirt. He's walked where we cannot, Romulus, he knows his way about, he has an A to Z of somewhere else. A

Sat Nav to the beyond and back. I'm sure some of them clouds I see through the hole in the roof at night above our hermitage he parked there ready for the next ride. I'm telling you true, I'm not on the exaggerater side. He'll never say a word of himself, but I will. He knows of yin he knows of yang he knows "Auld Lang Syne".'

Sledgehammer slowly putting up the scaffolding of another tale, pausing to tighten the nuts and bolts of it:

'Down the Auld Black Hog pub, drinkers only, all with faces like pirates. I was with the boxer Pelty McGinty and the wrestler Colonel Couqaliquie, we three knew we was in for some fisticuffs for absolute certain. You could have heard a sin drop in there that night . . .'

Turpin's voice came through. 'I like a coat with pockets. Look here – I've got a mini bar in this one here, with all them little miniatures.'

'Give some over here.'

'Get stuffed.'

'I'll have that whole coat off your back in a minute.'

'Try it.'

'Keep it down.' The steady voice of Baron.

'Eh?'

'We don't want them back.'

'No.'

'I don't care.'

'We doing this, aren't we?'

'Yes.'

'Well, shut it, then.'

More sleep, more quiet. More voices in and out.

Then, Sparkie, I think: 'No bastard gets tears out of me, he got hold of me and he said. "I don't pay." And he had a knife. Looked like a sabre to me in the lamplight. I said, "OK, OK, but at least give me something." I was thinking of the crack man. He won't take no excuses never. I can deal with knives better than I can with him. It's just if they put it to your throat, that little nick you get, I can't stand that. The sting of it and then the line of blood. Bastards.'

Another voice – was it Fawn? – I don't know:

'I like riding on the trains but it makes me sad, makes me think of going to the seaside, sitting on my daddy's knee, the clink of spirit bottles in the beach bag with my bucket and spade. The smell on him, the smell on her. When they leave you, you can't believe it at first, the first days, you keep thinking they coming back. Never quite leaves you, that feeling, don't you think? They set life up wrong when you little, they teach you it's *Jackanory* but it's not. They lie, everyone lies to you, they lie your little life away.'

More quiet. Laughter. Sleep. A voice.

'My second wife did the dirty on me. Never seen it coming, definitely saw it going though. Left me on the pavement without a penny piece.'

Then another:

'All over a crumpet or summat. He broke my Mum's nose. All over a crumpet or summat. He broke my sister's nose.'

A bit of an Irish song. Then more talk coming, fading in and out.

'My woodwork project for the year was to take away half the woodwork teacher's face with a chisel, a bow saw and a rasp. Would have sandpapered his nose off also but they had me all too soon. I went down and was never able to complete the project, but boys was free of him at least, the bastard and his vice . . .'

Distant talk, muffled talk.

'He said, "Is it shaved down there, little girl?" I said, "Not last time I looked, and I'm twenty-two." He din pull no knife but he battered the living daylights out of me. But I wouldn't cry, no fear, even when the boot was going in. I've been kicked by harder than him.'

And on the voices went, in and out, over and under, in and out like that for ages, and then suddenly I woke up with all their faces round me. I felt like Snow White. Then it was London.

Chapter Thirty-two

WE PULLED INTO EUSTON STATION. I QUICKLY PHONED GAB, to have him on alert with the taxis when we left the train. It was a long time ringing; then his voice came on the phone all groggy and my heart sank. He said he was ill but I could tell he had only just woken up. I felt sick. I felt angry. I hung up. I would have to let him go – not that he had been employed, but he had been an unspoken part of it. Not for much longer. What did it say in Suze's book?

Have a heart, but not a bleeding heart.

This was business, there was too much riding on it, no room on board for bloody slackers.

They all went mad, charging up the carriages to get off. On the way they came across Tickerty, kissed him and lifted him up to the height of a luggage rack, rolled him in there, left the little kicking fellah hollering. And then we all ran like the wind, off down the station, screaming like kids, me running with them, caught up in it. For a second I was in their world and right then I preferred it to mine.

Suddenly we were out the station. London. London whacked in, honking and whirling. I needed a taxi straight away or I knew all would be lost, I had to contain this journey.

We should have been in two taxis but I couldn't let that happen. No one would take us at first. A sort of boozed-up City type of bloke who Sparkie had been chatting up helped – pretended it was for him, then stepped away and we all piled in. The cab driver was an all right geezer though. Saw the funny side and squashed us all in, saying there wasn't much to Pup and Sparkie anyway, that they could count as luggage or a couple of umbrellas.

It was a mix on the journey, some excited, some cool. Turpin and Sparkie were going from window to window. Pup, perky, sitting on Boadicea's knee. Sledgehammer, flat nose to the glass, overawed, or ready to throw up? Romulus, eyes closed: what the hell was he doing? Rolo panting fit to bust. Baron giving a half glance here and there like he'd seen it all before, but it was at least a glance. I knew he was thrilled inside, deep. There was a glimmer in the dark eyes, bright, like the ping off a Fairy Liquid glass – no, wrong, not that – like a glint off steel, but a glint all the same. Boadicea was screaming and pointing things out:

'There's old One-Eye, the Nelson. Look up top, the peeking get.'

Fawn whispered to me that she was scared. I knew what she meant – that first feeling of London: the size, the swirl, the many faces – all that. And something deeper – a fear for your little self. It was a feeling all the way through, like a blade that tickled, a fear and a thrill flirting and fighting it out sort of thing, under the heart, like. Remembering my first visit with Rafe, the excitement still remained.

When we passed a homeless man in a slow traffic jam, someone shouted out the taxi window, 'Be a model, mate, they give you taxis.'

London spun us round some more and on we went. 'Let's swing by the Queen's pad, shall we?' shouted the Cockney driver; he was enjoying himself. We went round roundabouts like they was fairground rides. It started to rain.

But when we got there and piled out it had stopped and the street was sparkling, with rain, not jewels, but sparkling all the same. They all gasped a bit, then looked up at the building. It was massive. All necks cricked back. I had to catch Sledgehammer, he nearly fainted, good thing I was behind him. I knew I had to keep them herded, keep them together. This was the real test of my mettle now: stage two.

There was a second of hesitation, then Rolo suddenly slipped away from Romulus and took off in front, barking, and then they were off without me. I was like on the sleigh and the huskies were charging. There was a leap in my stomach, it was happening, my God almighty it was happening. The tension had kept me distanced from it but it was really happening now.

In the vast foyer, I got a kind of aerial view, vision, of us all, a little thrown scallywag collection scurrying after a lopsided dog.

We all tumbled into the auditorium, it was big. Romulus captured Rolo, then they were all subdued for a second or two by the vastness of it. It gave me a chance to get among them, but they all seemed to sort of fall in line naturally and walked in quietly, eyes roving everywhere. Then suddenly I could feel the pack urge to run and spread and explore and I hurried them toward backstage.

All around us were busy people doing last-minute check-ups, lights, etc., then as we passed everything fell into silence. Don't think they had ever seen anything like it. As we reached the stage, Lucy appeared. I could see from the off she was excited to see them all. She just stood staring.

'You all look incredible, darlings. Oh my darlings.' Then she was speechless. First time I'd known that. Not from shy-ness but, as she said later, a kind of brilliant shock. I could see in her eye a twinkle: it was better than she expected. They weren't sure who she was, even though I'd explained. They'd had enough of all that and were getting restless; they were starting to look around. I saw Sledgehammer beginning to drift, Sparkie too. I indicated to Lucy to hurry us through.

She came to her senses and then led us quickly backstage. I passed people putting names on seats along the front row. Did I read Jackie Collins?

I had them all secure backstage. Lispin came in – no, he didn't – he 'entered'. 'Where's these bloody barnets then?'

He'd put on weight but it suited him. Not sure what he was wearing, seemed to be wearing hundreds of things on top of things round things; all I can say was he was bright! And he smelt lovely. I ran over to him and into his arms. I started crying.

'Stop it, stop it,' he lisped.

Think he was about to go, too, so he quickly turned his attention to the crew. I saw the reaction I was getting used to now, a shock and a thrill together. Or, as Lispin described it later, a 'shockrill' or a 'thrillock'.

They didn't know what to make of him, it looked dangerous to me, no one was speaking. What we gonna do now? Then Lispin spoke.

'Look at you lot, by gad. I saw you in the article but by gad you're uglier in the bloody flesh.'

They all laughed.

'Right then, I'm told we've no time to lose.' He patted the stool then spun it seductively. 'Who's firsters on the turntable of tweek?'

No one moved.

'Come on, gents, ladies. Ladies, gents.'

Suddenly Sledgehammer got up and walked over. He sat down sullenly.

'What's your name?'

'Ned, but you can call me Sledgehammer.'

'Mine's Lispin, but you can call me Lispin. Right, let's have a butcher's.' He looked at Sledgehammer's head.

'Bloody hell, Mister Sledge, when was it last shampoozled,

this rascal? It's Lice in Wonderland. Here, you won't need gel. Nothing like good solid grease to sculpt with.'

They didn't know how to take him but they laughed, thank God, he could have just as easily have had his scissors to his throat or up his backside. He put his fingers in and moved Sledgehammer's hair about and looked at the scalp.

'Never seen a scalp like this one, Sir Sledge. I'm sorry, never, looks like a bombsite from the bloody Blitz. It's a veritable perm of scabs and cuts.'

Sledgehammer, quite proud in a way, began to point out marks on his head. 'That's where a bottle went, that. There, an axe.'

Lispin was making a million oooohs with his lips. 'I'll get the buffer out after, bevel it off.'

'Off with his head,' shouted Boadicea.

'Listen to Marie-Ann Twatnet over there! Can't wait to get my fingers into that pile.' Indicating her hair.

Sledgehammer was just staring at himself in the mirror. Don't think Sledgehammer had ever looked in a mirror for that length of time.

'Let me introduce you, Sledgehammer, this is your fizzog,' Lispin said. Sledgehammer just grunted. 'That's your very own mug. It's sort of Sid James meets Mick Jagger meets the north face of the Eiger. You gorgeous gargoyle.'

Suddenly he skipped over to Romulus. 'Squirt of Mr Sheen and he's done.'

To Baron, 'Oh pate-on-a-plate that one, easy, just a muz.' Winked at him and then on to Sparkie.

'Now, here's a pate-to-hate. What conditioner do you use, rust and lighting?'

And on he went like that. He floored them all. Then worked miracles on them.

Sledgehammer had sat there grim, thought he was going to flip, but when it was over he just grunted, stood up, looked in the mirror, and walked away a bit taller, I thought. Lispin even gave Rolo a brush-up. The job he did on them all was superb, shaped their misshapes in a way, left them wild but guided somehow. I can't say it, but they looked great, and none of them was complaining.

Lispin enjoyed it, said it was a tonic. He looked at me at one point, two tears in his eyes, and said, 'He would have loved this, you know, loved it. He'd have been all over them in his quiet way, grinning at all the jokes. Taking the greatest care. I still miss him like mad.'

I had been watching, enjoying it all but keeping it quick. Conscious of the plan. Lucy had won them over from the off. In some ways they were kindred spirits, she being the rebel drop-out, her knowing the streets. There was no point in rehearsing. She just showed them the catwalk, walked down it herself to the end then back, explained they'd have to get a new costume on then back down again.

Everyone was ready. As I'd explained to Lucy there should be no time lapses, we must stick to the schedule. She was going to do as we'd done on the shoot, match their own clothes with those of hers, let them twine. Gab suddenly appeared. Sheepish. I could see he was going in the wrong direction; as we were going up he was coming down.

'You should see it out there. Everyone's in, all the names, the faces.'

I peeped out and saw the crowds, banks of photographers, the seats rapidly filling up. Lucy was so excited, I could tell. She'd had success, loads now, but this was more what she believed in. Her clothes were wheeled up on racks, she walked along them, looking at the clothes, looking at our models; looking at the clothes, looking at our models; then suddenly she'd pounce, point at some thing, a dresser would have it out and she'd guide them to the model. It was amazing again, watching the transformation as I looked along the line. The thrill in the air was palpable, whipping, electric, then I noticed someone was missing. Who was it? It was Sparkie – where was she?

'Sparkie! Anyone seen Sparkie?'

Nothing from no one. Lucy caught on, Gab too.

'What's the matter? What is it?'

'Sparkie's gone.'

'She's probably in the loo, I'll check,' said one of the girls.

But she wasn't. We combed backstage.

She must have got out. My dread had hit home and was in my stomach, thumping lead.

We went to the back door. The bouncer there hadn't seen anything. Boadicea offered Rolo's services: 'He's good at sniffing out bitches.'

Then Sparkie just appeared, linking Lispin, waved at me and skipped back in line.

Lispin came over.

'What happened?' I said.

'Well, I heard the commotion and went out into the back alley, see if she was there, found her crouching between the bins. Said she needed something, she couldn't get no further without a hit of something. I've been clean for years, all I had on me was a little bottle of homeopathic medicine for my sinuses. I gave her that with a wink and a nod, like it was the greatest stuff there was. She got the top off and downed the hatch with the lot. Shook her head then come out skipping.'

He shrugged and laughed. I looked across at her and she was beaming. Bubbling up to a high and thinking she was sitting on a secret.

They lined up. It was time to go.

I nearly broke my fingers crossing them, then remembered Suze's words:

Forget luck, she follows work. She'll visit if she will. Work's the only thing you can do.

I gave a silent thanks to her.

And then the lights were up, then there was a hush like I've never heard in an auditorium; this was something unique, witnessed for the first time. The show was opening. The lights went down, a spotlight spin. Lucy was announced, Urchins was announced, a thrill fell through me. I looked at them all lined up backstage; they seemed a bit frozen in time. Then the music started up, Jackie music, the same she'd played for me by her pool, the big tune, the swooping, energizing one. I chose it. The big soul. Sledgehammer said, 'Let us on.'

A cry went up from the others. I knew the audience would have heard it, but it didn't matter.

I was at the door with the assistants and Lucy, 'Go, go.'

The curtain to one side, first down was Fawn. A gasp went up – her beauty and the shabby clothes and the beautiful clothes in fusion, they had never seen anything like it. Baron, next, he went on, walked a few steps, then stamped, never taking his eyes off the audience. It was like that for all of us, no one knew what they were going to do next and that's what was in the air. He stamped again, stopped, turned, and again. Sparkie was already on, her fast, deft way of moving, a flirt like they'd never seen before, that harsh-hitting sexuality. Romulus and Boadicea next with Rolo on a string, gliding down and around, ghost-like. Turpin shot on. He did upper-cuts all the way down, then spat, kicked his whistling boot up under a camera lens, froze there a second then back up the catwalk, then the whistling boots kicked up and down in a cancan, and down into the bloody splits! Pup ran on, darting about everywhere then off; Sledgehammer went down, sprayed them with a beer can . . . On it went like that, on like that, on like that; they were back, we had to dress them, Lispin on the hair, turn them, back out. Fantastic. It went by in a flash. The audience went wild. The music. Lucy was called on, she called all of them on, the roof went off. Never seen a response like it at a fashion show – never. Nobody had.

Backstage, corks were popping, champagne, people crowding in, hugging Lucy, wanting to hug the Urchins, then not sure, then doing it anyway.

There was a party afterwards, dancing. Turpin gave us a tune on the spoons; was there no end to his talents? A fight broke out at one point. I'm not sure who it was between, only that it was over in seconds and that the two enormous bouncers ended up unconscious on the floor like two dead whales, with little Pup sitting on one of them. On on on into the night.

People were coming up to me all the time – press, stars, TV, magazine editors, photographers – everybody wanting to talk about Urchins, use them, have something to do with them, give me a card. My bag was bulging with cards. It actually broke – no word of a lie: busted. Offers from all quarters, so many I forgot, so many 'Ring us please, please,' all that.

Then I felt something familiar inside, it was deep and beautiful, what was it? Oh I know, it was like the soul music, had someone put it on? Must have, it was impossible to hear anyway above the deafening, excited chat. Then it felt like the feeling was somehow outside of me, a presence. I turned and it was Jackie! Jackie Collins, she had just entered the room. She came toward me. I swear there was a silence. A slight slow motion in the room as all heads turned, but she wasn't aware of it, she was focused on me, coming toward me. I wanted to rush straight into her arms, but you don't do that with Jackie, she draws you in and you melt. It was all there again – the deep beauty, the look of wealth, the wealth of soul, the beauty, the look of a wonderful life lived. She smiled, took my hands and said, 'This idea, it's so unbelievable. How on earth did it come about?'

Before I could really explain, she was surrounded, people were all around. Photographers. Journalists, people. Men were drawn around her, as I suppose they always have been. I saw Sledge looking over, never saw him show an interest in women before, then all of the Urchin men came over. Shy on the outskirts, but she wanted to be introduced, then Turpin went straight through and kissed her hand. Then Sledgehammer, his big face slowly turning up to hers, taking her hand after Turpin, just holding it, then like in Beauty and the Beast, lowering his face to it so gently you wanted to cry at the tableau. She took Fawn's face in her hands: 'You, young lady, you are beauty itself. A face that can't keep still for beauty.'

Beauty to beauty, I thought. She was in London on business and had been leaving that night, then delayed the flight when she found out about the show. That she would do that for me . . .

'You've done something so few people achieve, you have done something original and you have done it all alone. You are something special.'

It was lovely to bask in her praise awhile – that was praise indeed to me, the most important. I tried to tell her what she had done for me, but I went a bit dumb again. Damn that

– what is it that comes over me like that? And then I did something I hadn't done for a long time, I blushed, a good old-fashioned burning one, and it felt good. It was a return of something, something of myself I thought I had forever lost. And then she left as she came, and the party kicked back in full roar.

It had been the icing on the cake for me, the stunning, brilliant, best day of my life. And I looked around and saw everyone so alive and genuinely moved by the whole night, and saw the Urchins were overawed but loving it, different already, confident, confused, confident, confused then confident. A way was opening before them. The tight grip of the day's plan was over, this last part I let go, I let them loose, but you know what, you know what, nobody ran.

Next day the media went mad.

Other shows pale away into precious pretentiousness

They were calling it the new look: 'Camera dangerous' – 'Raw fashion'.

It just caught on like wildfire.

Chapter Thirty-three

BACK AT THE MILL, I SAT AT MY DESK. IT WAS CLEAR THIS thing was bigger than even I had imagined. The phones were going constantly, people wanting to book the models, magazines, TV, papers wanting to interview them. And the Urchins themselves, I didn't need to phone them now, they all rang in constantly: 'What's happening?' – 'When can we do it again?'

It was clear I needed help. I'd prepared but not quite for this. I was expanding too fast. All I had in the office besides me was Mum, who kept coming in to move the furniture about every two days or so; I think it was a kind of Mum Feng Shui. She even went up and helped the Thai boxers hang a bag. What next? I opened Suze's book.

Draw from roots.

I couldn't quite work that one out at first. I didn't know if it sort of meant take people from my area, or use people I had worked with in London, get a load of Butanes up here. I was wondering about going down to my local job centre, see if they could help, when three things led me to the answer, and what an answer it was. Firstly, I came into the office after lunch to find Denise and Thinnie from Safeshop sitting there waiting for me. I sat behind my desk. Denise started straight in.

'I've decided I'll go with you.' She was straining to refine her accent I noticed.

'She made her mind up this morning,' Thinnie piped in.

'When do I start?'

'She's got a bikini in her handbag,' said Thinnie.

'Don't mind doing glamour.'

I couldn't help wondering if Igor had given Denise the time off for this she never gave me!

'She won't ever remove her bottoms though. So don't ask. We've noticed the successful ones never remove bottoms ever. Anyway, her boyfriend would kill her, if she removed bottoms; if bottoms was to come off, it would be slaughter most terrible I'm telling you now. He'd kill the photographer as well and everyone he could get hold of from the world of magazine publishing, and then anyone who'd seen it and anyone who'd stocked it even – libraries, say, doctors' surgeries, say.'

'OK, Thinnie, OK.'

'He's a footballer, you know. Semi pro, but there you go.'

'You can see him on the sports pages of the *Local Journal* every Saturday if you're interested.'

'So bottoms on. Though she sees not much wrong with a thong.'

'Right then, where do I sign?' asked Denise. 'Oh, and one other thing, I'll go with you but you've got to take Thinnie on too.'

Thinnie blushed at this and seemed to begin a bit of a protest. But Denise talked it away. 'I told her, she can do it. I told her if them scumbags you've been using can do it, anyone can. She's coming round to it now, particularly since Councillor "Roll-Me-Own" saw sense in it. Roll-Me-Own's a friend of mine and hers. He comes to the ciggy counter twice a week for his tobacco. He's a man of the world, he's well connected, he's well dressed, very generous with his advice. I told him about Thinnie doing it, and he laughed his head off at first, din' he, Thin'?'

'He did.'

'But then he thought about it for a while and he said, "Well, there was Twiggy." And there was, wasn't there? Then he remarked on size zero, which was . . .'

'. . . very contemporary of him,' Thinnie whined.

'Yes, I thought that, man of his age – but he's up with everything, Roll-Me-Own, impressive as hell he is, got an understanding of everything, more or less. I mean, I know he's a curve man himself, likes the fuller figure like most gents, he's said as much to me many a time, but he saw sense in it and that was enough for Thinnie.'

'I must say they gave me confidence.'

'Yes, so there it is, a Safeshop special offer, take one get two.'

They both laughed.

'Where do we sign?'

I was dumbfounded for about a minute. Then I managed to get something out.

'Look, I thank you both for coming in, but I'm sorry, I'm sorry – you're not what we are looking for.'

There was a stunned silence. Then Denise stood up. 'Oh, I see. Come on, Thinnie.'

Thinnie stood.

'Look at you, who do you think you are? Once a two-a-penny till girl always a two-a-penny till girl. Don't think I don't know how you lot was always jealous of me 'cause I was on Cigs. This is spite, init!'

'Don't lower yourself, Denise.'

'I won't. Perhaps if I slept in a public bog for three weeks, come in with a heroin needle sticking out me arm and puked up, I might have more chance. Come on, Thinnie.'

At that Denise turned on her heel and left.

That got me thinking about Safeshop again. I had been so involved I had forgot about them all.

The second thing happened later that day. The upstairs of a bus pulled level with my office window and I happened to glance out, and I saw Bet. She didn't see me, she was talking hell for leather, and half the passengers on the bus were cracking up. I was awed again by her force and personality.

The third thing was when I was opening the mail and I came across an envelope I hadn't opened from days ago. It was a card from Adam, congratulating me on the success of the show; he'd seen it in the papers. I thought about him and realized he had been a sort of silent, distant support through everything. Mum had been telling me not long ago that he had phoned often when I was ill, asking after me, even sent her a card of support, I was so out of it then I don't know if she told me about it or not at the time, but she reminded me of it recently.

I then got to thinking about Safeshop and the skills they had and I thought about *drawing from roots.* It became so clear. What about drawing from the talent I knew? I wasn't thinking about London but closer to home – what about taking from Safeshop? Yes, why not? No, it wasn't possible – but why not try and take from that good and talented crew? For starters, Adam would be just the greatest manager for the office.

My mind started to really investigate it, filling all positions from there. Bet, Bet would be a great PR, imagine her dealing with press, media – they would never have met anything like it. It would be so different and unexpected, in keeping with Urchins, and apart from all that, a hoot. She'd be great in the field, but I'd need someone back here. It would have to be Joan from the newspaper stand, she knew all the newspapers and magazines, knew them all back to front. She could deal with all that. Bless, Bless could do us a website. Finances, oh yes, Little Lily Lottery, a whiz with anything to do with money, that careful collector of lottery money for the syndicate. If you won you got your winnings worked out to the penny. Sometimes it was a penny. Quiet Alice – not sure what she would do but knew she'd find a place useful and true.

Then – oh yes, not Safeshop, but my roots all right – what about Solemn Ted as our driver? I'd heard he'd retired from the buses. The more I let it unfold the more sure I was. Bookers? Well, me, and then perhaps Maureen – she was bright and confident. All this natural talent that was hardly noticed, drowned out in the bleep of the tills, I could encourage, and get meself a fantastic staff.

Could it be possible? Of course it could, what am I saying? Look what I had just done, a mere till girl, took a bunch of homeless people and then set the whole fashion world alight.

I took a glance in Suze's book just before I contacted them. It said:

Start with a solid centre.

So I started with Adam, who thought it through and then agreed there and then. As for the rest, it wasn't easy. Some of them needed a confidence booster. Not Quiet Alice though, who, with a sweet in her mouth, mumbled, 'Reet,' or Bet, who said, book in one hand, fag in the other, 'What will I have to do?'

'Meet people, go to parties. Just talk mainly.'

'OK, when do I start? Will I need a new mini or two?'

Or Joan, who just had to consult her stars first, then she was on for it.

The other person I really wanted to involve was our Dawn.

I went to talk with her; we'd never quite made it up since

the trouble. She was alone now with the children. I hated to see her like this. She'd let herself go, put a lot of weight on.

'Do you want a cup of tea?'

'No, I've come to ask you, will you work with me?'

'What?'

'I need someone to do the writing for me – marketing stuff, ads, everything.'

'Why not hire somebody proper? I can't do that.'

'I don't want to hire a firm, I want to use people I know. I know you can do it, and you'll be fresh and do it with heart.'

'I—'

'I'll pay you well, Dawn.'

'What would I do?'

'Write. The natural thing that you've always been able to do – write.'

She looked at me then burst into tears. 'It's what I've always wanted to do.'

We were off. First thing Adam did was sort out all our models with a home. We put up the rent advances and the security and they were all placed near by to us. They got constant work. Media went mad to use them. And media loved working with our Bet. She was amazing, she had them all eating out of her hand, they loved her. Mini-skirted and bold. At first I was a bit afraid she might let us down, stay home for the Beano, all that, but no, she was always in first thing. You'd hear her swearing on the stairs, panting and puffing her way up, but she wouldn't take the lift.

'I don't like lifts,' she'd say. 'Anyway, them stairs is good for me,' though she'd have been finishing a fag off on the way up. 'Look at the pegs with all this exercise, toned up, sculpted now, every muscle a go-go.'

And she'd turn her calves this way and that, and they *were* good.

Joan set things up with the papers, magazines, telly, then Bet rocketed in. Quiet Alice just used to turn up late morning. She didn't even expect to be paid, always looked surprised when I gave her a pay packet, just came and cleaned round and made tea for everybody and offered out sweets and looked out the window, and in the same way she'd been at Safeshop, she'd be gently nudging things back in order without you even noticing it, maybe guiding Sparkie out the room if she was getting too mouthy and slipping a sweet in her gob, or helping Mum move a filing cabinet. Sometimes she'd go for a ride with Solemn and the model, like a kind of quiet minder.

Bless would ring in excited at something he'd added to the website. In fact, he rang in a bit too often really, but it was OK. I couldn't even understand what he was on about most of the time but I understood it when he'd give us a rundown of how many hits we'd had from all over the world – it was in the millions! Our Dawn was great, her copy about the company was class and fresh. Heartfelt always, no sickening slick polish. It was lovely to watch her blooming. 'All them years, what have I been doing?' she'd say, and shake her head.

More and more the model world was being rattled to the core. The big magazines couldn't wait to get one of the Urchins on their front covers; we had them fighting over it. In the end Baron ended up on the front of *Vogue*, Fawn on *Cosmopolitan* and Sledgehammer in *OK*, would you believe? He had them in his home doing shots of his little flat. He was so proud of that place, everything was always immaculate.

Adam was brilliant in the office. He had everything organized and he kept tabs on everyone. Occasionally jobs would come in and you couldn't find one of them, then we'd send Solemn Ted out. He'd always track them down. He was great, still solemn, but there was the beginning sometimes of a twinkle now in his eye. And it was great when he dropped someone off at a shoot and got out to open the door in full Teddy-boy regalia, rock 'n' roll sounding out from inside.

And the change in the models was astounding. It was like I always thought: it was decline in reverse, sobering up instead of taking to drink, coming away from drugs rather than going into them. I wondered where they would all end up – as vicars, nuns, or saints perhaps.

Everyone wanted Urchins. There was the occasional incident; it was to be expected with people who had been so damaged. Someone might lose it and trash a photographer's studio, but they'd shoot on through it, trashing and all, and the pictures were so great and the publicity so fantastic the company who hired them would willingly pay for the damages. With our lot they always got controversy and amazing pictures, with our lot it really was a realization, it was like the death of the pose. Everyone wanted our models.

We were a success. They dealt with it all great, considering.

As I said, there were incidents, like when we were called to a shoot Sledgehammer was on. We rushed out there, he'd thrown a big photography lamp through a window. They'd got the shot, they weren't that bothered, it's just that he wouldn't move, sat on a box. If anyone came near he snarled at them like a lion would.

We got everyone out the room and sat with him. Came out he was depressed. It was his flat. We couldn't understand it, he loved his little flat more than life itself. Seemed he just couldn't stay in there any more. We talked about finding him somewhere else, but it wasn't that. What had happened is that every time he did a commercial (he'd started doing adverts, very successful they were too: Sledge says, basically Sledge endorsing products) they gave him the product. His flat had begun to fill up with leather sofas and televisions and washing machines, many of the things not even out of the boxes, and these were the things that were forcing him out of his home. He didn't know what to do. It was getting him down. He had even started sleeping out again a couple of nights. It was ironic that a man who had had nothing all his life and lived on the street desiring these things was now being put on the street by the very same things. He was being swamped by everything he had ever coveted and now he sometimes had them in threes.

We talked him off the box and persuaded him out the studio. He was shame-faced, saying sorry to the little assistant there. He took her hand. She stroked his forehead, almost like he was a buffalo.

We went straight to his flat and helped him clean out. We

gave a lot of it to the homeless centre. He came down with us and couldn't get out. He was mobbed and then covered in kisses by the fat cook, still calling after him he was the handsomest man in Christendom.

Sparkie had taken to sparkling mineral water, can you believe, and her need for drugs had fallen away. She didn't have time, she said. Some bloke tried to force a drink down her and she broke a bottle of champagne over his head. He was related to royalty and we heard later he asked her to marry him. She wouldn't, but she went down to his estate for a weekend. They were doing drugs and, when she refused, one fop tried spiking her drink. She was too smart for that, took a shotgun and went gunning all round the house for them; they were all cowering away. The pheasants had a day off that day, she shot out all the windows and blasted the stuffing out of a Queen Anne chaise longue in the drawing room.

Then she hitched a lift back with a lorry driver who recognized her from the papers and the lads' mags; he couldn't believe it. He was hooting his horn at all the passing lorries and pointing to her. Had her talking down the CB to his buddies, telling them who she was. Asked her to marry him. Then wouldn't let her go till she'd scratched her autograph, her name in twelve-inch letters, across the bonnet of his truck. He said he'd never wash the seat again. There's a truck out there called Sparkie. Such a long way from the shivering street corners she used to one time walk.

Baron took to the life early on; came in one day and said he'd bought a shop. Smart operator. Did the job, got out, gave no trouble as long as no one gave him none. Hung out with footballers, rock stars. Heard he'd broke a marriage up, between some actress and her billionaire husband, and then dropped her; it was hinted at in the papers, no names mentioned. I was never sure what he was up to; he often appeared in some interview we knew nothing about. Never came near the office. I hadn't spoke to him for ages. He just took the name of the job, or some woman would answer and take it for him, more likely. Went his own way, set up his own publicity sometimes. Had the soft blue tattoos removed from between his fingers, not sure if he had his nose altered too. When I saw pictures, something had changed in his face. It was rumoured at one time he might be considered for the next Bond.

It was mad the way it was going, the speed of it was unbelievable, from begging to Bond. And they weren't losing it; it was going in reverse as I predicted. They'd seen it all, been to the bottom, and nowhere further to push but up and up.

Turpin, now he was a catwalk favourite. A performer. People would turn up just because Turpin was listed as a model, the general public too, sometimes fighting for tickets. He was a favourite on television interview shows too. One fashion house, and this was unknown, had him as the sole model: he came on, went off, came on again, like a quick-change artist. No one ever knew what he was going to do. Sometimes he'd come on on his hands or backward on all fours barking at the audience. Or he might snatch a woman up from the audience and kiss her passionately. Kept the whistling boots on, trademark, and for luck, he said. He could do the splits or anything, he was so physical. Turned out he'd been a gymnastic champion. Marks and Sparks had designed an overcoat called the Turpin. They wanted him to advertise it. Far cry from the old street days when the M&S shopgirls used to smuggle out sandwiches to him after hours.

Romulus did great, as you can imagine, for strange ads, anything surreal, and he was one of Lucy's favourites to use. She felt he went well with her work, sent him down the aisle in long white suits and robes, always with Rolo on a lead. That was his gimmick: Rolo had to be with him.

Boadicea got bigger and bigger in physical presence and character. I can't describe what I mean – not fatter, though she ate for England, Wales and Ireland, but her presence, the space she filled; bigger like someone unfolding a wonderful canvas of a painting flap by flap, and on it goes, everyone gasping at the beauty of the thing as more is revealed. She was popular but could only work alone; if they put her with other models her hair eclipsed them. Romulus and her lived apart now. He was one of the first to go to London, took on a tiny place in Bloomsbury that had belonged to a famous Victorian occultist. Boadicea didn't want to live anywhere, she loved going from hotel to hotel with each job. Always with the windows wide open. We got a complaint once because she'd left the windows of her room wide open all night in a storm and it had trashed the room, whirled the room up, toppled things, broke things, filled it with leaves. She must have slept through it – or danced with it, knowing her.

Pup, he was a real favourite of the ladies' magazines. They all fussed over him and loved dressing him up in baggy jeans and such. There was always a big turn-out at a shoot by the ladies when Pup was in for a job. I always liked Solemn to take him or, if in London, someone to accompany him. Often we'd go to collect him and he'd be in the editor's office, asleep on a chair with a drink next to him, while she was holding an important meeting, having everyone speak in whispers so as not to wake him. He may have been there hours, everyone tiptoeing round him, she just liked him there. I don't think he was ever quite sure where he was or who was who or really still sure what was happening.

Fawn was our true star. Cover after cover, catwalk dream, she grew into more and more grace and elegance on her way to being a true supermodel. She gave a lot of her money away – any cause, any sorry story and she was asking Adam to send a cheque.

Now is the time to make sure success does not eat you. Look to yourself.

Adam and I were getting really friendly. It was so good being with him, everything was clear and solid. Never been able to depend on anything like that before. He was there, really there. We spent most of our time together and he loved the agency as much as I did but we kept a respectful distance. One night though, at one of our late meetings at the mill, to this day I don't know how it happened, but we kissed. It was

307

almost like we missed each other. Neither of us was sure if it had happened. Then the meetings began to turn into dates.

I really liked being with him. It was . . . It was just the way his cuffs came out from his jacket sleeve, it was so many things. His clothes were comforting, well put together, his aftershave, everything, it was all done right. Nothing was out of fashion or in fashion. But this was not boring. He cut a fine figure. Overcoats. Jumpers. Hair right. Everything felt clear and fine when you were with him. No chaos. And I could feel his love for me, and it was respect too. I was taken into his world and I would be looked after – anything that entered his world was looked after. I've been loved in the past – I think, anyway – but this was different. I felt genuine respect, not just body stuff. We went to good places – pubs with fires, solid restaurants. A drive. A walk through a village. It was so, so nourishing. And I knew he was there, looking after everything. The desks were clear each night, both his and mine. You knew he slept well and good.

Chapter Thirty-four

EVERYTHING AT LONG LAST SEEMED ROSY IN THE GARDEN. I loved nothing better than going up the mill stairs, settle in before the phones start ringing, but no matter how early I turned up I could never get there before Adam with his sweet cup of tea.

It was about this time a letter arrived from HM prison. It was from Rafe. Ironically, I'd been reading the last chapters of Suze's unfinished book; basically it was about making peace with everything. And here was Rafe's letter, asking my forgiveness.

Dear Crystalline,
I don't know how to start this letter or what you must think of me now. I don't think I have the right to even contact you. I lay it in your hands to do with as you please. You may not have even got this far into the letter but I am going to continue. This is not a begging letter,

you know that's not my style. But it is a plea for your forgiveness . . .

It went on. Telling me how he's changed through the therapy he's had in the prison, how he's been inspired by me and Urchins. He wants to use his skills now to help others, sees his mistakes. How he has an idea for charity, for the prison to set up a fashion show in there, on the lines I had developed with Urchins, using the inmates.

I didn't show the letter to anyone at first, I just went off with it on my own. I thought about Suze, I thought about the good that had happened to me. I'd had a chance.

He'd dragged himself up, he'd had time to repent. I knew if I told anyone they'd tell me not to but I decided to let him go ahead. Use our resources, have our support, go ahead – but I didn't want to meet him or be involved. It would help the prisoners, hopefully, in the way it had helped our people, and it might help Rafe. I believed his letter. I went out into the office and announced it. Bet turned away. I held up my hand before anyone spoke. Adam was going to say something then didn't, even looked like Quiet Alice was going to say something. I saw Joan was about to speak. I said, 'Joan, I don't want a prediction on this one.'

I talked to Adam. I said, 'Listen, I want to do this thing but I don't want to see him, we'll just help.' So we did.

Then word got round Urchins was doing a prison project. How it got round, I don't know. Everyone wanted to be in on it, get in this time on the first wave; we were a company that could do no wrong. It started to build. All the main fashion houses came forward, vying to be the first in there. I began to feel a bit nervous about it, it was a project getting too big too soon. It was only s'posed to be us offering a little help in organizing.

The press got hold of it; it was all over the papers. They wanted to televise it but the prison authorities didn't want that, mainly because of Rafe's protestations. I thought that was noble of him. Here was his chance to really use this for self promotion but, throughout the whole thing, that genuinely didn't seem to be his goal. It made me feel I was right, it was like he had really changed. From what I heard he worked really hard too, organized everything. Prison came alive, I believe. Even down to the building of the catwalk in the prison workshop.

Bet went as our representative. She told us it was mayhem just trying to get in there, giant lorries turning up packed with racks of clothes from Armani, Paul Smith, Gucci, Versace, rolling in through the gates.

'It were like a bloody lorry park and limousine show-room forecourt had got blended. They were all in the prison yard and car park and lined up along the street to the gates. Honestly, it were like five circuses had arrived at once, and everyone honking horns, a veritable horn orchestra. Solemn of course turned the rock and roll up. We were OK, I don't mind, brilliant for me to have a bit of Buddy of an afternoon, like, but it was bedlam, love, I'm telling you.

'Oh them in the big house, they just weren't really ready for it, I tell you true, hadn't expected owt like this. Press was at the gates five deep, flashbulbs a-bursting, telly vans and cameras and mics almighty, fans, passers-by, a right rum scrum. The poor old nick, I'm afraid, had broken the bloody Boy Scouts rule: they were not prepared.

'We got through the gates eventually and Solemn dropped me off and I joined the queue to get in. Funny being in a queue with posh people, they not used to it. They OK if it keeps moving, like along a red carpet for a premiere or up a staircase and into the ball – the only pause they have to make is to give a little wave or a pose and smile into the camera – but they've had it when they are stock still. They don't know what to do. Everyone goes a bit quiet and twitchy, suddenly, like, self-conscious. Unusual seeing them like this – just a few models every now and again going at it like statues, to whom of course standing still is an occupational hazard. Not sure what the delay was – I think they were trying to check everyone's individual invite and identity and all that – there was just too many of us, they must have given up in the end, because things started moving and, when I finally reached the doors, any security checks had been shortened to a sort of a bouncer's nod.

'We were ushered in through the prison by guards at first; it were quite thrilling for all the glitterati. See them giggling and wide-eyed as the doors were opened and clanged and locked behind them. Some wags demanded to be strip-searched. We just poured through, a shining river of glitter and suits and shimmering shoes, echoing along tiled corridors. It was a very old nick, I bet Sherlock himself had banged a few up in there. Had that shiny brick tile effect like you see in old Victorian hospitals or swimming baths, and all the posh voices echoing off the roofs and floor.

'It was a bit claustrophobical – I got these horrible feelings like what would happen if we was all heading to be gassed or poisoned or summat. Half the fashion heads of London gone in a stroke, drugged to death. Still, they were doing a pretty good job of that themselves.

'So many of us moving, you couldn't see where you were until you arrived; so many expensive scents I was nearly throwing up, singularly each scent superb, together a pong. We entered a sort of makeshift reception area. We were met by their best-behaved prisoners on their best behaviour. Hair plastered down. Totally out of touch with fashion. In fact, I'll wager they was wearing the same gear as when they was imprisoned. You could tell when each had come in by their civvy clothes. It was like the history of toughs' fashion from 1960 to the present day. One thing they all seemed to have in common, though, was that their trousers were half mast.

'Each was on their absolute bestest behaviour, trying their hardest, polite and muttering. Again, no way did they expect so many people, so much fuss, and for some of them you could see in their eyes it was like, tits, lads, tits, tits everywhere you turn. Tits is here. I mean, they don't get the Beano here, do they? I was keeping the pegs pretty much out of view, even on a bit of old boiling fowl like me they was a prize for these poor sex-starved inmates, slobbering sinmates.

'Honest though, and I hate to say it and I know it wasn't the intention, but all these people had come because they thought it was Urchins, the latest Urchins event. And you name it, they were there. I thought I'd come a bit incognito like, lowered me mini hem and everything, but to no avail. My neck was aching and my cheeks nearly falling off from all the head-nodding and smiling as people made a point of letting on to me and letting others know they knew me and by association were well in with Urchins.

'Then we all spilled into the main recreation hall or dining hall or summat. There was a faint whiff of lags' lavvies and corn beef and wet leather for some reason, and Victorian sweat, which set a lot of the women off giving themselves another poof of perfume, and that rose like a gorgeous cloud above us, lying on top the other smell like petals on dirty water.

'Otherwise, I was impressed. A big stage and catwalk had been put together. Lights, good sound system. The catwalk was the longest I had seen; it went right through the auditorium – we almost stepped on it as we came in. Served as well to divide the hall, and on one side was us, the other side, I presumed, would be them, the inmates. The best seating was reserved for us, all uniformly set out seating, their side was a bit scraggly, a row of plastic chairs would suddenly go wooden, then what looked like a church pew for a bit, then office chairs started. Every department must have chipped in some furniture; people must have been standing up all over the prison.

'I kept trying to put folk straight about it not being an Urchins event but nobody was listening.

'"Wonderful Urchins should be doing this."

'"What other agency would be here?"

'"See it, all these beautiful people against a prison background, perfect Urchin ethos, a massive reverse version of the tramps in Armani."

'"Marvellous! What next from you wonderful lot?"

'I'm like, "No it's not actually Urchins. It's the prison, we just giving some support, some . . ." But you know what it's like, they'd gone by then.

'There was drinks for us. I could see the inmate who passed mine to me didn't want to let it go; his eyes followed it all the way to my mouth. I recognized the one had to be Rafe straight off, he was in and out the crowd, in and out the lighting and sound people, the ushers, everywhere. He had this shiny brilliant suit on, he'd obviously raided the stock. He was pristine all over, let me tell you, like newly trimmed. Some people he obviously recognized. Many he must have worked with, but he was careful, you could see he didn't presume, just toe-testing the water here and there, didn't want to push it. Flitted, just giving everyone the polite required respectful time, then off again. He was like someone driven by electricity, or operated by someone else across the hall pressing control buttons. Few times watching him I half expected him to take off and circle above us a couple of times and then land upside down, his legs whirring in the air, till someone righted him and then he'd be off again.

'All of a sudden, there was a silence as individually each of us became aware that the inmates were being let in. Solemnly they took their seats in rows – bet there was some slavering going on at all them jewels just a hop, skip and a jump and a thump away. Once they was settled, we all sat. And there was a sort of heat I can't describe, not heat that makes you hot, but a heat taking the air a bit, like a Cagney film. Could have been too many people in one room, could have been always like this, could have been that glutton tension taking all the oxygen.

'Then the Governor took to the stage. Honestly, he only looked about sixteen, I always thought governors was like hard old headmasters. He thanked everybody and all that, but you could tell he was a bit overwhelmed by the number of people and the rich and the beautiful and the powerful and the beautiful powerful packing out his pissy old prison. You could tell it had peppered up his speech in praise of Rafe with something extra.

'He went into how Rafe had brought this about by sheer determination, had been involved in every level of its realization and incorporated every department of the prison, supervising and encouraging the inmates to make the catwalk, organize and set up the lighting, even down to making sure he was in the kitchens, placing the cherries on the buns for the catering. That it was great to bring such opportunity to the prison and to his fellow inmates and for charity . . . and so on and on. Then he passed the mic over to Rafe, who played shy, mumbled some praise to the prison and thanks to all who had come but suddenly damn well cleared up his voice to send out a ringing thanks all round the hall to you: "Thank you to Urchins and Crystalline, I say this is their event," then back to mumblations. Tell you what, he intended everyone to hear that. The Guv' had a tear in his eye, he was some soppy bloody Guv' this one, and he called into the mic too, "Thank you, Urchins."

'Then Rafe stepped back, signalled to someone and the lights were out for a second – scary being in the dark with a few hundred prisoners not ten yards away – then a spotlight went spinning around and across the audience. Half the prisoners ducked. Then music. Then a puff of smoke from under the catwalk and the show began.

'It was the same Urchins formula – rough faces in beautiful clothes – but they were all men. Some were real hunks, handsome. None of them could move though, awkward most of them, could see them doing it in their heads: "Walk. Wait. Stop. Turn. Take jacket off. Throw it over shoulder. Bloody hell. Now back."

'And they were all regimented and drilled like that, not the free form of Urchins. Think Rafe had seen to that, he was right at the side mouthing their instructions to them, then a hand raised to conduct the lights, the music. Bet he would have liked to have done the whole show on his own if he could have. I was enjoying it though, it was my favourite music – Beano Latin as I calls it.

'I noticed Rafe was starting to gradually speed things up a bit, counting them up and down a bit quicker, sort of getting off pace with the music. They started to get a bit confused. A couple of real heavy blokes bumped into each other at one point. I saw Rafe with his head in his hands. But I was watching him careful and there was something unnatural in the gesture, a movement with the finger like a signal or something, a twisting of his ring, a serpent ring.

'At this the two started fighting, but this seemed kind of concocted to me, seen plenty fights on a Saturday night but this didn't ring true, and instead of the music going off it went up about a hundred notches, bloody deafening, disorientating. One of the blokes threw the other offstage into the audience of prisoners.

'Suddenly everywhere they went up, chairs were flying on stage, but to me it all seemed on cue, counted in just like the models had been. But there was certainly nothing artificial about the fighting of the inmates in the audience – bloody Nora, it was terrifying. The guards went in. Then smoke started pumping from under the stage in massive amounts. We were all coughing and crying and choking with smoke and fear. God, were we really being exterminated?

'The guards were good, though, they quickly contained them. Then the lights went off. Suddenly there was a panic and we all headed for the door in the dark. We started getting out. The guards tried to stop us but we were running for our little lives. They had to get the doors unlocked or there would have been a crush. All the glitterati battered and spilling out into the yard. There was call for calm but everyone ignored it.

'Disgruntled, hair gone, hats half off . . . And Rafe and

three mates were away. No one knew at the time. They'd just slipped under the catwalk, followed it to the door, waited for us to pass and slipped out into the moving crowd – already dressed in designer clothes like the rest of them, Rafe bewigged, I believe – out into the car park. A plant or two of his must have been in the audience – and they were away. False passes just waved as we were let out. Like in *The Great Escape* they crawled free but instead of a tunnel of dirt, they crawled in Gucci suits under a fashion catwalk, under the very glittering high heels and souls of those he knew. It was simple, sodding simple, too simple to sound true: the dirty, three-faced bastard had got free.'

At that Bet burst into tears. 'He got free on your back, Linda. Oh, dear, dear Linda. I think it's my fault somehow. I was there to protect you, somehow.'

Apart from fear, and anger, I didn't think much about it in terms of the agency until the next day. God, the press coverage was terrible. The news made out it was us.

The backlash lashed, and how it lashed. After that, the phones pretty quickly just stopped ringing – except for papers and media wanting a quote. Bet and Joan tried to straighten it out but couldn't get our side in, all the press wanted was some more dirt to pep up the scandal.

Dawn put together a statement from us for the press. It was brilliant, a perfect balance to it, she really was good, but they didn't print it or quoted from it wrongly. The media didn't turn on the models, thank God, but they turned on me all right. They said I was earning vastly exaggerated amounts from exploiting homeless people. That I kept all they earned and only gave them spending money.

Denise had given an interview to a paper. Must have done it to get a few bob or revenge, probably both. She said I'd told her she was too healthy-looking and curvaceous, that she should go on the street for a few months.

Then there were other rubbish stories about girls from good families going on the streets and doing drugs just to get in to see me. Crazy tales suggesting that we helped with the escape. Others that it was a big publicity scam and we would be releasing the escaped prisoners on to the catwalk at our next show. Next show? That was a laugh. We couldn't get anything. Companies we had done favours for in the past, even they didn't want to know. Even the great Lucy, though she wanted to help, her hands were tied. She was under big financial pressure and her backers didn't want anything to do with us. It had all gone too far and we were clumped in with it. It was our name the papers quoted, it was us the fashion houses held to task.

It was about this time also that some of the models started to be poached. Baron was the first to go. Left with a wink, went to a top London agency. Sparkie too, still driven but not twitching now, not driven by drugs and booze but by her own ambition. At least she couldn't die of that. Pup got involved with music, asked to front a band, made a few records. The first was called 'There's A Lorry Out There Called Sparkie'.

Romulus and Boadicea fell out; I believe they fought for

custody of Rolo for a while but then Romulus threatened to do a ritual and that was it, the dog was his. He drifted away from modelling, just did the occasional shoot for those occult coffee-table-type books. Last I heard he had become involved with a number of wealthy women and the odd celebrity, as adviser or something. You'd sometimes see a picture of him walking with his hands behind his back, all in black, Rolo at his heels, around a leafy garden square in some old part of London, accompanied by some fawning celebrity.

Boadicea met a rich man and we never could find her again. Sledgehammer went to Paris and became an icon. Turpin went on a reality TV show and became a millionaire. Fawn, lovely Fawn, was the only one who stayed, and she was the one who was most pursued. In the end I made her go. We were doing nothing but holding her back; none of the big companies wanted to use us now. We were still picking up the odd third-division job, but she was worthy of more.

The accounts started to show a loss. I couldn't bear to close the business, not for myself but for the others in the office – everyone had worked so hard. Little Lily Lottery was up every night for a week trying to balance out the figures, make something work, but it wasn't feasible, it was no use. Eventually I had to let the staff go. By taking nothing myself I managed to scrape up some sort of severance pay for them, but an envelope came back the next day with Alice's money still in it; she wouldn't take a penny.

Bet did well. She had made such an impression on so

many of the media people she dealt with there was talk of her hosting her own TV show. Love to see that.

Little Lily Lottery used her severance pay to fund a trip for her and her husband to go to Las Vegas. She had worked out a little mathematical plan to beat the systems – Little Lily Lottery in Las Vegas! In fact that was the title of Pup's second single. Who'd have thought he was aware of all these things, but he must have been taking it all in as he slept.

Our Dawn was offered work by other companies, but she turned everything down and went home to write her first book. Joan bought into a newsagent's with her sister in Cornwall, called it Zodiac. Solemn and Quiet Alice got together. Set off into the sunset in his car to lead a quiet and loving life. I heard later that they decided to get married. He wanted a simple wedding, but Alice spent her savings in getting them over to Memphis to get married in a little drop-in chapel near the home of the King.

Adam kept trying to get me to close the agency but I couldn't, kept it going long after I should have, and because of that I lost everything. Flat, money, the lot. Went without going bankrupt though, didn't owe a penny. Didn't have one either. I always say, if Suze's last chapters had been there I'd have made it.

Chapter Thirty-five

THE DAY WE WERE CLOSING I WANTED TO BE ALONE. I SENT
Adam home. He didn't want to leave me but I insisted. It was
quiet all around, just the last creak of the Thai boxers' bag upstairs. I heard the boxing students leave, the rattle of the great
lift. Then I heard the Thai boxer himself lock up, and then his
feet on the stone stairs; he always ran down. Mine must have
been the only light on.

I thought I heard a noise out in the corridor. Went out.
Nothing there. Then was sure I heard something on the floor
above, went up to the next floor, switching lights on as I went.
I called out one of those 'hellos' like they do in thriller movies,
don't know why, just fell into the role. No one called back, as
they never do in thriller movies. I went up one more flight, up
unswept stairs, up where the lift don't even go.

It was dark, the lights didn't work; only light was what the
moon could squeeze through the dirty windows and a bit
thrown up from the stairs below. The dust caught your throat

straight away. It was black and dirty up here, probably un-touched since the mill days.

The first door off the corridor was heavy and old, steel, badly rusted away and sharp in loads of places; you could cut your fingers. It was ajar but not wide enough to see into the room beyond. I gave it a little shove. It easily opened further. Rust spat out from between the hinges as it creaked. They were about gone, it would be off soon; I must report it to the owners. Through the gap I saw the mill room beyond. Cobwebs covered the doorway. I didn't like to step in, and the dust inside was literally inches thick, coming up light blue in the beam of moonlight that cut in.

It was a vast room with rusty metal pillars. Reminded me of the first photo shoot I had all that time ago when me mum said it was like the mill without the machines. But there was one machine left in there, I could make it out at the far end of the room, an old rusting machine, half the front panel miss-ing, showing all its insides, like iron intestines. A machine like the ones Gran's nimble, fixing fingers might have gone into.

I now imagined the place full of machines, the women all working, thinking of Grandma there. It felt suddenly very real: I was there with the immense noise, the smell of oil, the rows of women, and me gran there, beside the distant machine, like in her picture, her beautiful hair taken up on her head, but she was calling to me, calling something important, like a warning, but I couldn't hear her for the massive, massive noise of the machines. She was beckoning now, it was urgent, really urgent, I was leaning forward a bit to listen.

Suddenly I was flung against the wall by strong hands, punched in the face quickly about three times. I tasted blood in my mouth, the room span, came into focus, span, came into focus and then I was thrown to the floor. Somehow I caught my balance – all those days on my feet, who knows – I didn't go down and I ran, ran forward into the room, got the door shut.

I struggled with the lock, it had an old sliding bolt on it, just as I felt the push against the other side I got it across. My hands were bleeding from the sharp and rusting edge of it. I turned, looking for a way out: there was another door across the room. I ran to it, was so dark in here, only the moonlight. I could hear the door being thumped on, kicked. I got into the farther room, but it was only a small storeroom and nothing beyond that – pipework, brick; through the dirty windows just the canal below.

I could hear the constant kicking getting more ferocious, the door beginning to give with each thud; I could sense it. I struggled to shut the door to this room but it was completely seized up, I could do nothing with it. I went back into the mill room – nothing, nowhere to go. I hid behind the machine. I wasn't breathing, holding everything in. Suddenly the door came off its hinges completely and went down in a thick rising cloud of rust and dust and through it a figure came. I tucked in tighter, heard them pass the machine, go into the storeroom. At that I took my chance and charged for the now open doorway to escape, but they were upon me before I was even halfway across the room and had me around the neck from behind and then flung to the ground. My face was in the thick dust, I was choking from the force of his grip and from fear like I had never felt. I looked to my side and I saw a pair of stack-heel boots. No. I looked up and my spinning vision settled on the face of Rafe.

'Nay good screaming. I've checked twice, there's nay one about an' anyways, I'll rip your tongue out by the roots if you scream again.'

I made to try and get up and he pulled a long knife out of his pocket and slashed it at me. It just missed, swished through the air. I couldn't breathe for fear.

'What do you want?'

He laughed, but it was more like a snarl. And again the whispers, the bollocking in whispers, the anger in measured, calm whispers sharper than whisky.

'I want what I had before ya ruined it.'

'Me?'

'Aye, you. Bitch.' He leaned forward with the knife. 'I took you from nowhere and made you a star and you ruin me.'

'No.'

'Shut up. No one would touch me after that time you made me slap you. Had to go back to Glasgow to work. Set up me own agency. It didn't work out; naybody would work with me. I started getting into supplying escorts, then whores and girls for skin flicks. Those bitches had me in and out the nick.'

There was something about the stack heels, worn, lopsided, planted in the dust. It came back to me – the cash and carry. The shooting, under the shelves.

I blurted out. 'Was it you? The shooting, the—'

''Course it was, darlin', who else? Ya thicker than I thought. Came down this way once to supply some girls for Sugarstealer, thought I might look you up while I was here. As luck would have it found out about his little mission to blow your boyfriend's brains out. I went along, couldn't wait to have a shot at you. Nearly blew the whole thing – they really punished me for that. What's another scar or two? I didn't care. If only I'd hit you instead of the Cadbury's Roses. Knowing my luck probably got the coffee cream.'

He turned the knife again.

'Back up there in Glasgow, one of my "models", I s'pose you could call them that, started playing up like you did, but I'd learnt my lesson. Didn't even let her get going, I whacked her down. They put me away, don't know why, I let her live. She did lose an eye though, but there you go.'

He held his finger up to the light and I saw the serpent ring again. 'Her slut eye came out on it.' Looked at the ring again. 'What would it bring away from your face, I wonder?' Kissed the ring.

'Like Suze, that was yours, was it, on her cheek?'

'Aye, Suze, well branded. Suze was the best though, she was entirely mine. I always had her completely, but you even got to her, didn't you, eh? At the end there, even she started playin' up, would ya credit it, after all I'd done for her – you lasses. Nay, ya can't have that can ya?'

'So it wasn't suicide.'

'Well, I wasn't there, she did it herself. What can I say, except there's sixty ways to skin a slag.'

327

He screwed the serpent ring into the side of his own head, as though it was burrowing in, as though he had burrowed into her head. Then he grinned.

'So things haven't worked out too well for you. You should have called on me. I was always there. Ah well, no one said the model world was easy, did they?' He came closer with that knife. 'Did they?'

I shook my head, terrified.

'Urchins,' he spat. 'I couldn't stand it, seeing you prosper like that. Then I hatched the escape plan, the catwalk to freedom. You were too thick to see that, weren't you! Eh! Eh!' I nodded. 'Now I'm going to take what you owe me.'

'I have nothing.'

'Oh yes you have.' He started to undo his belt, came towards me. He put the knife at my throat, thrust my legs apart – those hands again, their final controlling move. No. No. I looked away and at the machine beside me, into its open insides. A part of my mind was drawn deep into its workings, almost calmly figuring it all out, as the other part of me raged in fear and blind panic. It was like it couldn't resist the mechanics, or was it the only way I could cope, because what was happening was just too terrible to bear? In a flash it had it all worked out for me: the interconnectedness of the parts, what held what, how bits loosened, what drove what – I had never known such focus, and all in a second. I could have stripped it down, swapped parts and reassembled it there and then, but all too soon my distraction was over. I was wrenched back to the dirty factory floor, as Rafe struggled to get my trousers undone, then just ripped them open. The knife left my throat for a second. He looked up. I thrust my finger into the tidgy triangle with all my might, pushing him back with it. He fell against the wall, choking, gasping, eyes popping. I jumped up. He was struggling to stand, coming round. I sent my fingers into the machine: would the big bar above the cogs loosen just as I thought? Could my fingers find it through the rust? Rafe was up now and coming toward me. Suddenly I felt it shift, it came clear in my hand. In one continuing movement I turned and hit him over the head with it. He went out. Beaten by Suze and me, standing over him at last.

Chapter Thirty-six

COLD MORNING, EARLY, EARLY MORNING, DARK AND COLD. I'M running from the car park to get in as fast as I can, chasing my frozen breath. Inside, it's a quick change into my checkout overalls, then straight through the aisles and into my seat behind the till. I can feel all the watchful eyes and all of them on me. I look up. Someone with a clipboard looks at me then turns and says, 'OK, everyone ready now. Quiet on set.'

I'm shooting the second series of the highly successful daytime soap *Checkout*. I play the main character, Joyce the checkout girl. The advert director – remember him? came through. When he got his first series he tracked me down. I look over to see Adam with our baby girl. He waves. Happy to be house husband for a while.

'OK, and action.'

The conveyor belt starts up and I start to check the shopping through. Supermarket to Supermodel to Supermarket.